Eliza
Stanhope

Eliza Stanhope

Joanna Trollope

E.P. DUTTON New York

First American edition published 1979 by E.P. Dutton,
a Division of Elsevier-Dutton Publishing
Company, Inc., New York

For information contact:
E.P. Dutton, 2 Park Avenue, New York, N.Y. 10016

Library of Congress Catalog Card Number: 78-74023

ISBN: 0-525-09750-3

10 9 8 7 6 5 4 3 2 1

FOR DAVID

Eliza
Stanhope

Part One

1

From her window, Eliza had an uninterrupted and exasperated view of them. The lawn rolled away, bland and green from the wall of the house to the ha-ha, only broken in its plushy sweep by the ilex walk, whose curve intruded gracefully on the left-hand edge. That was clearly what her cousin, Julia, and her cousin-in-law to be, Richard Beaumont were making for.

Cousin-in-law! That was the horror of it. Not only did Julia intend, with what seemed to Eliza awful deliberateness, to marry this man of truly remarkable dullness, but in so doing she never seemed to think what it would mean to Eliza to live without her. They had been together day in, day out all Eliza's life, and Julia appeared to give no thought at all to the selfishness of her marrying. Eliza claimed that she could not bear the man Julia was to marry, but in reality what she could not bear was that Julia was to marry at all. There were plenty of excuses she could muster to obscure the fact, and some of them she actually believed. She knew people married as Julia was presumably about to do, for money and position, but she cherished a fierce conviction that it was only really justifiable to do it for love. Knowing nothing about either love or marriage did not make her remotely cautious in expressing her views most vigorously.

Eliza lightly beat her fists on the window-sill, carelessly crushing some small, exploring golden tendrils of wisteria which, encouraged by the unexpected warmth of the day, were crawling tentatively around her window. She narrowed her eyes and riveted her glare on the pair on the lawn. Julia

7

would have been pleased with the gracefulness of her own back view, the hem of her spotted muslin slipping over the grass in little rushes like water behind her. She was tactfully – no, Eliza decided, tactically – wearing the Indian silk shawl Richard Beaumont had given her a few weeks ago, but it was obvious to her cousin, from the indifference with which she let it slip from her left shoulder, that it was not of significance to its wearer. Richard had given it to her in the small parlour, while Eliza had sat sewing and smouldering as chaperone in the corner, and Julia had said:

'But how charming! How positively – interesting! What taste you have!'

And Richard Beaumont had beamed complacently, and then had been embarrassingly anxious to demonstrate the shawl's merits, its colours, its intricacies, the wonderful exoticism of its birds and flowers. He had placed it with doting incompetence about Julia's shoulders, turned to Eliza for confirmation of its qualities, and bowed himself out in the state of unmitigated gratification that comes from a sense of perfect generosity.

When the wheels of his carriage had ground away, Julia fingering the shawl as if it were a reptile, said, 'It is hideous, isn't it? The jewels of the East should be left where they belong. It looks absurd in Hampshire.'

'So,' said Eliza crossly, 'did you. All that simpering and hypocritical gratitude –'

'Ah,' Julia said airily across her disapproval, 'true. But there is much at stake. If the path to Quihampton and Royal Crescent and that pretty house in London is paved with Indian shawls, I must endure to walk it. Eliza,' she said commandingly, 'must I not?'

'I would not,' said Eliza fiercely. 'It is such folly. He is such a dull man, such a foolish man.' She cried in despair, 'He cannot even ride with much confidence!'

Julia had laughed. Eliza's energy was legendary, both physical and emotional, although her cousin frequently pointed out that she wasted most of the latter in indignation. Eliza would do battle over anything. Julia would not. She was, at this moment, turning into the ilex walk, replying with perfect conventionality to Richard who, measuring his own stature by her apparent approval, was visibly expanding in her company. They stopped in the first dappled stretch of shade while he said something with great and ponderous earnestness and Eliza saw Julia's downward glance, pout, and toss of curls in reply. It was just as well, Eliza thought, that Julia's own wit gave her such an amount of private pleasure since Mr Beaumont had none to please her with.

They were gone. Even the heavy block of shadow made by Richard's shoulders and the high roll collar of his coat had fragmented and dispersed among the leaves. Sighing heavily, Eliza sat down by the window and leaned her sharp chin on her folded arms. It was all quite impossible. Julia, her much-loved and enjoyed Julia, was, it seemed going to throw away her looks and wit and charm upon this dolt, this amiable buffoon.

They had spent the last five years, those girls, shrieking with mirth over Richard Beaumont, and had invented a game of forfeits to each other every time one of them had failed to avoid dancing with him at balls and assemblies. Eliza's aunt had often caught her mimicking his walk behind his very back and had inflicted the worst punishment of all, that Eliza might not ride for a week. And now there might be no more shrieks and giggles and wonderful avoiding games round the pillars in the Assembly Rooms. Incomprehensibly and – even more, it seemed to Eliza – disloyally, Julia had agreed to marry him, and Julia claimed that the only disadvantage of the arrangement was that it had put Eliza out of temper.

Eliza got up. Although she was not actually confined to her room that May afternoon when she longed to be riding out with her uncle to visit his tenants, her aunt had made it perfectly clear that her behaviour at dinner had been shameful. Her attempts to catch Julia's eye, her small imitations of Richard Beaumont's table manners, had all been beadily recorded by her aunt. As they rose from the table and she attempted to slip behind the sheltering bulk of her uncle, the axe had fallen. Mrs Lambert was entranced by the fact that her Julia would become in time a baronet's wife and also, being a perfectionist in trivia, required from all her dependants a faultless outward manner. Appearances bore for her an ultimate importance, and her niece Eliza had been to her a constant cross in this respect. To the best of her unimaginative ability she had reared the child as her own, and felt herself repaid most thanklessly. Eliza's attitude to Richard Beaumont was inexcusable.

'Wait!' Mrs Lambert had ordered.

Subdued, Eliza waited by her chair while her usual ally, her uncle, slipped cravenly from the room with a volley of winks and gestures.

'You know what I have to say to you.'

Eliza considered pretending ignorance, decided it would only delay the affair, and dumbly inclined her head.

'Such impudence, miss! And to a man not only of excellent family' – there was a pause; Mr Lambert, to his wife's distress, always heartily referred to himself as a farmer – 'but to whom you now owe respect and affection.'

'I do not feel either respect or affection.'

'Have you not heard of duty? Have you so little control over your giddy head you cannot school yourself?'

Eliza raised her head.

'I should like Julia to be happy, Aunt.'

'Happy? Happy? The notion is absurd. What has happiness to do with it?'

'He cannot even make her laugh –'

'Laugh? That is all you girls think of. Laugh indeed. I despair of you, Eliza. And I am most displeased. I had imagined that dreadful incident the other day might have taught you a severe lesson.'

Eliza kept a resentful silence. Her aunt appeared to have exhausted the small vocabulary she felt fitting for reprimand, and after fidgeting incoherently for a moment or two, picked up a volume Julia had left on the window-seat.

'Take this and occupy yourself with it until I send for you.'

Eliza looked down at it. It was in French, which was unfortunate, but it was poetry which made up for the language. Her aunt stood waiting for an apology. It could not be done. Eliza dropped her the smallest curtsey and sped to her room.

She had been allotted her bedroom all those years before because it was too small for any other use. It might have made a dressing room for her uncle, except that the great dressing table upon which his manservant would lay out fresh sets of clothes, and remove the evidence of a day's hunting from others, would have had to have several inches sawn from its length to be accommodated. As it had belonged to his father, Mr Lambert regarded the suggestion as sacrilegious. So Eliza's the room became, furnished only with bed, washstand, closet and desk, the whole dwarfed by the great sash window which was its glory, and which was necessary to the outside of the house for perfect symmetry.

Eliza put a chair back under the window, propped her book on the sill, and sat inelegantly astride. Her bruised feelings derived some comfort from this tiny and unseen defiance. She began to read the poems, relieved to see that they were not concerned with the soul or heart of man for once, and then was gradually delighted to discover that most were in praise of Napoleon. Eliza was enraptured by all action, and who achieve more action than soldiers?

> *On parlera de sa gloire*
> *Sous le chaume bien longtemps*
> *L'humble toit, dans cinquante ans,*
> *Ne connaîtra plus d'autre histoire.*

She beat time lightly on the chairback. *Gloire*, indeed! How could you achieve *gloire* as a girl, even if you were frequently the toast of the hunting field? There was no talking of Eliza Stanhope in awe beneath the humble thatch, except to thank her for bringing calf's-foot jelly. Anyway, people seldom thanked her, only scolded.

She reflected on what had happened a few days before when she had concocted an idea at breakfast whose charm had quite outweighed the possibility of its also being shamefully bad behaviour. She had sat, bursting with impending mischief, while Richard ate his way solemnly and methodically through a meal sufficient to last him three days. If he was conscious of Eliza's ill-suppressed derision, and the light of sheer naughtiness in her eyes, he gave no sign but chewed thoroughly on, rising every so often to carve himself another helping with the dedicated precision of a surgeon. Every time he got up, Eliza went into a perfect pantomime of ponderous chewing and thorough facial scrubbings with her table napkin, continuing to mimic just long enough for her victim to be perfectly aware of what she was doing as he turned from the sideboard with his refilled plate. At length, Mrs Lambert, unable to control her niece by frowns and mouthings of extreme ferocity, dismissed her summarily from the room. Eliza, pink with over-excitement, claimed she had not finished her toast.

'That is of no consequence. Perhaps a little hunger may have a reducing effect on your spirits. Pray go upstairs and wait for me in my boudoir.'

The pink in Eliza's cheeks turned to scarlet at the humiliation of being treated like a child, especially in the presence of the despised suitor for her cousin's hand. She opened her mouth to protest again, but then her eye was caught by a warning gesture from her uncle. What she would not do for her aunt, she would for her uncle. Fiery-faced, she went quickly out of the dining room, firing her Parthian shot by giving the door a slight but defiant slam behind her.

Half obedience was quite enough for Eliza. Having left the room as bidden, she had no intention of waiting in her aunt's boudoir. She would instead go to the stables and do what she had schemed to do. It was a lovely morning and her choking feelings subsided a little as she crossed the cobbles under a clear blue sky while her uncle's white pigeons flew in graceful formation above her. A groom was holding Mr Lambert's horse, ready saddled, and in his other hand he held the reins of the grey mare that Eliza loved to ride herself, though the mare was considered big for a girl to manage. She broke into a run. The groom grinned amiably at her.

''Mornin', miss.'

''Morning, John. Why is Bess saddled?'

John's grin widened.

''Tis for the visitor, miss. He'm goin' out with the master. The master said to give 'im Bess for she won't play 'im up.'

Eliza knew full well that one did not gossip with servants, but her blood was up.

'Mr Beaumont? He cannot ride, John, he has no more skill than a sack of potatoes!'

'Master's orders, miss.'

'I might have wanted her myself this morning,' Eliza said indignantly.

' 'Tis my orders, miss.'

Eliza detected a note of sympathy in his voice. She took her chance.

'May I just hold her, John?' She hoped her tone sounded slightly pathetic.

He passed the reins over.

'I'd be glad to let you, miss. Give me a chance to oil this old boy's hoofs before the master comes out.'

Eliza waited until he had clattered to the opposite corner of the yard and was bent over, mercifully with his back to her, with brush and oil pot. Slipping Bess's reins over her arm, she moved quickly to the horse's side and, supporting the stirrup and saddle-flap on her forehead and out of her way, she deftly loosened the girth a dangerous number of inches. Bess lowered her head and blew out gratefully. John came back across the yard and retrieved his charge, and Eliza, gleeful now, skipped into the nearest loose box and awaited results.

They were beyond even her expectations. Richard Beaumont, an apprehensive horseman, approached Bess gingerly some minutes later, encouraged by Mr Lambert with reassurances of Bess's reliability. He put his large, well-kept hands reluctantly upon the saddle, bent his left leg for John to take, pulled vigorously upon the loosened saddle and fell with a cry back upon the cobbles, hurling the groom to the ground with him. Eliza, stifling delighted giggles, watched him entranced as he lay like a large ungainly beetle upon the ground, his hat rolled off, his breeches torn, and his face working like a codfish in bewilderment and indignity. Her triumph was short-lived. Having picked up and dusted off a Richard bruised both in body and feelings, Mr Lambert had rounded upon his groom with a volley of invective at his carelessness and slovenliness. Eliza was horrified. Not for a second had she thought through the ultimate consequences of her action. She watched in anguish for a moment as John, his face twisted with uncomprehending misery, tried to protest his innocence, and then, chin up, head high, she left the shelter of the loose box and crossed what seemed an endless stretch of ground to confess to her uncle. It was very awful, for he had never been really angry with her before. Worse, he made her apologize to Richard Beaumont, which she was aware of doing with a very ill grace, and then, worst of all, he sent her in to her aunt.

'I shall leave you, Eliza, to tell the story in entire truthfulness.'

Eliza's memory skated quickly over that interview, and she diverted her gaze and thoughts back out of the window.

She looked out to the horizon and saw it filled only with Julia and Richard Beaumont. They had crossed the ha-ha to the fat meadow beyond where Mr Lambert's Jersey herd browsed decoratively in the sun, Julia's pale muslin entirely fitting, and her shawl not in the least so, among the May grasses and the golden cows. Richard Beaumont was guiding her reverently and unnecessarily among the hummocks in the grass – hummocks she had known since childhood – and she, her shawl dangling forgotten from her shoulder, was coyly holding buttercups beneath his chin.

A week ago Eliza had caught Julia alone in the dusk in the small parlour, with the candles and the moths, and had said, 'Oh, why do it, Julia? You could marry anybody, you know you could. Why all of a sudden, like this? Why him? You know what we have always said about him –'

'He will never cross me. Or chide me. He will give me London and Bath and several carriages and pay for my amusements, and one day he will make me Lady Beaumont.'

'But so could a thousand others! Henry Leslie is heir to a baronetcy and Richard Peel has more money than the rest of the county put together – and John Knight-Knox has two lovely houses even if they are falling down – and they *all* want to marry you!'

'Ah,' Julia said and raised a hand.

'Well?'

'Sit down. And put down everything you are carrying else you will only fidget.'

Eliza deposited a tangle of embroidery wools, two books, her whip and a very small horseshoe upon the table. Julia looked at the horseshoe. Eliza, anxious not to deflect her from her explanation, said hurriedly that it was from the old donkey upon whose grudging back they had all first learned to ride, and who was being pensioned off in the orchard.

Julia said, 'Shall you keep it?'

'Of course.'

14

'I cannot keep anything. I have not the energy. Do you not sometimes think that I am the idlest creature you ever met? I am only witty because I cannot stir myself to be serious.'

'You certainly yawn a good deal,' Eliza said.

'Do I not?' Julia said delightedly. 'I am a positive glutton for yawning. It is an absolute pleasure. I am sure that if I tried a little I might have a little viscount or a fledgling duke or even – though this is very ambitious – a man of considerable intelligence, but I cannot stir myself. Richard Beaumont has come along, and I am a little bored, I do confess, and I will have him.'

'He has not,' Eliza pointed out, 'come along. We have been tripping over him for years. And he is just as dull and idiotic as he was when I first met him. I was fifteen and you were seventeen. We thought he was a perfect fool, with all his talk of estates in the Cotswolds and the title, such as it is, and London society – and I for one still do think him a perfect fool.'

'My standards,' said Julia agreeably, 'are lamentably low.'

'I could hit you,' Eliza said miserably.

'Pray don't. One day you will want to be married and – '

'I shan't.'

'Oh?'

'I don't think,' said poor Eliza, 'that anyone will much want me. Aunt says I am so rough and rude and cross and even dear Uncle, when I pressed him, said I did have charm but it was the kind he usually looked for in puppies.'

Julia was not to be perturbed. No amount of reference to 'Lady Beaumont of Boredom' had the smallest effect. Eliza could not comprehend how Julia could remain unoffended by her suitor's clumsiness. Even at this moment he managed to look foolish helping Julia over the stile at the bottom of the ha-ha. He was endeavouring to swing her over like a small child, his hands beneath her arms, and as she was nearly as tall as he, it was scarcely possible. Long indigo shadows were beginning to inch across the lawn as they came up the incline of the ha-ha, and in and out of the bars of shade they moved, the future Sir Richard and Lady Beaumont, watched with indignation by Eliza from her window, and with gratification by Mrs Lambert from the drawing room below.

Julia came to Eliza's door some minutes later and demanded her presence in the drawing room.

'Is it to play something?' Eliza enquired hopefully.

'Only at conversation.'

They went down the shallow staircase together in the thickening light, and Julia led the way gracefully into the drawing room. Eliza, anxious not to remind her aunt unnecessarily of her presence, chose an obscure seat, but Richard Beaumont found her immediately.

One of his most irritating characteristics, Eliza decided disagreeably, was his eternal readiness to forgive. It seemed to her the sign of a weak mind that someone could be mercilessly mocked and almost badly hurt and then be so ready to be reconciled with his persecutor.

How delighted he was to see her, he exclaimed in his full pleasant voice, and how sorry he had been about her indisposition that had prevented her from joining the delightful walk in the unexpected warmth.

Indisposition? Eliza shot an enquiring glance at her aunt and was answered with a bland smile.

'Such a delightful walk!' said Richard Beaumont again.

'I saw you,' Eliza said. 'It looked it.'

'The air, Miss Stanhope, the flowers, this charming valley. Used as I am to the bleak uplands of Windrush, this greenness, this lushness is entirely – is quite – quite – '

'Green,' said Julia.

'Exactly so!' he said triumphantly. As Mr Lambert entered the room, still dusty from riding, Richard added that he came from sheep country and thus was no judge of cattle but that it seemed to him that the Jerseys out there in the meadow were undoubtedly superior to others of their kind.

Mr Lambert grunted, kissed his wife, beamed upon his daughter and his niece, and with a 'See you for tea no doubt,' uttered without enthusiasm to Richard Beaumont, left the room again. The time crawled interminably. Candles were brought, conversation ebbed more than flowed, and Eliza tried to beguile the creeping minutes by sorting her aunt's wools. Mr Lambert came in at last and rang for tea, paused, then rang again for toast and butter, sat down, realized that Richard Beaumont was in his own customary chair so got up, glared, rang again to remind Fanny to bring cream, and resumed his unfamiliar seat to fidget until reprimanded by his wife. Tea came, and with it the welcome ritual of pots and lamps, dishes and cream jugs. A sudden animation born of relief seized them all. Richard Beaumont, awkwardly upon his knees charring toast before the fire, assailed his host once more.

'Well, what of Napoleon, sir? Shall we not have peace eternal do you not think? Is not the threat to Europe entirely gone, sir? Is it not a relief he is confined to Elba?'

'Not at all,' said Mr Lambert ungratefully. 'As a result I am besieged daily by fragments of our army wanting work. I have none to give them. They are only fit for the army, nothing better.'

'Poor things,' Julia said. 'They do not even want what they ask for. We would give them a few shillings and a cottage and a regular life after a life of a few shillings and gin and no family responsibilities.'

'I hope he will escape!' said Eliza, buttering toast for her uncle.

'Nonsense, my dear,' he patted her hand. 'He is confined to an island, heavily guarded. Nobody wants him back.'

'I expect the French do,' Eliza persisted.

Richard Beaumont, anxious to rescue her from what might become a tight corner, little realizing she never minded being in one, said, 'Should he come back, dear Miss Stanhope, it might please my brother at the least!'

Out of the pool of disinterest that spread after this remark Mrs Lambert said faintly, 'Your brother, Mr Beaumont?'

'Yes, indeed, my brother Francis, my younger brother. Do you believe, Mrs Lambert, that my younger brother Francis always swore he would not take to soldiering. He said he wished to live quietly in the country all his life, and think and write, I believe he said – and here he is, my younger brother, actually patronized by the great duke himself!'

A spark of dim interest lifted Mr Lambert's head from his dish of tea.

'Wellington?'

'None other, sir,' cried Richard Beaumont with delighted

emphasis. 'Francis is no more than thirty and has served so gallantly under our great commander in Spain that he has not only earned his notice –'

'Yes?' they all leaned forward.

'But his praise!'

They leaned back again.

'He is a wonder, Francis!' cried his brother, letting a blackened piece of bread fall from his fork into the ashes below. 'A wonder! So unassuming, but so gifted. Noticed and commended by the great Duke of Wellington two days after his thirtieth birthday, but has his manner changed as a result of it? No, indeed! To meet you would never know he was a soldier at all –' Here Eliza's face showed disappointment. 'No side, you know, no flash. Indeed –'

'Why', said Julia, 'have I not met this paragon?'

'He has been home but these three days –' at which point, fork and bread both fell in an ecstasy of excitement at the notice taken of his conversation. 'I would have brought him, my dearest Julia, but he is – he is fatigued,' said Richard Beaumont euphemistically, remembering Francis' manner ('Indeed I shall not come. Can you not arrange even a little matter like a wife without a second opinion?').

'Another time,' said Mrs Lambert, her mind passing with pleasure over the connection with Wellington. 'We would be so charmed.'

'Charmed,' said Julia and yawned.

Richard was instantly contorted with alarm that he had fatigued her that afternoon.

Under the cover of his booming concern, Mr Lambert said to Eliza, 'Our Mr Beaumont is said to be in every way a mirror image of his late and unlamented mother. Could there be two such images, do you suppose?'

'If so,' said Eliza, 'it is no small wonder their father is said to be a recluse.'

They smiled complicitly at one another.

'A picnic, perhaps!' Mrs Lambert cried. 'He might join us for a picnic when the weather is more certainly favourable.' Her mind ran on pies and napery and early strawberries from the glasshouses on the south wall. 'The barouche – landau –' She paused. The cushions, after last summer, were not entirely as she would wish, but Mr Lambert's new chestnuts were so pretty, so well matched. Perhaps it would not signify about the cushions. A raised pie, cold crust, her own chickens. The numbers struck her suddenly with satisfaction.

'It will be delightful,' she said with finality. 'Your brother will provide a companion for Eliza.'

2

Francis Beaumont, largely overlapping a hammock beneath the walnut tree at Quihampton, was not disposed towards making an effort for his brother Richard. He was fond of that hammock. It had been given to him by a very drunk sailor one night in an inn in London, and the sailor had claimed incoherently that the hammock had been used by himself aboard the *Temeraire* throughout the campaign that culminated in the Battle of Trafalgar. Francis doubted this but would have liked to believe it.

His brother Richard sat uncomfortably on a stone seat, whose dampness he quite rightly suspected, and eyed his brother resentfully. Francis' closed eyes and faint smile, his swinging right leg and the inevitable, maddening motion of the hammock, all contributed to his irritation. Perhaps Francis would become more amenable if he knew of the reputation which, thanks to his loyal brother, he enjoyed among the Lamberts at Marchants. On second thoughts Richard doubted such knowledge would influence him in the least. Richard found both his brother and his father quite unmanageable at times.

'I cannot see your objection!' he cried, beating his large hands together. 'I am only asking you to undertake the smallest social duty for my sake and you –'

'Go away, Richard.'

Richard sat doggedly on in silence.

Eventually his brother opened his eyes, and said with obvious control. 'Listen, dear brother. I have no objection to coming on an inspection tour of Miss Lambert. Indeed, since I shall have her as my only sister-in-law, I am more than interested to meet her. But I have been home only two weeks for the first time in three years, during which time you have travelled back and forth to Hampshire like a demented gadfly. To me it is an utter pleasure to be here and to order my own day to my own choosing. All I beg is that you will give me some weeks to reconstitute myself and then I will accompany you on whatever romantic mission you care to name. If you were a woman, Richard, I would beg you not to scold.'

'But, my dear brother – '

Francis closed his eyes again.

'Not another word. But,' a thought struck him with pleasure, 'since Miss Lambert is to be as a daughter to him, why not take Father picnicking in Hampshire?'

With a snort, Richard got up, nervously feeling the seat of his breeches, and moved away across the grass. Mrs Lambert, once the idea of a joint visit by both Beaumont brothers had firmly settled itself in her brain, had been obsessively persistent in wishing to name a date for that visit. In fact, thought Richard injuredly, she was the only person in either of the two families about to be united by his and Julia's marriage who showed the least interest in, or approval of, the arrangement. His own father had looked up scowling from some document and said, 'Marry whom you will,' which was scarcely encouraging. Mr Lambert appeared to regard him with amiable indifference, his own brother with feelings not much warmer and, as for the little Lambert niece, her animosity was the most obvious thing he ever saw. Not that he minded – Eliza Stanhope was a mere chit of nineteen or so – but it was not pleasant to be regarded with such odium by any pretty girl. Richard stopped and gazed morosely into the lavender hedge where stout bees, oblivious of his afflictions, were callously busy. Just like his own relations, he thought, and tramped into the house.

His father had been watching from the library window, not because he derived any anxiety or pleasure from an altercation between his sons, but because he could not help brooding with an almost passionate delight over the return of Francis. Francis knew this and was always grateful his father seldom spoke of these intense feelings, or if he did, in

21

the most veiled and acceptable terms. Francis was a devoted son, but like many men, he disliked the sensation that he was the apple of any one eye. It was, he was quite aware himself, the chief reason why, after his placid, stupid mother's death, he had left his Cotswold valley and joined the army. He hoped very much, observing his father's silhouette in the window across the grass, that he would not have to have the same performance all over again. He was surprised how bleak and stiff the house had become without his mother's presence, and surprised at himself to realize how much he had been looking forward to the cosseting and comfort of home. It all ran like clockwork to be sure, but cheerless clockwork. Perhaps, he thought, I shall have much to be grateful to Richard's Miss Lambert for we clearly need her here, if only to think of some other sustenance than beef and other ornament than pipe-racks. He remembered his father, hurling handfuls of pot-pourri into the air with cries of contempt ('Dead petals? Dead flowers? In my rooms – never!'), and he wished he had defended his mother more. It was little wonder people regarded his father as an ogre since he took so much trouble to behave like one. In fact, there had been much speculation as to how such a misanthropist ever came to have wife and sons at all.

Sir Gerard Beaumont, as the world had rightly suspected, had married for purely calculating reasons. Quihampton had been in his family now for three hundred years, and the possession of it at the age of thirty upon the death of his forbidding father filled him with the only passionate delight he was to feel, with a single exception, in the whole of his lifetime. The house, the park, the valley, the outlying farms and cottages, touched upon some black vein of primitive possessiveness in him that absorbed all his emotions and left none to spare. After three years of his inheritance he realized that as the last of his line, Quihampton would cease to be Beaumont land upon his own death and so, with the sole thought of finding himself a breeder of sons, he set out to find a wife. He disliked mankind, but of all of it he most disliked women, and so he chose the most anonymous and unexceptionable member of her sex that he could find. She was youngish, healthy, biddable, uncommunicative and rich. She gave him two sons and twenty years of dull loyalty, and he repaid her with alternate bouts of bullying and neglect. The fact that without her he would never have possessed this adored second son, who was to rival Quihampton in his father's narrow and savage heart, entirely escaped acknowledgement. All that Sir Gerard could think of was that Francis had not been born first, the heir to Quihampton, and this accident he regarded purely as his wife's carelessness. She died exhausted when Francis was twenty, and the world rightly judged Sir Gerard an ogre.

The ogre was, for him, quite jovial at dinner. He had spent a large part of the morning in the cellar, finding a claret worthy of Francis. It was one of the few things, Francis had said, that had made the Peninsula bearable, and in that heat, of course, there was no difficulty in bringing it to blood heat.

'As our blood was mostly on the boil, the wine matched it perfectly.'

Sir Gerard, carving a great sirloin with absolute precision said, 'And how do you propose to occupy [yourself now?'

'You, too!'

'Eh?'

'Richard is sure I am in want of occupation too, sir. He has been belabouring me with requests to accompany him to Hampshire.'

'He seems to want,' said his father, as if Richard were not in the room, 'to marry some girl there.' He paused. 'Milk and water county.'

'Miss Lambert –!' began Richard hotly in defence of his beloved.

'Is a paragon, Father,' Francis said smoothly, treading heavily upon his brother beneath the table.

'Know her?'

'Not yet, but I shall quite soon. I am being worn down by my brother.'

'I've been that for years,' Sir Gerard said unkindly.

'Do you not think, sir, that Richard should bring her here?'

'Certainly not!'

'But it will be her home, sir.'

Sir Gerard growled faintly.

23

'Sufficient unto the day is the evil thereof. It would in any case be impossible to have her here without some chaperone, and I will not have the house overrun with women. The household servants are bad enough.'

'When they are married, sir,' said Francis unwisely, 'not only might they wish to live here, but Richard's wife might well require her own servants, so would it not be best to accustom yourself, sir?'

Sir Gerard, his mouth full of beef, bulged and went purple. Richard gave Francis the imploring glance of a spaniel, and Francis with a cry of 'Too much mustard, sir!' leapt up to thump his father on the back, and hold a glass of water to his lips.

'You know,' said Sir Gerard in a thickened voice, 'that I never drink it.'

'Now then, Father, you tell me what I should to do occupy myself.'

'Memoirs?' said Richard hopefully.

His father snorted.

'I kept journals all through Spain,' Francis said, 'and they make dull reading even to me.'

'I should regard it as a privilege,' his brother said gravely, 'if I might see them.'

Sir Gerard raised his glass.

'I was unaware you could read, Richard.'

There was an unhappy pause.

'I might redesign the garden for you, sir.'

'I am quite content with it as it is, but if it would amuse you –'

'The *idea* amuses me. Nobody has touched it since Good Queen Bess. All that yew and those parterres and box hedges.'

'When I am married,' Richard said in a voice higher than he intended, 'Julia and I will divide our time btween London and Bath.'

'Pleasuring!' his father said with derision.

'Miss Lambert's qualities are seen to great advantage in society.'

Sir Gerard flung himself back in his chair and rocked with laughter.

'Have you shown Father her likeness?' Francis said, who

24

that morning had been privileged to attend a small ritual of locket, glove, miniature and curl of chestnut hair.

Richard shook his head and made elaborate mouthings to the effect that he did not wish to.

'Do my garden, then!' Sir Gerard said abruptly. 'Give it up entirely to potatoes, if it would please you. But do not go away again just yet.'

Francis got up quickly to fetch another decanter.

'I promise to go no further than Hampshire, and even that,' he added with a warning glance at his brother, 'not yet.'

'Where's her picture, then, Richard?'

'In my room, sir.'

'Describe her then!'

'She is quite tall, sir, of excellent figure and bearing, quite beautiful, sir, with a considerable air and a good carriage, sir –'

'Is she a horse or a woman?'

Francis looked across the table at Richard's red, doubtful face, and felt a pang of pity.

His father said, 'Have you seen the portrait of this centauress?'

'No, sir,' said Francis, suddenly gathering resolution, 'but I am soon to see Miss Lambert in the flesh. I said I would only leave Quihampton for Hampshire, and I will keep my word. But I shall go with Richard this week to meet her.'

He avoided the absolute gladness in his brother's eyes and launched into a soldier's anecdote. After all, this week or three weeks hence, what difference did it make, and he would insist upon riding as the exercise would do him good. To his surprise, Sir Gerard said no more about Hampshire or Julia Lambert except to mutter to Francis as they left the dining room.

'Put him off, Francis, if she don't do. I'll not give this house to a girl who don't do.'

Alone in his room in the spring darkness later that night, Francis began to regret the sudden impulse that had made him agree to go to Hampshire with Richard. He lay on his pillows among the familiar dusky shapes of his bedroom and wished very heartily that he did not have to leave it. Richard might have thought, he mused resentfully, what it was like

25

to have clean sheets and quiet days and freedom from duty after three years of campaigning in the oven of the Iberian Peninsula. But then Richard was in love, and love made men unimaginative of others' wants and needs.

He shifted comfortably and folded his arms behind his head. The owl that used to call all through his boyhood was still vociferously busy in the deep blue darkness out there. No, it could not be the same owl, it must be a child or grandchild of that owl.

He wished idly that his affection for his brother was not such a dutiful thing. It would be wonderful if it sprang from truly irresistible and spontaneous feeling, and not from pity and familiarity and the ties of blood. It should be, he decided, like the love he felt for Pelham. He had met Pelham Howell at Oxford. They had become firm friends, and Francis had quickly developed the habit of spending a good deal of time in the Howells' comfortable cheerful house near Newbury. Francis reflected that he and Richard had nothing in common, no shared experience beyond their childhood, whereas he and Pelham had everything in common. They had been bought their commissions in the army together, they had fought together in the Peninsula, they had both suffered desperate moments fearing the other dead. Even at the thought of Pelham, Francis found himself smiling with pleasure in the darkness.

A sudden and happy idea crossed his reverie. He would persuade Richard to go via Newbury, and he would call on Pelham and entice him to go with them to Hampshire. Richard was bound to have chosen a girl as dull and worthy as himself with, no doubt, a family to match, and at least he might enliven his time there if he had Pelham with him. No household could object to having Pelham, so amusing, so personable, so very skilful with the mothers of pretty girls. In fact, Francis considered, if you included Pelham in the scheme, a visit to Hampshire might be a very pleasurable affair indeed. Smiling contentedly, Francis rolled on to his side and fell asleep.

Francis thought he might be given another day of idling in his hammock, but it was not to be. Richard was at his door early the next morning, face and boots gleaming, with the news that he had despatched his man to Marchants at dawn

to warn Mrs Lambert they would be with her by noon of
the following day. He had wanted to travel at great speed
since the distance was less than a hundred miles, but Francis
insisted that they should break their journey at Newbury.
He had won on that point, but lost on that of riding. Not
only was his elder brother an indifferent horseman, but he
had just purchased a new gig, and clearly the image of
himself bowling dashingly up to Mr Lambert's door in it
was not to be resisted.

Francis breakfasted with what seemed to Richard exas-
perating slowness.

'There is no need, dear brother, to eat such a quantity.
The King's Head will supply us admirably tonight.'

'As a soldier,' Francis said, helping himself to more ham,
to his brother's despair, 'one learns to breakfast as solidly
as one can. One never knows when food is to be seen again.
Especially when fighting. The problem is usually catching
breakfast. I shudder to think of the number of breakfasts I
consumed ... which were squawking around ... a farmyard
... but an hour before.'

All this was uttered between mouthfuls.

'I would dearly like to be going to my hammock now,'
said Francis sadly in conclusion.

The pressure to leave was irresistible. His gloves were
found for him, his cloak laid in the gig, his boots given a final
burnish. He could not even linger to bid farewell to his
father since Sir Gerard had left instructions that he was not
to be disturbed. He was scarcely seated beside his brother,
his man hardly mounted behind them, when Richard
touched his bays and the gig was going. Francis looked round
to say a silent good-bye to Quihampton, its steeply pitched
grey roofs clustered among the dark outlines of the yew
trees and hedges, but he did not see his father watching from
an upper window.

At Francis' special request, they drove via Oxford.

'It was a place I thought about almost as much as home
when I was away.'

It did not disappoint him. Late May was perfection. They
dined modestly at an inn on the river and fed the great trout
below them on pieces of bread. Then they lay beneath an elm
and Richard told Francis how he came to be in love, and

27

how it had taken him three years to summon the courage to speak, and how entirely astonished he had been when he was accepted. Francis tried to remember her from his other life, before the army, but he could not. He could remember nothing of any Lambert, not even Julia's two brothers whom he was informed he had hunted with.

'And there is a niece,' said Richard painfully.

'Ah?'

'A Miss Stanhope. Miss Eliza Stanhope. She is a very good horsewoman.'

'And?'

'She is perhaps nineteen or so. A pretty child with graceful movements and,' here the blood surged into Richard's face, 'abominable manners!'

Francis smiled.

'She is a perfect minx. She has no idea how to conduct herself in society, and no thought for the feelings of others. She is most immature.'

'Do I gather,' Francis said, 'that she and Father share similar views about the engagement?'

'She is quite impossible! Rude to the point of insolence, and imitates me when she thinks I am not aware of her.'

'Is she not reprimanded?'

'Continually. She is quite irrepressible. Her behaviour will, at least, if it does nothing else, serve to convince you of the devotion I feel for her cousin. The house would not be tolerable else.'

Francis got up and brushed grasses from his clothes.

'What a tiresome child she sounds.'

They drove slowly to Newbury over the great, swinging downs and through comfortable villages. As the light mellowed and faded over the countryside, Francis felt very keenly that even if he was not going to enjoy himself at Marchants, the journey alone had been worth the trouble of leaving his hammock.

They slept at the King's Head, and Francis woke at first light, as he was used to do, to the sound of small hooves on the cobbles. The street was full of fat sheep. Francis smiled fondly down on them, fat, comfortable English sheep. Their passing woke Richard, too, and as the day was again wonderfully fine, it was agreed to start immediately.

Richard was in a fuss about the diversion to collect Pelham, but Francis pointed out that his brother was in his debt.

'I have come with you precisely when I most wanted to stay at home, so you must indulge my whim of wishing to add Pelham to our caravan.'

Then, as Richard began to speak, he added, 'I shall not jolt another mile without him.'

Richard, absorbed in refuting this implied insult to the springing of his gig, objected no further. Before the Howells had finished breakfast, sprawled carelessly about their dining room in the manner of houses where energetic men reign supreme, the Beaumonts came speeding up the drive. Pelham, his mouth full, sprang up from his chair, scattering a pair of lurchers who had camped upon his feet, and rushed out in welcome.

'My dear Francis, what a truly magnificent surprise! I cannot think that I have ever been so gratified to see anybody. Oh, and Richard. Good morning, Richard. And what a splendid one. Come in, come in. Mother's idea of breakfast is enough to bring tears to a soldier's eyes. Mother! Mother! Look who is come!'

Through the welter of bounding dogs and booming Howells, Richard, somewhat discomfited by this rousing reception, saw his brother being most soundly embraced by a stout and rosy woman in a riding habit. When she had kissed him copiously and felt him all over as if civilian life might have impaired his physique, she came over to Richard and shook his hand most cordially and gave him a plate of game pie in one hand and a tankard in the other.

'Are you come to stay with us? I do hope you are come to stay, indeed I do. We are so dull, only the seven of us, and the General does so need diversion when he has to do without a campaign. It will amuse him splendidly to have you here. Do stay, my dear boys, do?'

Francis, with slight sidelong glances at Pelham, explained the solemnity of their mission to Mrs Howell. As if echoing his earlier words to Richard, she shouted with laughter (in a manner, thought Richard, that was utterly foreign to Julia) and cried, 'Can you not choose a bride without your brother, my dear boy? Must you have his approval for that?'

Stiffly, and with some discomfiture, Richard exlained that the choice was made, he merely wished to display his beloved's charms to his own brother. Pelham's face lighted up.

'So, Richard, you are to put her through her paces for Francis, and he will be permitted to run a knowing hand down her fetlocks and count her teeth.'

Despite their mother's mock frowns a roar of approval rose from the Howell brothers. Richard, unutterably upset at the analogy with horseflesh being drawn twice in two days, did not join in. Pelham was instantly contrite.

'My dear fellow, I mean no harm. I am a clumsy creature to be sure and I beg your pardon. To show you have forgiven me, will you let me come and kneel at the shrine with you both? I swear to behave with utter propriety, I do indeed.'

'That,' said Richard, 'was the purpose of our coming to you.'

'Splendid! Give me one quarter of an hour and I shall be ready.'

Pelham bent briefly towards Francis long enough to say 'What sport!' and was gone, thudding up the stairs and shouting for assistance.

Mrs Howell looked at Richard's troubled countenance and said to Francis, 'I shall be severely displeased if you do not control Pelham. I only permit him to go on the strictest understanding that you discipline him soundly. He has more spirits than he knows what to do with. I rely upon you, Francis.'

Francis bowed and smiled and went to urge his friend to hurry. It seemed that Richard's patience had been tested long enough. It was, however, to be tried still further for Pelham insisted on bringing his horse, and by the time mount and rider were noisily assembled before the house, Richard was miserably convinced that they would be late. In a medley of shouts and cheers of encouragement the gig moved off, Pelham riding docilely behind as a testimony to how well he meant to conduct himself.

More downs, more uplands, more great skies as they drove steadily south through Kingsclere and Overton, Steventon and Axford. South of Alton the landscape became gentler and prettier, and by the time they were spanking up the drive to Marchants, Richard could contain himself no longer.

'Is it not quite faultless pasturage?'

Francis looked about him at the moist green fields, the May blossom, the cropping cattle, and nodded. They topped a rise in the drive and Marchants lay before them, rectangular and handsome, afloat on impeccable lawns. There was evidence of prosperity and meticulous housekeeping. Mrs Lambert would have been gratified to know that Francis thought to himself that he had never seen door furniture blaze so briliantly as did the knocker and handles upon the twin leaves at Marchants.

The gig was led away with copious instructions from Richard, the doors opened and the brothers and Pelham were taken across the hall to the parlour. Chatter died away as the door opened and Mrs Lambert came forward.

'My dear Mr Beaumont, how charmed we are. Such a pleasure. So good of you to travel so far again so soon. And to bring your brother. Mr Francis Beaumont, how do you do? You do us great honour coming like this. And your friend – any friend of yours, Mr Beaumont, you know! How do you do, Mr Howell?'

Francis bowed. A tall, handsome girl with lovely indolent eyes was moving slowly towards him.

'Julia, may I present my brother, Francis.'

He bowed again. There was a great deal of sunlight in the room and it was difficult to see her clearly. She was saying calmly, 'How strange! You are not in the least alike.'

She smiled her slow, wide smile. Francis bowed again. It was clearly not going to be difficult to like her.

'Richard was born under a more generous planet, Miss Lambert.'

'Ah!' she said. 'Then you have had to make your advantages for yourself.'

'I have indeed, Miss Lambert, and my only regret is that a planet might have chosen much better for me.'

Mrs Lambert, ringing for servants, patting cushions and altering the positions of certain sweet peas in the bowls around the room, stopped long enough to say apparently to the shadows by the window, 'Come forward, Eliza dear, come and introduce yourself.'

31

Eliza, quite taken aback by Francis' appearance being so utterly different from his brother's, came from her corner slowly, trying to readjust her prejudices as she came. In the presence of Francis, she did not seem to have enough courage to glance with her usual bold contempt at Richard. She had not spoken a word yet, and Francis already looked at her as if he disapproved of her a good deal. In the confusion of the moment, it did not occur to her that this was entirely natural and also her own fault. Mrs Lambert propelled her forward, hissing instructions in the most audible of asides.

'Good day, Mr Beaumont,' Eliza said.

Richard bowed slightly and smiled even more slightly, but if his smile was a meagre thing, the good-looking, brown-haired man behind him was beaming broadly. He held out his hand and said helpfully:

'I am not a Beaumont. My name is Pelham Howell.'

Eliza nodded gratefully, but aware of that other presence very near, exuding some sensation that made her most uncomfortable, could not speak. Her aunt put a hand upon her sleeve.

'Mr Francis Beaumont, may I present my niece, Miss Stanhope.'

To her horror, Eliza felt herself growing hot. Tears of mortification pricked at her eyelids. Why should she be so afflicted in front of a perfect stranger, and anyway, why should she care about the opinion of any stupid Beaumont? She raised, with difficulty, a scarlet and defiant face and opened her mouth to speak. No word came.

Unsmiling, but with great friendliness, Francis said, 'I am delighted to meet you, Miss Stanhope.'

3

The plans for the picnic were awe-inspiring. Francis said to Richard that his future mother-in-law should have been a general. Two days were spent making sufficient preparations to feed and amuse at least fifty people instead of a mere six, and then, upon the actual day appointed for the expedition, the party woke to leaden skies and running gutters.

Mrs Lambert was in despair. Her lamentations resounded throughout the house. Despite the weather, Mr Lambert had no difficulty in persuading Francis and Pelham to ride out with him, and they slipped away together before their plan could add to the loudly voiced miseries of Mrs Lambert. Julia took Richard to the library, placed him in a wing chair, and proceeded to draw him, not being in the least offended when he fell gently asleep. And Eliza climbed the stairs to her room, pushed a chair against the door handle, and sat wretchedly upon her bed.

Last evening, Francis Beaumont had turned to her after cards and said, 'I hope you will ride with us to the picnic tomorrow. I hear much of your reputation as a horsewoman.'

Today he had apparently quite forgotten that remark and had gone out with her uncle without considering her for a moment. She had longed to ride with him, if only to show him that there was something she could do with skill and quiet competence. The rest of the last two days had been an unmitigated chapter of disaster for her, and the strange mortification she had felt when he first arrived had not so much abated as increased. She could not seem to feel at ease, and above all she longed to. She was used to amusing the family, indeed they looked to her for it, but she somehow had not dared to in front of Francis. She had even stammered once or twice in replying to him, and what was worse, appeared to say the opposite of what she wished to say.

He had leaned forward at dinner the first night and said, 'After three years of male dining, I cannot tell you what pleasure it is to see faces of the gentler sex across the table. A truly miraculous contrast to the company of soldiers,' and Eliza, meaning to say that she could not imagine female company preferable to what she imagined the dash and brilliance of military conversation, replied rudely:

'I cannot think why.'

She had blushed again, of course, after this. She seemed to be blushing continually these difficult days, and if it had not been for the charming and spirited kindness of Pelham Howell, she did not know how she should have got through them. He was so easy and so happily comfortable to be with that he only seemed to throw into miserable contrast the gawky discomfort she felt in the presence of Francis Beaumont.

That is why she had felt so sure that if only they could ride together, this terrible constraint would ease, this clutch at her throat loosen. She tugged at a lock of hair that had slipped to her neck, and tried a few of her time-worn arguments to herself.

'What difference does it make to me what he, I mean, what any Beaumont, thinks of me?'

'It does not signify, they will go home in a day or so.'

'I have done nothing wrong, why should I feel so ashamed?'

She sighed. It was of little use. For some reason which as yet she could not wholly fathom, Francis Beaumont, by his mere presence in the house, made her feel childish, ashamed, clumsy and poor company. What was worse, he clearly found Julia quite the opposite. She had observed them talking together delightedly, Richard watching like the admiring spectator of a skilful game, and had pressed her lips together hard and gazed at her lap until the humiliating lump in her throat had dissolved.

She had a sensation that Julia should not laugh and whisper with Francis, and an even keener feeling that she did not like it that he appeared to like doing so. Pelham would divert her, usually.

'Come now, you look quite the maiden aunt, your face

quite black with disapproval. You will have to learn, Miss Stanhope, that soldiers are entirely irresistible to women, there isn't one in the universe who can withstand our charm, not to mention our uniforms. Come out into the garden, and I will bore you with tales of my conquests, how I left half the female population of Spain weeping their black eyes out as I rode carelessly away, and at the first sign of a yawn from you, I shall challenge you to a ferocious battle at bezique.'

Grown men like Francis, of marriageable age, had hardly entered Eliza's consciousness before. Her cousins, Julia's brothers, were playmates to her, romping like great dogs; she had never thought of them as men whom women might want as husbands. Julia's suitors, too, amiable though they might have been, were targets for mimicry rather than people to be taken seriously. It had not occurred to anyone at Marchants that Eliza's concept of humanity was shockingly narrow, and her affections limited to her own family, and only to some members of that. She had come into the household too small to walk, and had grown to be something of a court jester, a fixture like the long-case clock in the hall. Apart from her bouts of temper, no one had even corrected her much until Richard Beaumont had come along and roused such passionate feelings in her opinionated bosom. No one observed she was jealous of Richard for taking away the companion of a lifetime, any more than they saw that Francis' good opinion was something she longed for ardently because she was suffering the pangs of first love. She was only aware of an enormous frustration, and the household in general of her mood, which quivered on the edges of rage and the borders of tears.

If only he had remembered the suggestion to ride! She was sure that if she could *do* something, take some action, she could shake off this black misery. Her hair was now down in tendrils all over her shoulders she had fidgeted with it so, her slippers were off, her muslin crumpled. Her hair, of course was the trouble, she thought, clutching at straws, even if it wasn't truly red, red hair of any kind was an affliction to its owner. Nobody with red hair was ever even-tempered, everybody knew that. Julia was always saying it. So was her uncle. How easy it must be to be fair! It clearly was easy to be brown, one only had to think of Julia. She pulled the remaining tidy locks to her shoulders, and began to brush it fiercely, counting a hundred strokes until her scalp was tingling.

She could not sit still any longer. She tied a ribbon hastily round her hair and went quickly down the back staircase they had always used as children. Raised voices could still be heard from the kitchen quarters, no doubt Mrs Lambert still mourning over her hampers. There was a cloak hanging on the wall by the cellar door, and as it was already wet, Eliza felt no compunction in making it even wetter. She threw it over her dishevelled head and sped through the conservatory to the garden. Keeping close to the house, she managed to edge around the lawn to the entrance of the ilex walk, and then the thick leaves thankfully hid her.

She ran. The mossy grass was spongy under her slippered feet, but the ilex held most of the rain off her head. The hem of her dress began to slap wetly against her ankles, but her face was cooling in the damp air, and her feelings with it. The walk ended in a semicircle of rough flagstones, a bench from which to admire the prospect, and a flight of steps down into the ha-ha. Eliza stopped running in the last stretch of shelter and looked about her. It was not in her nature to retrace her steps ever, so, despite her drenched feet and ankles, she did not consider going back to the house the way she had come. Instead, she heaved the cloak, which luckily seemed a very large one, further forward over her head, wrapped it as tightly as she could and descended the steps into the ha-ha. There were several advantages to this plan of action, the first being that no one, unless looking out from the second storey of the house, could see into the bottom of the ha-ha, and as only the servants dwelt in the curious wedge-shaped rooms up there, she had little to worry about. The second was that at the far end of the ha-ha, she could scramble out screened by the beech hedge and get to the stableyard behind it. A visit to the horses, Eliza thought, would be comforting. She began to creep along the ha-ha, deriving growing pleasure from her elaborate game. If she was discovered she would be scolded for getting wet and no more, but her enormous stealth was no amusement unless she could pretend the risks were much greater. A few cattle, pressed against the fence in the ha-ha, lowed gloomily at her.

She reached out a hand from her cocoon and patted their broad wet noses.

At this end of the ha-ha there were no steps. It was blocked, like its sides, by a grassy wall. By digging her toes into the bank and thus being able to reach the stout trunks of the beech hedge, Eliza managed to haul herself out, slipping only once, which left a sticky clod of mud adhering to the cloak. Once up she gained the stableyard easily and found the grooms whistling and rubbing down horses with twists of straw. Her uncle must be back, there was his hunter, and the grey mare whom he always lent to visitors. Eliza went from stall to stall, nodding and smiling to the grooms who were so used to her presence they hardly noticed her. At the end of the row, she went out into the yard again, and then into the dusky darkness of a loose box where Julia's pretty chestnut was recovering from a strained tendon. It was a friendly little thing. Eliza climbed into the manger at its head so that she could talk to it properly while it ate the hay from round her, making no objection to having its sustenance sat upon.

There were voices in the yard outside. A servant's voice said:

'I'll see if you left it in the stall, sir.'

Boots tramped off on the cobbles. Other boots followed them and turned back. Eliza, her face pressed against the chestnut's cheek, the hay tickling maddeningly in her nostrils, felt a sneeze inexorably mounting. In anguish she rubbed the bridge of her nose, held her breath and shook her head violently. It was of no use. She sneezed. The boots came nearer with quick decisiveness, the door was opened to admit the dim daylight, and a man looked in. There was a small sound of amusement, then he leant back out of the doorway and shouted:

'Don't worry, Tom, I've found my cloak.'

Then he put his head back into the loose box and added as if to himself, 'And, what is more, it is inhabited.'

Eliza gazed miserably at Francis Beaumont.

'I – I'm very sorry,' she said.

He came forward and peered at her, crouched damply in the manger.

'Sorry? What about?'

37

Eliza's teeth began to chatter.

'T-taking your cloak.'

'You were very quick, I will say. I had hung it up but five minutes for Tom to take away and brush.' He looked at her muddiness and extreme wetness.

'Where have you been, Miss Stanhope?'

'Oh, just out. . . .'

'Evidently.'

'I needed to be – to be outside. I wanted something to do.'

'Why did you not ride with us, then? Weather is clearly not a deterrent to you.'

'I thought –' Eliza stopped. To cry at this point, and add tears to the dirt and damp and the bedraggled hair, would be the final humiliation.

'You thought,' said Francis helpfully, 'that because I had not repeated my hope of last evening, it was not still my hope. What a silly girl you are, Miss Stanhope,' he added gently, 'not daring to speak up, running about in the rain, climbing about in the stables. Come, we must dry you.'

Eliza sniffed.

'I cannot go back like this. Aunt –'

'Aunt will know nothing of it. You can remain shrouded in my cloak, and if we meet anyone, you shall say you have been showing me the stables. I am sure there is some way you can slip to your room.'

He was like a kindly schoolmaster. Eliza sniffed again, and was lifted down, straightened out and offered an arm.

'Come,' he said.

She dared a very brief glance at his face. He was smiling, but she could not tell if he were laughing at her.

'I love to ride,' she said, more vehemently than she had meant to.

'So do I. But I cannot believe you sincerely love getting soaked to the skin. Why, Miss Stanhope, do you run in the rain and crouch in mangers when other girls are prudently in-doors, pressing wild flowers and practising their instruments?'

'Aunt says I am wild and rude and rough. I expect that is the answer.'

'Does your character delineation distress you?'

Eliza reddened. 'Yes,' she said and for the first time that answer was true.

When they reached the house, rich smells from the kitchen told them that Mrs Lambert had, in her own way, tried to compensate fully for the failed expedition. Eliza paused by the small staircase.

'I can go this way.'

Francis bowed slightly and lifted his cloak from her shoulders. She ran lightly up, and he stood watching, rather hoping she would turn. She did not. She remembered at the top that she had not thanked him for his sympathy, but when she looked down, he was gone.

English summers being what they are, it was possible to salvage the picnic plan on the following day. It was hardly a morning of cloudless skies and hazy distances, but the air was warm and still and the sun, if not brilliant, did at least shine intermittently. Selborne had been fixed upon as the spot which would allow the young people, cried Mrs Lambert, the chance of exercise in walking up the beech hangers.

'In that case,' said Julia, smoothing the folds of her parasol, 'you must count me as an old person. I cannot endure to walk uphill. Indeed some days, I feel I cannot endure to walk at all.'

'When we are married, my Julia, I shall ensure you do not have to walk a step.'

'You will need a sedan chair in the house, then,' Eliza cried, 'which will be exceedingly awkward upon the stairs!'

Richard Beaumont, always vulnerable to the possibility of Eliza's malice, turned a severe gaze upon her. To his amazement she coloured slightly and said hastily, 'Oh, Mr Beaumont, I meant no mockery. Or if I did I only meant to mock Julia.'

'To which mockery, Eliza, I am quite indifferent. I should relish a chair to carry me about the house. Think of the joy of never having to cross the drawing room again.'

They set off at last, a cold collation of gargantuan proportions accompanying them in hampers. Eliza, to the surprise of the entire party, elected at the last moment to ride with her aunt and cousin in the landau. Mrs Lambert, settled across the faded cushions, thus preventing their diminished glory from being visible to the discerning eye of any Beaumont, regarded the arrangements with something near complete gratification. She gazed about her complacently, noting how well the gentlemen looked on horseback, although perhaps Mr Beaumont showed slight signs of apprehension; how becoming to Julia was that particular shade of lilac, and how pleasing it was to see Eliza at last in that yellow muslin which had cost at least nine shillings a yard.

Ten miles through newly leafed lanes, and Selborne was reached. It was admired, exclaimed over, the yew tree in the churchyard remarked upon, the village urchins provided with pennies, and a spot settled upon where the splendid curve of beech-clad hills might be properly admired.

'If only all bivouacs,' Francis Beaumont said, his wine glass upraised, 'were as glorious as this, we English should be the scourge of the earth.'

'Are we not, in any case?' Eliza demanded.

'Quite right, Miss Stanhope! Most properly corrected. Of course we are. No other kitchen but an English kitchen could produce a pie like this!'

Mrs Lambert delightedly pressed him to have more. She was disappointed that so little was being consumed. There was, indeed, a lack of natural animation about the party as there often is after a postponement. The edge of excitement is taken off an event, anticipation can take no more stretching. Conversation was desultory, never general enough to give the gathering impetus. No remark caught fire. Dutifully they ate the early strawberries, but there seemed, after all the praise that had been lavished before, no adjectives left to award them. A lull followed their consumption, during which Mr Lambert stretched himself beneath the hedge and proclaimed his intention to sleep by firmly closing his eyes and becoming deaf to his wife's remonstrances.

'Who will walk with me?' said Francis to the remainder of the party.

'Not I,' said Pelham. 'I am so wonderfully surfeited that I intend to follow the splendid example of my host. Unless, of course,' he added, turning with a smile to Eliza, 'you would consent to walk with me?'

Encouraged by his pleasantness, Eliza laughed and shook her head and said the responsibility of taking his over-burdened frame up the beech hanger was too much for her to share. Suppose he fell, burdened by his intake as a medieval knight was by his armour, and she could never get him to rise again? Pelham said she was extremely wise and that he was really fit for nothing but slumber and then bowed and smiled broadly at her again, and vanished behind a clump of elms on the edge of the field.

'He will be snoring in two minutes,' Francis said with affection. 'He has the greatest capacity for profound and instant sleep of any man I have ever met. Well, now, and will the rest of you surrender to torpor, too, and leave me to fidget and chew grasses until you are sated?'

Julia announced her intention of sketching the church, Richard his of carrying her stool thither, and Mrs Lambert of overseeing the repacking of the hampers. Eliza looked tensely at her lap.

'Will you walk with me, Miss Stanhope?'

She assented at once, too eagerly she thought, and he helped her to her feet. She looked anxiously around to see if Pelham had observed her fickleness, but the elms quite concealed their slumbering charge.

'It will make a pleasant change, will it not,' he said *sotto voce*, 'to walk dryshod?'

'But not quite such an adventure.'

'I shall accept that as a challenge.'

The path from the meadow went steeply up among the trees. Francis, pausing to say he had not realized how steep the hill was and perhaps she would like to reconsider, found that he was wasting his breath, for she was moving quickly and easily up the slope beside him. They continued in silence until they reached the summit where a view worth climbing for awaited them. Francis found a fallen beech and motioned Eliza to sit upon its silvery trunk.

'I am glad to have a chance to speak to you, Miss Stanhope, for there is something which presses rather heavily on my mind.'

Eliza, instantly afraid that he wished to speak of Julia, did not reply. After a pause he went on.

'I hope you will not be offended if I speak to you very freely for someone who has known you but a few days. I hope you will regard it as something that an elder brother might say to you.'

Eliza hoped her face showed none of the disappointment that sank like lead into her heart.

'Please go on.'

'I am disturbed by your profound dislike of my brother. That is the essence of it. I would like to know if there is some real reason why you do not wish him to marry Miss Lambert, or is it just that you have no sympathy with him.'

It was most unjust of him, most unfair. He had framed a question to which it was quite impossible to reply. Of course she had no real reason, but how could she tell the man's brother that she bore an instinctive dislike to Richard Beaumont? It was especially unfair because she had only that very morning resolved to subdue her feelings and had managed to give Richard the outlines of an apology for some remark. She looked up with some indignation.

'It is not right you should question me thus.'

'It is perfectly right,' he said calmly, 'I am as anxious for my brother's happiness as you are for your cousin's. If you know in truth that she does not care for him at all, and will make him wretched, I wish to know. As a man in love, Richard is not as aware as other men, and I must be his keeper.'

Eliza cried sharply, 'What are you trying to say?'

'Simply that I suspect a plot. I fear that you and Miss Lambert have set a trap for my brother. You schemed to catch him and you have, but you, Miss Stanhope, cannot keep your malicious delight in the success of your plan from showing.'

Eliza sprang to her feet. She was shouting.

'How dare you suggest such a thing? How dare you give us such characters? There is not a word of truth in what you say, but if you want the truth I will tell you. Julia chose to marry Mr Beaumont, and I, only I, did not think him good enough. And I still do not! I have begged and begged Julia not to marry him, she will be frantic with him! But a plan to trap him! Trap him, of all men! Who would *want* to trap your brother?'

Francis was standing before her, white with fury.

'Richard told me you were an impossible chit. He was entirely right –'

In a wild gesture, Eliza raised her right arm, and it caught Francis a glancing blow on the cheek. She had not meant to hit him, nor had she meant to lose her temper. But both were done now, and in a frenzy of despair, she stumbled away from him down the hill, the resolutions of the morning in pieces, the lovely harmony of yesterday destroyed.

The drive home was awkward at the very least. It was all too evident from their faces, returning to the picnic a hundred yards apart, that some altercation had happened on the hillside. Julia, it is true, could not quite be bothered to inquire, and Richard was incurious as long as no difficulty touched his beloved. Mr Lambert managed to subdue the paragraphs of queries rising all too visibly to his wife's lips, and Pelham summoned all the good nature he could muster and flung himself into the task of diverting Mrs Lambert from her niece.

Later, jogging beside Francis through the lanes, he said quietly, 'What's up?'

'That child,' Francis said with fury, 'is everything Richard said she was. Immature, spoilt, ill-judged and wholly careless of others' feelings.'

Pelham edged his horse to ride shoulder to shoulder with Francis.

'Nonsense. I think her delightful. I cannot remember when I last met a girl of such frank and unaffected charm and such delightful spirits.'

'Her frankness,' Francis said, 'led her on that hillside to claim that Richard, my brother Richard, is not good enough for her cousin.'

Pelham let out a shout of laughter, then clapped his hand to his mouth, eyeing the bulk of Richard trotting ahead of them.

'It is no earthly use, my dear Francis, to get on your high horse about that. You know full well that a good part of you agrees with her. Secondly, I do not believe she would state herself so baldly and, thirdly, I admire a girl with affections she is prepared to champion.'

Francis tried to recall Eliza's exact words to him among the beech trees. She had certainly said that Richard was unworthy of Julia, but how had she come to say such a thing? Had he by any chance driven her to expose her innermost feelings on the matter? No, indeed not, he had merely said that he would like to see her able to behave more civilly than she did towards Richard. And was that not

43

an insufferably pompous attitude for a man of merely thirty to take to any girl? Certainly not, she had led an impossibly cloistered life; indeed it was almost a duty to let her profit by his ten years' advantage of her. He remembered suddenly.

'She struck me!'

Pelham's reaction was to howl with laughter, bent forward helplessly on his horse's neck, oblivious to Richard craning anxiously round to see if he were indisposed. He recovered after some minutes to turn his delighted face upon Francis and say 'Below the belt?' before doubling up again with mirth. Francis, initially outraged, considered riding forward to join his brother but then allowed his sense of ludicrousness to prevail over his injured dignity.

'It hurt,' he explained to Pelham.

'Good girl,' said Pelham approvingly and challenged Francis to a race along the verge of the lane to catch up with the carriage. Glancing sideways, he saw that Francis' expression of outrage had gone, but that he looked undoubtedly perplexed.

Eliza went straight to her room upon arrival at Marchants, and no amount of beseechings through the keyhole could bring her out, or even draw a syllable from her.

Unease sat heavily upon the evening downstairs, with Francis suffering alternate pangs of guilt and anger, Mrs Lambert enduring far worse gnawings of curiosity, and Pelham and Mr Lambert frankly missing Eliza's enlivening presence. For her part she had cast herself fully dressed upon her bed and cried and cried until she was exhausted.

Late in the evening a heavier tread than the slippered feet of Julia or her aunt approached the door and paused. Eliza, tense upon her damp pillow, waited, hardly breathing. After several minutes, Francis said, 'Miss Stanhope, may I speak with you?'

His voice sounded strained and unhappy. She could not reply.

'Please,' he said.

She seemed frozen to her bed. She lay in an agony of she knew not what, until the tread of boots went slowly away down the staircase. She slept feverishly and heavily that night, and when she came down in the morning, Francis Beaumont had gone.

44

4

July the tenth was fixed upon as the wedding day. Mrs Lambert was thrown into an ecstasy of arrangements. The preliminary list of guests yielded two hundred names, which did not include Sir Gerard's suggestions as he appeared not to wish to offer any, and which threw her into agonies since the church at Marchants would sit no more than a hundred and twenty. The silk for Julia's dress, purchased after interminable consultation, proved to have a minute flaw in it and must thus be returned, and there was no doubt whatsoever that the best of the roses would be over by the second week in July. Messages and packets, boxes and bales came and went in an increasing procession, and Julia smiled upon it all as it none of it concerned her in the least.

Through the bustle moved a most unhappy Eliza. The first anguish had abated, but not the shock of losing her temper so utterly nor the bitter disappointment of being misunderstood by someone whose good opinion she craved above all else. She tried thinking resentfully of his behaviour, which was initially some solace, but all her weary endless mental turnings always now ended in the fierce regret that the quarrel had ever taken place at all. Night after night, wrapped in one of the cashmere shawls Julia had discarded in favour of the new splendours of her trousseau, she paced up and down her little room going over and over that brief and savage exchange, blaming and excusing, now here, now there and always shuddering with misery at the memory of Francis' insult. Impossible chit, he had said. And perhaps, thought Eliza, battling with self-knowledge for the first time, she was. Or at least had been, for she was so changed now, so entirely changed. She wondered if she could ever feel older and more weary than she now did, her mind always fundamentally oppressed by the results of her temper and stupidity. He had been terrible to her though it was not all her fault, but his terribleness only showed he thought no more of her than that she was an impossible chit.

In the middle of June, Richard Beaumont arrived with a new and splendid carriage to take Julia to Quihampton for the daunting task of meeting his father. Eliza had to admit in Francis' favour that he had clearly said nothing to his brother, since Richard treated her with a new and oppressive kindliness. Julia had wanted to take Eliza with her, but in alarm Eliza had declined and Richard, in vast embarrassment, had indicated that as his father was used to his own company, strangers, especially female strangers, were not given an exactly royal welcome. He had almost thanked Eliza for remaining at Marchants. She watched them drive away one Tuesday morning, was dreadfully agitated all the time they were gone, and with fearful apprehension saw them return a week later.

The visit had been a tolerable success. Sir Gerard had failed to find fault with Julia's looks or manner and had almost admitted that she was as bearable a woman as could be found. She had sat calmly and amiably in the parlour or garden embroidering very slowly, never speaking unless spoken to and smiling often.

Richard reached a peak of adoration, and almost came to embracing his father when Sir Gerard said, 'Handsome creature. But I cannot conceive what she wants with you.'

Eliza pressed and pressed her for information about the visit, but since Julia had no notion of what she craved for, got little satisfaction. She learned the size of Quihampton and the land, but not how Francis looked; she learned the layout of the rooms, but not how Francis seemed; she learned about the number of carriages and horses, but nothing that Francis had said. Those long nights of pacing had shown Eliza one thing most clearly, and that was the state of her own heart. Once realized, she even felt a grudging sympathy for Richard Beaumont, at the same time envying him passionately for the gratification of his love. Julia might not return his devotion, but at least she did not insult and detest him.

At last, after a whole evening and morning at home, Julia said, 'Eliza! I quite forgot. I have a letter for you somewhere. What did I do with it? There, I told you all that if you travelled me about I should fall to pieces, and I have. I cannot remember where I put that letter.'

Richard found it eventually in her workbasket, and Eliza almost snatched it from his hand. She waited in the room with a poor pretence at unconcern for a few moments and then fled into the garden.

Dear Miss Stanhope,

I am sorry not to see you with Miss Lambert. I had hoped to speak with you so that we might resolve the difficulty we seem to have got into. I trust our difference caused you no distress.

Yours ever,

Francis Beaumont

Eliza was aghast. She did not think she had emotional energy left for any more tears or wretchedness, but it seemed she had. So cold, so distant a note. There was not even a word of apology or real concern, just this stiff little missive which would clear his conscience, no matter what it did to hers. She tore the paper into tiny pieces and scattered them in the rhododendrons. The last spark of hope, an emotion most difficult to kill, died and Eliza made a resolve that she would try to put it all behind her. She longed *not* to make that resolution but Francis Beaumont had left her no choice.

There were by now but three weeks to the wedding, and the ensuing busyness coupled with the fact that nobody at Marchants was particularly observant of emotion, enabled Eliza to get through the days with comparative inconspicuousness. Julia might have noticed, but her absorption in her new clothes and rooms and carriages was total. Her aunt remarked vaguely that Eliza seemed more manageable of late, but then a wild child is bound to grow up one day. Her uncle did his best to be out of the house from dawn to dusk. So Eliza passed her time fetching and carrying, folding shawls, writing letters and making enough lists to paper a mansion. While doing all this, and unless especially absorbed in calculating some figure of the total and exorbitant cost of getting married for her bewildered uncle, she thought about Francis. Of course she could not keep her resolve of not thinking about him at all, even if she could usually save herself the worst pain by not remembering the worst moments.

The night before the wedding was a calm evening, warm and lovely and silent. In some senses, Eliza felt Julia had gone already.

She went to help Julia dress, for all the neighbours of consequence were invited that night to dance or play cards according to their taste, and Mrs Lambert had insisted that it was as important for Julia to look her best among them as it was to appear radiant the following day. Julia, her maid, and the curling tongs were in disharmony before the glass.

'Let me,' Eliza said.

The maid was dismissed and Eliza set to work.

'Do you feel alarmed, Julia? I am sure I should. I should hate to be the cynosure of all eyes.'

'You do not seem', said Julia with mild malice, 'to hate it much in the hunting field.'

'That is quite different,' cried Eliza defensively. 'That is because of what I can do, not because of what I am.'

Julia did not seem to find a reply obligatory. She sat in silence for a while, gazing at her own calm and handsome face. Then she roused herself, and with a huge effort said:

'I have been meaning to congratulate you, Eliza.'

'Oh?'

'Yes. I have meant to say, oh, these three or four weeks, how much more pleasant life has become since you controlled your silly feelings towards Mr Beaumont!'

How middle-aged she sounded. Eliza thought. Quite the sort of remark Julia would have scoffed at anyone for making six months before. Did the prospect of marriage automatically turn you into a matron?

'He has remarked upon it to me,' Julia said. 'You think him unobservant, but I can assure you he notices much. It used to put him out considerably when you behaved so impossibly.'

At the sound of the last word, Eliza's eyes filled with tears

48

which she did not trouble to check as she knew Julia would never notice them.

'You must come to us,' Julia said, 'when we're in London or Bath. Bath might bring you out appreciably. You must regard it,' she added with the warmest touch of her old affection that she had shown for weeks, 'as your second home.'

Then she brushed Eliza's cheek with hers, took a last satisfactory look in the glass, and went smoothly from the room. Eliza, with a sensation that not a soul in the world, except perhaps her uncle, cared in the very least whether she lived or died, followed at a distance. Her muslin looked, she thought, extremely girlish behind the elegance of Julia's newly donned silk. And she had become too thin of late, she knew that. Absurd to care, of course, about either muslin or thinness, and she never used to give a fig for either, but now everything was different and what used to be of great significance was not so any longer, and vice versa. She looked down over the banister at the familiar gathering below and wondered sadly if those were the people she would see year in, year out until she wore a cap and silk mittens like old Miss Cantripp and was pointed out as an unparalleled example of old maidenhood.

At the foot of the stairs, her uncle met her.

'Do your best, my dear. I know you don't care for this sort of thing any more than I do myself. Just hold on to the fact that by this time tomorrow the house will be ours again.'

'Of course, Uncle.'

'We shall have some splendid times this summer, you and I. We shall ride ourselves into extinction, you've hardly been aboard a horse these four weeks, have you? No wonder you're looking peaky. Now, off you go and make sure no young man monopolizes Julia.'

She gave him a smile of absolute gratitude and affection and watched him go off, all resolution and no inclination, to a phalanx of dowagers. She was immediately captured by John Knight-Knox. He was a handsome, healthy, insensitive Englishman, who had known both Eliza and Julia since girlhood, and was one of a steady band who had pursued Julia amorously for the last two years.

'All alone, Miss Stanhope? My dear Eliza, this won't do. Think what an advantageous position Julia's marrying puts you in! That should stop you moping!'

'Emotions are not that logical, Mr Knight-Knox. Julia and I are not interchangeable in people's affections.'

'Mr Knight-Knox, indeed! Pooh, Eliza, you need taking in hand! Come now, you cannot be so cast down over Julia's going that you can scarcely be civil to an old friend?'

'I am sorry, John, I did not mean to be cross. I think I am probably tired. You cannot imagine the campaign that has been organized for this wedding. I think even the most veteran soldier would be tired.'

John Knight-Knox laughed heartily at this and led her away to dance. His place was quickly taken by several others, all of them behaving with a gallantry Eliza had not known they possessed. She felt a good deal better as a result, she had to admit, and when the dreadful moment came, as she knew it must, of the Beaumonts' arrival, she had no inclination to faint at all. This slightly disappointed her. She saw what must be Sir Gerard, tall and handsome and unsmiling, led quickly away by her uncle to the card room. She saw Richard go eagerly, beaming, through the crowd to Julia and Mrs Lambert. Then she made herself see Francis. He looked as big and imperturbable as if nothing out of the ordinary had happened in Hampshire before. He stood in the doorway easily, casting his eyes slowly around the room, inevitably caught her anxious glance, bowed and let his gaze travel on. Then he seemed to recognize a face and went forward into the crowd. It was Henry Leslie he knew, Eliza thought, quite shaken by the fact that their being in the same room again passed off so uneventfully. How did he know Henry Leslie?

Then a voice said, 'Are you not dancing, Miss Stanhope?' and she turned to find Pelham Howell standing at her elbow.

It had not been difficult for Pelham to obtain an invitation to the wedding and its attendant festivities. Mrs Lambert had been, like most matrons before her, captivated by him, and had needed no urging to include him on the list of guests, even to the extent of excluding some small local squire in his place since the church was so cramped. Pelham had played up to her admirably, had sought her out the moment he arrived with the Beaumonts, told her that it was difficult to distinguish which of the Lambert ladies was to be the bride, and had then gone instantly in search of Eliza. He saw her standing alone on the edge of the dancers searching the room for someone, so oblivious of her surroundings that she was on tiptoe and craning her neck this way and that in hopes of her quarry. He did not much doubt whom she sought and resolved to surprise her with his presence.

She jumped when he touched her as he spoke and then coloured, and Pelham felt a surge of gratification.

'Mr – Captain Howell!'

Her tone and her blush were all he had hoped for.

'I am going to capture you, Miss Stanhope, before any more Hampshire farmers have the chance, and I warn you that I am most unlikely to release you.'

There was no doubt, Eliza thought, that it was a delight to be found by him. Her spirits lifted measurably at the sight of his familiar, good-looking face and at the air of impending gaiety and adventure he carried about with him.

'I hope it will be a comfortable captivity.'

'Hardly. It promises to be extremely energetic. The comfort depends entirely upon the manner in which you treat the gaoler.'

He led her on to the floor and bowed with idiotic flourishes, and he made her dance with such speed and flamboyance that she forgot about Francis Beaumont for at least fifteen minutes together. Between dances, Pelham escorted her with absolute determination.

'Nobody here is capable of looking after you like Captain Howell, ma'am. Will you have an ice, or a seat in a dim corner, or a walk on the terrace, or another dance, or a game of cards? The only proviso to your choice is that, whatever you choose, your act will be heavily accompanied by me.'

It was impossible not to feel better. Laughing rather than dancing made Eliza feel she would like to rest for a moment. Not much of a moment of course, just enough to recover her breath and relieve her aching ribs. On the way to an obscure sofa, chosen by Pelham, she saw Francis again, and he paused, Fanny Leslie on his arm to say:

'I hope I find you quite well, Miss Stanhope?'

But he said it with no more than common concern. The anticlimax of his coming, Eliza thought, was almost harder to bear than the indifference of his manner.

Pelham instantly observed a shadow fall across her countenance. He took her elbow in his warm and confident hand.

'What troubles you?'

His face wore an expression of genuine concern, and the sight of it made Eliza fight back the rising lump of misery in her throat and say, unsteadily:

'I think I just need some air. In any case if we do not go out we shall be squandering the scent of the roses whose durability has preoccupied aunt these last three weeks.'

It was indeed easier in the dark. They leant side by side on the stone balustrade of the terrace, and Pelham was charming and funny and attentive. Gradually the small, hot ball in Eliza's chest began to disperse itself. After some moments of solitude out there, footsteps came out of the house, hesitated then came forward with sudden resolve.

'Don't look round,' Pelham said.

'Ah,' said a voice, 'just whom I was seeking. Not you, Pelham, for once, you would not serve my present purpose in the least. I am come to ask if Miss Stanhope would –'

'No, Francis,' said Pelham, his hand on Eliza's wrist in the darkness, 'Miss Stanhope would not. Miss Stanhope is being admirably entertained by me and has no wish whatsoever to desert my company for yours.'

Eliza laughing and struggling to find ways of demonstrating to Francis that she was overjoyed to see him come without conveying any hurt to Pelham, managed to say nothing coherent before Francis said, with a little edge to his voice:

'It is most unlike Miss Stanhope not to express her opinions for herself with extreme vehemence. You must have cast a spell indeed, Pelham, to make her so submissive. All the same, I will endeavour to attract her attention for a moment only. Miss Stanhope, will you dance with me?'

Intent upon refuting the first half of Francis' remarks before she accepted the second, Eliza opened her mouth and said with vigour, 'No indeed –' and then stopped in sudden confusion.

There was a tiny, highly charged pause, in which Eliza's gasp quite drowned a sharp intake of breath from Francis. Almost simultaneously Pelham gave a shout of delight.

'There's your answer, my dear Francis, given with the lady's adorable frankness. Now go your way and leave me to the delightful task of pursuing mine.'

Eliza thought she had never heard feet sound so furious as Francis' did, striding back to the house. In a daze of misery and self-reproach, she heard Pelham say, 'Now you have no excuse whatsoever for not dancing with me again,' and allowed herself to be led back towards the house in the wake of that enraged tread.

It was, perhaps blessedly, the last dance. The fiddlers in the corner were sawing away with the last surge of energy shown by men who know release is near. Eliza, craning her neck again among the dancers, saw Francis talking to Julia and instantly wished she had not looked. She saw her uncle wave encouragingly to her, and her aunt smile at her with true fondness, and every time she was turned by Pelham she observed, out of the tail of her eye, Julia's pale silk and Francis' dark-clad figure still very close on the edge of the floor. As the dance ended, Pelham spun her like a top so that the room flew past her in a kaleidoscope of all colours and no shapes, and brought her to a giddy halt, her hands in his against his chest. They were both panting, Eliza's eyes were shining, and her hair had escaped completely from any discipline earlier imposed on it. Keeping his eyes upon her as long as possible, Pelham slowly bent his head and kissed each of the hands he held.

'I shall look forward, Eliza, to seeing a great deal more of you in the future.'

For some reason, her eyes smarted with tears, and then she told herself that perhaps men like Pelham never mean gallantry to be taken seriously, and so she swept him a profound curtsey and pointed out that he had only to wait a few hours until their next meeting in the morning.

'That,' he said, 'will be a deal too long.'

Then he offered her his arm and looking flatteringly down upon her rumpled head all the way, led her to her aunt.

'Captain Howell! My dear Captain Howell! I have seen

nothing of you all the evening, positively nothing! Pray, tell me, you have been well amused?'

Pelham bent over her hand.

'Madam, I was never so well amused in my life before.'

Then he straightened, bowed, and with a last glance at Eliza, left the room.

Well, Eliza thought, wearily climbing the stairs behind her aunt and cousin, what did it matter really. As another old Miss Cantripp or Mrs Knight-Knox, or even at best Mrs Howell, the future looked equally unsatisfactory either way. Of course, she thought with irritation, it would be wonderfully enlivened by visits to Bath to be 'brought on'. Oh, bother Julia, bother Richard Beaumont, and a thousand times bother his brother. She put her head down gratefully on her pillow and slept instantly.

She had to be woken on the wedding morning. Her aunt was already at fever pitch despite the fact that brilliant sunshine had removed half the matters she had predicted would send her white with worry. At twelve o'clock Julia was arrayed in white silk, with Eliza's assistance. At half past twelve Mrs Lambert was arrayed in lilac silk with Eliza's assistance. At one o'clock Eliza, with no assistance, dressed herself in white silk gauze, curled her own hair and went down the staircase with Julia, holding up the snowy folds of her cousin's dress out of the way of any dust that might have dared to intrude since the last cleaning that very morning.

Into carriages they climbed and to the church they went.

It was a truly impressive cavalcade, and Julia very much the star of it all, entirely beautiful and composed, with pearls and diamonds in her dark hair and never a tremor of lip or hand. Eliza sat opposite her in awe, and noticed that her own hands were shaking and her own inside felt hollow and insecure, and wondered how Julia could take so momentous a step with so little outward reaction. Was it, Eliza wondered, more or less momentous to marry a man one did not love? It was, in Eliza's view, almost wicked to do so, but was it to a greater or lesser degree awe-inspiring? She considered, helplessly blushing as she did so, how she would feel if it was her wedding morning, and she was about to marry Francis, and decided that it would be unendurably exciting but that it would not daunt her because she loved him. But Julia, patently not loving Richard, did not look at all daunted. Eliza was dismayed to think that someone she loved so much could put possessions on the plane where other people hoped to find love.

There was an enormous crowd outside the church. The whole village had gathered, and from the look of the crowd, neighbouring villages, too. Julia dismounted from the carriage with perfect elegance and gracefully acknowledged the cheers and flung posies. Eliza stumbled in her wake, nearly fell, was rescued by a footman, and received a cheer from the villagers. Julia glanced backwards with a tiny frown of annoyance then moved forwards smoothly to take her father's arm. The footman bent quickly to pick up Julia's train and thus avoid further mishaps, and put it competently into Eliza's hands. The sound of the organ rose, and the little procession moved between packed pews up the short aisle to the altar.

Thus, on July the tenth, 1814, Julia Lambert promised to love, cherish and obey Richard Beaumont in the presence of their families and friends at the Church of St Andrew, Marchants, Hampshire. Captain Francis Beaumont was best man, the bride's mother wept copiously out of sheer delight, and the groom's father expressed neither approval nor disapproval of the union. As bridesmaid, Eliza stood in the aisle only feet from the best man's impervious back and was thankful when the ceremony was over.

She could not decide whether she minded more that Julia was marrying at all or whether it was that she herself was not marrying Francis Beaumont. Her uncle, glancing sideways at her from his pew as she stood behind Julia in the aisle, thought how very young and lonely she looked, how very unlike his usually irrepressible niece, and how very carefully he would look after her when all this wearing and expensive nonsense was over. He loved and admired his suave daughter, but she did not touch a spring of protectiveness within him as his niece did. The bridal pair, blessed and united, turned to go down the aisle, and Mr Lambert saw Francis Beaumont move with the kindest of smiles to offer Eliza his arm and then saw his sudden perplexity and annoyance as Eliza, head bent as she concentrated on some inner wrangle with herself, ignored him completely and followed her cousin out into the sunlight. Mr Lambert stepped out into the aisle towards Francis who was gazing in some resentment at Eliza's retreating back.

'She never saw you, my dear boy. Don't take it to heart. She is very distressed at losing Julia's companionship, you know, it is taking up all her thoughts.'

Francis said with indignation, 'She did see me, sir, she could not have done otherwise. I was but a few feet from her. I fear she dislikes all Beaumonts most acutely, and has transferred her special disdain from my brother to myself.'

'I think not –' Mr Lambert began earnestly, but a press of people and his wife's urgings drew him away from Francis out of the church.

Outside the church, Eliza realized that she should have allowed Francis to escort her down the aisle. Her fantasies of him as bridegroom rather than best man had been so seductive that it had quite driven etiquette from her mind. She swallowed hard and wretchedly, and looked about desperately for him to apologize to. There he was, coming out of church, nearly a head taller than most of the other men, and wearing so stormy an expression that her heart failed within her. Think how scornful he would be if she were to go to him now. Even her dauntless spirit failed. Anyhow, she thought, squaring her shoulders resolutely, it was a tiny error, a trivial mistake, and if he minded about such a petty thing he was the lesser man for it, indeed he was.

She climbed into the carriage with her uncle and aunt and jogged home to Marchants, her aunt in prattling satisfaction with Julia and her new son-in-law, her uncle watching her benevolently. Pelham was ahead of them to hand Mrs Lambert down.

'Promise me, madam, that you will not marry off the second delightful young female inmate of this hospitable house without consulting me.'

'Oh, Captain Howell, sir, you are quite shocking! Did you not hear him Eliza? Quite shocking, is he not? Now, Captain Howell, take Eliza and find her refreshment, she looks utterly done up. Of course,' she added *sotto voce* to Pelham, 'she does dote on Julia, you know!'

Pelham nodded, and took Eliza's arm within his own. Mr

Lambert gave them a nod of satisfaction and braced himself for the second tidal wave of society within twenty-four hours of his customarily secluded life.

'Are you fatigued?' Pelham asked Eliza.

'A little, but more in the emotions than the body. I have never been to a wedding before when I wished – when – when I hoped so that the bride would be happy.'

'With all due respects to that particular bride,' Pelham said firmly, seating Eliza in a corner from whence she could not easily escape, 'she will make quite sure that she is happy. I know you love her dearly, but I should spare an ounce or so of sympathy for Richard Beaumont. I fear he is going to need it.'

Eliza's expression hovered between suspicion and incomprehension.

'Nonsense,' she declared roundly. 'He is more fortunate than he could ever have hoped to be. She is a thousand times too good for him.'

Pelham leant against the wall beside her.

'I would die with gratification to hear you defend me in such a way.'

Eliza said, entirely without coquettishness since her mind was so full of Julia, 'Then you must study to deserve my love as she has done,' and Pelham, quite overcome by the implications of this remark, had to move away, ostensibly in search of refreshment for them both, but in reality to calm himself. As he came back through the crowd, his hands full, Francis stopped him.

'And who is the second helping for?'

'None of your business, my dear Francis. We have never chased the same woman, and, please God, may we not start doing so now.'

'Tell me,' Francis cajoled. 'I always like to inspect your taste.'

'It is wild and sweet and red-headed. Now let me pass and get on with the most entertaining wooing I have ever done.'

'Wooing?' Francis asked abruptly. 'Wooing Miss Stanhope?'

'And what is that to you? I thought you had washed your superior hands of her.'

Francis said, 'I have not much choice to do otherwise,' and

57

his tone was so suddenly dejected that Pelham looked at him closely.

'Francis – Francis, could it be that your vanity is a little piqued?'

Francis opened his mouth to confess that it was more than his vanity, closed it again and nodded as nonchalantly as he could. Pelham gestured with a full glass to the long windows, against one of which Fanny Leslie was prettily silhouetted.

'Fertile ground over there, my boy!'

Francis smiled.

'Apart from a pretty face, she has not much else to offer. Never mind, I shall feed the morale on such pasture. I wish you joy of the firecracker.'

'You might say so in a less gloomy tone. But I care not. I am about to divert her from the loss – which to my mind is no loss – of her cousin Julia.'

Francis nodded, 'Richard is going to have his hands full.'

'Let it be a lesson to us. When we choose a pretty woman, may we make sure she is also good.'

'I don't believe she exists,' said Francis, and went off in pursuit of Miss Leslie who had been holding a pose for his benefit a good ten minutes or more.

Eliza had seen them talking. She accepted champagne from Pelham, but suddenly did not feel like drinking it, so placed it unobtrusively beside her on the floor.

'Is – is Mr Beaumont, I mean Captain Beaumont, enjoying himself?'

'Not much, I think, and certainly not one hundredth part as much as I am.'

'Is he not – very sociable?'

'Oh, indeed he is sociable, very much so. . . . I believe he likes mankind almost as much as it likes him, which is to say a vast amount. I do not believe he has an enemy.'

'Oh,' said Eliza in a small voice.

'He is dearer to me,' said Pelham with a wave of his glass, 'than my own brothers. If I were more like Francis Beaumont in character, I should find living with myself a very pleasant business indeed.'

Eliza sniffed.

'And he is wasted,' went on Pelham, 'on that pretty, silly creature over there. She does not know how undeservedly lucky she is to have his attention. We waded knee deep through broken hearts in Spain on Francis' account. Why are you not drinking?'

'I do not seem to feel that I want to.'

'What do you want to do?'

'At this moment,' said Eliza truthfully, 'I should like to run away somewhere.'

'May I accompany you?'

She could only laugh. Mrs Lambert came up to them, satisfied to see Eliza so happy with charming Captain Howell, and said that Julia needed her cousin's help in changing her dress.

'No doubt, my dear, she would like to have a little last word.'

Eliza went upstairs to assist the change from white to blue silk. Julia hardly appeared to notice she had come but went on serenely giving instructions to her maid for the repacking of the last few items.

'Shall you miss me?' poor Eliza said at last, twisting her cousin's glossy curls around her finger.

'Shall you not be here, then?' Julia asked in mild surprise. 'Do you mean not to be here if I should need you?'

Eliza remarked to herself that Julia might have said 'want' rather than 'need'.

'Oh, I shall be here,' she said aloud, and added lamely, 'all the time.'

'Well, then,' Julia patted her arm with a large cool hand, 'what is there to worry about? You may be sure that I shall send for you.'

Then she swept out of the room and downstairs, and shortly afterwards, leaning on her husband's arm, was taken away from Marchants for her wedding journey.

After their departure, the crowds melted away into the afternoon. Among them somehow, Sir Gerard Beaumont and his son melted, too, unnoticed by Eliza. Later still she ate a much postponed supper with her aunt and uncle, during which her aunt conducted a monologue of utter satisfaction with everything, and her uncle gave her sympathetic glances. Then she and he played cards together, she held wool for her aunt's winding, tea was brought and drunk and midnight fell at last upon the strangely silent house.

5

July the eleventh dawned warm, grey and still. Eliza woke
with a sensation of emptiness and lethargy, her head heavy
and her mood in sympathy with it. She breakfasted alone in
the parlour, her uncle already being out and her aunt
preoccupied with the packing up of all Julia's wedding
presents. She ate little and slowly, gazing unseeingly out at
the level lawn and the gentle fields, and the soft dove-
coloured sky. There was to be morning after morning of this:
still, quiet, empty days broken only by the hunting season
and occasional visits away. She felt as if a glass bell had dropped upon her suddenly, imprisoning her, shutting out all
noise and warmth and activity. Years and years had passed
in her adolescence, it seemed, when she had not had to
consider what the next day would bring since, with Julia's
company, it always seemed to bring something. Now Julia
was not only gone but estranged in spirit by her marriage.
Parties and balls would continue, she was sure, but what was
the point of going to them alone with her aunt and uncle,
and having no one to discuss them with in delighted whispers afterwards? She crumbled her toast dispiritedly, sighed
and rose.

Her aunt found her immediately.

'Eliza, dear, how fortunate to find you. The crystal and
porcelain, my dear, are not to be trusted to the servants. The
packing, you know. Would you, Eliza dear? How truly kind.
You must support me, now, must you not? You are the only
daughter I have left. I shall feel Julia's absence so keenly,
truly I shall. Now, the crystal is to be packed in the chest
by the window, and the porcelain – ah, that reminds me!

Porcelain! Did you ever see Fanny Leslie look better than yesterday? Of course, I thought Julia's wedding showed almost everyone to their advantage, though none more than my dearest Julia herself. Now the porcelain in this chest, dear Eliza, but not the tureens. They must go in this separate box. Can you imagine what I am to do with so much food not eaten? I shall be obliged to take it round the village. Perhaps, Eliza, when this small task is done, you would oblige me?'

The small task occupied Eliza alone for most of the endless morning. She wrapped and packed and cushioned and wedged and not even a servant came into the room. Her aunt could be heard calling commands, her uncle did not appear. Alone and dejected she worked on, with no distraction, until the gleaming stacks of Julia's new possessions were safely stowed away for carriage to London and Bath and Gloucestershire. It must be wonderful, she thought fiercely, to be mistress of one's own household, not an object of charity in someone else's, to be able to give orders, do only the tasks one wished to do, and set the scheme of life to one's own inclinations. It seemed to her that she had spent the whole of the last two months helping to arrange the mechanics of a new existence for Julia, while her own life was only altered for the narrower. If she were a boy, Eliza thought pointlessly, she would run away to sea. As it was, being merely a girl, she would only run away to the garden.

She put a shawl over her shoulders, but she hardly needed it. The strange, quiet day was warm and soft and clinging. She walked slowly over the lawn, crushing the speedwells and daisies that starred its surface, and paused at the edge of the ha-ha looking enviously across at the stout, contented forms of the yellow cows in their deep pasture. Everything out there was exactly as it had been all her life – the fields, the hedges, the small hills, the cows, the church tower, the dovecote roof – and it was only she and her circumstances that were so utterly different. It seemed unbelievable and awful that Julia had really gone for ever and that she was now the only young person at Marchants. She seemed quite trapped. She hoped that in her desire to gain freedom she did not make some desperate mistake. She seemed after all to have a predilection for doing just that.

She turned slowly to the left and made for the ilex walk. As she was about to pass under the first trees, a servant came out to her from the house and informed her that a Captain Howell had called and asked to speak to her. Mrs Lambert had said she did not know her whereabouts but at that moment Captain Howell had seen her from the window and had asked for his message to be delivered. With suddenly flaming cheeks, Eliza said that she would see him in the library, and refrained from glancing towards the window that must reveal him.

She came into the library so quietly that he did not hear her. He was standing by the table, spinning the globe with one finger, and humming quietly to himself. Eliza wished very much he had not come. Inexperienced she might be, but not so devoid of instinct that she did not realize the probable cause of his coming back, so soon after the wedding, with the air still thick with romantic associations. She did not at all know how to handle him or even how to get any further forward into the room than the rug inside the doorway. He looked up at last, and started slightly at the sight of her.

'Miss Stanhope! Why did you not announce yourself? We must have wasted at least five minutes!'

He came across the room, and took her hands in his and looked down at her with much more fondness than she was comfortable to see.

'Do you wonder why I have come back?'

'Come back?' she said stupidly.

'Indeed, yes. Captain Beaumont and I were halfway back to my home at Newbury – '

He stopped. The mention of Francis' name affected them both painfully. Pelham had had the first near-quarrel ever with Francis that morning and was still not tranquil after it. He had announced his intention, over breakfast at the inn where they had put up, of going back to Marchants that morning, and he had seen a cloud cross his friend's face.

'What's up, Francis? Do you not sanction my going back in search of happiness?'

'I do not,' Francis said.

'What steps do you propose to take to stop me?'

'All that I can.'

'Well, I shall steel myself and probably disregard you. But before you hobble my horse and hide my breeches, I should like you to be civil enough to tell me the reasons for your violent objections?'

A sort of convulsion passed over Francis' face. He seemed once or twice to be about to speak, opened his hands wide several times only to bunch them into fists, and after a considerable struggle with something within said thickly, 'You go, my dear Pelham – of course, you go. No business of mine. You go, indeed you must.'

Still gesturing inconclusively, he moved towards the door of the inn parlour. Pelham caught him by the arm.

'Are you mad? What do you mean? One moment you are prepared to commit any crime rather than let me go, the next you are waving me away with tears in your eyes. What is the matter?'

Abruptly Francis wrenched his arm out of Pelham's and said furiously.

'Cannot you leave me alone? I said go, did I not? Well, go, and as soon as you may.'

'Shall you wait for me here?'

'No,' said Francis, and slammed the door.

Pelham had then ridden to Marchants in a considerable state of perplexity, only encouraged by his confidence in Eliza's kind reception when he arrived. She was looking pale, he thought, looking down at her now, and there were smudges beneath her eyes. When he had said Francis' name her eyes had widened for a second, and he felt the hands in his give an involuntary jerk.

'Can you spare me a few moments?'

'Oh, yes.'

'You are tired this morning.'

'I feel – I feel oppressed, Captain Howell. I expect it is the unaccustomed quiet after the gaiety of the last few days.' She sounded unconvinced.

'Is it your cousin's going?'

'Oh, yes, among other things – I mean, yes, it is, indeed it is, I shall be so solitary without her –'

Pelham took her to a sofa by the window.

'What other things?'

Eliza, tears rising, shook her head.

63

'Will you not confide in me? It is possible that I could help you. I cannot, I confess, bear to see you distressed.'

Eliza, unmanned by his kindness, allowed the first tear or two to slip down her cheeks.

'It is just – it is simply that I have ruined all chances of gaining the – the good opinion of someone whom I would do anything for.'

Pelham took her hand, and waited, in growing confusion of mind.

'I have been rude where I meant to be civil, unsympathetic where I meant to be kind. I have behaved like a silly child who does not deserve the – the regard of an adult. I have – oh, Captain Howell, I am so unhappy!'

He drew her to him, and she rested her head on his shoulder to cry in comfort. After a pause, he said gently, 'I do not believe you have been any of those things.'

She sat up, damp and crumpled, and said with vehemence, 'Oh I have, I have, indeed I have. You have seen me being so! I cannot think why you are so kind to me when you have witnessed most of my behaviour yourself!'

Looking directly at her now, understanding began to steal into Pelham's mind. Without thinking he said softly, his eyes still on her face,

'Francis Beaumont!'

She nodded.

'No one knows. That is, no one but you knows, and I beg you to make sure that no one else ever does. Cap– he would laugh at me if he knew.'

Still stunned, Pelham said nothing for a while. It all fitted, of course it did, the pieces of the pattern were there but he had chosen not to see it. A small part of his bruised mind told him to be grateful that he had not declared himself, for at least he retained a position of some strength.

Eliza said, 'I am sorry to burden you with this when you came to cheer me. Please try to put it out of your mind, it was most selfish of me.'

Pelham stood up a little unsteadily. He looked down at her, her face washed clean by crying, and was doubtful that he could bear to stay in the same room with her another moment if he could not hold her to him as his own.

The moment of parting seemed to intensify all his feelings.

She rose, too, and smiled a little faintly and said, 'Will you come back soon?'

Pelham swallowed. 'Of course. Forgive my being so – so uncommunicative. Of course your confidence is no burden to me, on the contrary I shall treasure it. I would be more than glad to come back in a few weeks, more than glad.'

He bent, took her hand and kissed it lightly.

'*À bientôt*, Eliza.'

When the door had closed behind him, Eliza sank down on the sofa. She felt a simultaneous sense of desolation and a relief that her pent-up feelings had had some escape. She looked out of the window and saw him ride slowly down the drive, a more sombre figure than he had ever cut before. With a pang, she remembered the reason she had supposed him to have had in coming. Had she been right? Did he come to propose to her? And, if he had, how had she received him? By bursting into tears and telling how much she loved someone else. Eliza's cheeks grew hot, and she watched miserably while the slow horseman diminished to a dot in the distance down the long straight avenue of trees.

Pelham considered riding all the way to tire himself thoroughly, but decided that he would use the next night to lick his wounds before he returned to his boisterous family. He plodded on through several miles of overgrown lanes, hunched in thought, and when the Stag's Head came in view, with its gables and half-timbering that he had left with such optimism that morning, he could not quite remember how he had reached it. He thought as he dismounted that it was foolish to remain here and ruminate on what might have been, and that what he needed was a diversion, so he resolved to rest his horse and himself a few hours, dine late and push on for Newbury in the long summer twilight. He handed his horse to the ostler, and tramped indoors. The place was very quiet in the early afternoon, even the dogs asleep in secluded corners, and Pelham got some satisfaction out of banging his way upstairs on the uncarpeted boards of the staircase.

He opened the door of the room he had taken the night before and found Francis sitting at the table by the window. Francis spun round at the sound of the door flying open, and his face wore an expression of barely concealed anxiety.

65

Pelham crashed on to the bedside and began to pull off his boots.

'I thought to find you gone.'

'I changed my mind.'

'Evidently. Give me a hand with these.'

The boots off, Pelham fell back across the bed and lay with his arms outstretched and eyes closed. Francis scanned his face for signs of glad triumph and saw none. Pelham opened his eyes.

'I failed.'

'Failed?' Francis tried to keep a note of gladness out of his voice and was not successful.

'Failed. Or to be more accurate I did not even attempt what I had gone to do, because I had proof that I would be unsuccessful.'

Francis clasped one hand with the other to prevent telltale shaking.

'I am sorry for it.'

Pelham eyed him sceptically from his prone position.

'I do not think you are, or even should be. When I have finished telling you what I am about to tell you, you will have no reason on earth to be sorry for anything.'

'Tell me,' Francis said quickly.

'Sit down then. I cannot be heroic with you towering over me in that way. The news I have for you is that even if I had got as far as proposing to Eliza Stanhope, she would have turned me down because she is in love with somebody else. And the climax of my information is that the somebody else is you.'

Only then did Francis sit down, and with a suddenness that made objects in the room dance in their stations.

'Oh, my God,' he said, his face in his hands, 'Oh, my dear God.'

Pelham raised himself on his elbows.

'I think I deserve more gratitude than the Almighty.'

Francis got up and came to the bedside, then bent over and clasped Pelham's shoulders. His face was quite transformed with incredulous joy.

'I do not know how to express the gratitude I owe you.'

'I had much rather you did not try.'

66

'I shall not, I promise you, but I should like you to know that I feel it.'

Pelham sat up.

'Nobility would not become either of us, my dear fellow. Now go away and leave me to reconcile myself to the notion of taking second place in the hearts of those I love most dearly – an affecting but honourable prospect.'

The door closed behind the jubilant Francis. Barely a minute later it opened again.

'Pelham?'

'Mm?'

'Are you entirely sure that it was me that she – she had in mind?'

'Horribly so.'

'Pelham?'

'Go away!'

The door closed more softly this time. Francis stood at the far side of it for some moments in a trance of thankfulness. Then he descended the stairs with a resolute tread on his way to the stableyard. Halfway there, he collected his wits and began to consider what he should actually do. His first impulse was to leap on horseback and make for Marchants in as short a time as possible, but then he reflected that by the time he got there, it would not be the most opportune moment for breathless proposals. The Lamberts dined early. However hard Francis rode they would be well on the way towards embroidery and card time and thus he would not be able to see Eliza on her own. The Lamberts would also be forced to ask him to put up for the night and might well be disinclined for more company after the wedding, quite apart from the bewilderment they might feel at the sight of a second suitor in the space of a single day spurring up the drive in pursuit of Eliza's hand. He would, if he wished to make the interview all he had begun to dream it would be, wait until the morning, when he would possibly be calmer and she would be free to see him. It chafed him to wait, but wait he must. Every moment with her so far had been in some measure mishandled, and he must and would see to it that tomorrow's was as perfect as he could devise. In addition he owed more than he could contemplate to Pelham, and must not forget him in his own excitement.

67

He would therefore wait. If when Pelham rose he wanted company, Francis would provide it, and if on the other hand he only wanted solitude, Francis would make himself scarce. So, his decision made, he sat himself down on the mounting block in the yard, and gazed into space and gave himself up to the delightful contemplation of what the morrow would bring.

July the twelfth, Eliza decided, opening her eyes in the dawn to look at it, looked no better than July the eleventh. The same quiet, still day was promised, the same air of frozen existence, and of course, she had fossilized her own life still further by being so clumsy with Pelham the day before. She argued with herself that she would only have refused him even if he had proposed, but a small voice told her that he had at least promised some escape route from future monotony. She rose reluctantly, preferring even that action to the alternative of her reflections, and thought as she surveyed herself in the glass that she looked as if she had lain under a stone for several weeks. Some pallor might be becoming, but not this transparent paleness. She dressed lethargically, hoping very much that this mood of deadening dullness would vanish as abruptly as it had arrived.

'We shall ride today!' her uncle declared later at breakfast, observing her looks.

She smiled at him gratefully.

'I should like that.'

Her aunt frowned. 'My dear, I need you with me, indeed I do. I cannot possibly achieve all I must this morning without some assistance, it is most selfish to consider I might.'

'It is not Eliza's whim to ride,' Mr Lambert said firmly, 'but my command that she does. There are ample days ahead, my dear, for her to help you all she may.'

Eliza went upstairs to change into her habit. Gratitude to her uncle made her able to be gracious to her aunt.

'I shall try not to be all the morning about it, Aunt, and then I can help you before dinner.'

Mrs Lambert was touched. 'Ah, my dear, perhaps you are to become a daughter to me after all and be the support that my Julia was.'

Eliza reflected on the inaccuracy of this remark as she laid her muslin on her bed and took down her habit. She could not remember Julia proffering even the smallest service to anyone all her life long, but then partings did seem to have a wonderfully forgiving effect on the minds of those left behind. Picking up her gloves and whip, she left the room and slowly descended the staircase.

At the foot of the stairs, standing together on the marble squares of the hall, were her uncle – and Francis Beaumont. Eliza stumbled, saved herself with a little cry, and saw Francis spring up a few stairs towards her, his arms outstretched. They both composed themselves, Francis retreating to the hall, Eliza stepping down holding the banister tightly in one hand and the hem of her habit in the other.

'I am to be deprived of your company after all, my dear,' her uncle said comfortably as she came down, 'Captain Beaumont is most desirous of an interview with you, and as he has come many miles for that express purpose, it would, I think, be discourteous to refuse him.'

Eliza started to say that she would not think of refusing him, stopped, coloured, and said instead,

'Shall you mind riding alone, Uncle?'

'In this instance, my dear, not in the least. I wish you a pleasant morning and hope to see you, Captain Beaumont, at dinner.'

Francis bowed. When her uncle had gone, Eliza said hastily, dreading the silence that was left behind, 'Would you care to rest after riding so far?'

'Not in the least,' Francis said.

Eliza was unable to meet his gaze. Whatever he had come for she could not envisage, but she was determined to conduct this interview with all the coolness she could muster.

'Shall we walk in the garden, then?'

'Nothing could please me more, Miss Stanhope. May I take your whip? I should feel safer if you were not armed.'

Eliza flushed scarlet, handed him her whip, then turned with hurried steps for the garden door. He caught her up quickly, and they crossed the lawn together, a yard apart, in silence.

As they turned down the ilex walk, Francis said with difficulty, 'It is uncommonly good of you to see me.'

69

'I thought,' Eliza said, without turning, 'that you had gone.'

'I had. I went ten miles and could go no further, so I have come back.'

Choosing to ignore the implication of this remark, Eliza said, 'And have you brought your father with you?'

'No. There was no point. It is a purely personal reason that has brought me back.'

Still she would not help him.

'Did you not think the wedding a great success?'

'Indeed, I did. In almost all respects it was exactly what I would have wished.'

Misunderstanding him immediately, Eliza turned sharply.

'Ah!' she said, her colour rising, 'so you have come to find fault again, have you?'

Francis came quickly forward and tried to take her arm, but she moved away.

'Please, Miss Stanhope – please Eliza, I have come for no such thing, I have come for quite the reverse reason. I wish to apologize to you for my abominable behaviour to you, and to beg for your forgiveness. I think in some mad moment I had even thought of asking for your friendship, but I see from your reception of me that it was a foolish hope – '

He stopped. Quite unconsciously, she had begun to listen to him intently and was gazing at him with a sort of desperation.

In quite a different tone, Francis said, 'I am not an ogre, Eliza, in truth I am not. Nor am I a mannerless boor or an unfeeling brute. I have come to confess to you my – my terrible mistake.'

Eliza's clenched fists went up to her chin.

'Mistake?' said Eliza hoarsely. 'You made a mistake? You cannot. It is my prerogative. I am the one who makes mistakes.'

'Only,' Francis said, 'delightful ones.'

He came right up to her and imprisoned her fists in his grasp.

'Would you let me speak, Eliza – and not hit me? Or at least not hit me until I have done?'

Eliza said faintly, 'I do not like to be reminded.'

'Nor I. That is why this conversation shall be utterly unlike the other. Come.'

He drew her towards the stone seat at the end of the walk and placed her gently upon it, holding her hands in his warm grasp since unaccountably she seemed to tremble.

'Look at me.'

She shook her head.

'I cannot.'

'Please. It would help me a great deal. I want to know if I am angering you, since it is my fervent wish never to displease you again.'

His tone was so much more than friendly that Eliza could not help but look up with a quick eagerness. Francis put his arm along the back of the seat. He smiled suddenly.

'It is perfectly absurd. I mean that *I* am perfectly absurd. I rehearsed this speech for several hours yesterday and for ten miles riding back today, and I find I cannot possibly utter it.'

'Perhaps you could just tell me about your one mistake,' Eliza said. 'It would console me for all mine.'

'Yours – '

'Yes, yes,' she said with some impatience. 'You know them by heart, lack of judgement, lack of self-control, lack of feeling, temper – '

'Mine was temper.' Francis said quickly. 'I suddenly became furiously angry for what proved to be quite the wrong reasons, and in the midst of my anger I found I was venting it upon the one person to whom I wished to show quite the opposite emotions – ' He leant forward, suddenly releasing her hands and beat his fists upon his temples:

'Oh, Eliza, Eliza, I am telling you what I want to tell you so shamefully badly. Perhaps if I were less in love I could describe it better.'

Eliza sat with her eyes tightly closed, terrified that this happiest of dreams should indeed prove to be only a dream.

'Whatever your reply to me,' Francis went on, his voice a little shaken, 'it will not alter those feelings. If you wish me to go, if you understandably regard me as intolerable, if as I say you wish me to go, I will do so instantly, but I – '
He stopped, and then cried with sudden anguish, 'Oh, Eliza, I would go, but I had so much rather not!'

She relented upon the instant. Was it not, after all, better than any fantasy she had cherished all those weeks of misery? She found she could not say much, but she let him pull her to her feet and hold her against him with such a force that she felt her lungs bursting for air. He did not kiss her then, but held her there, his cheek against her hair and told her how wretched he had been, how he had written her twenty letters after the picnic at Selborne and torn all twenty into shreds, and finally sent the twenty-first, only to regret it bitterly. He told her how he had counted on her coming to Quihampton, how he had planned to show her the cherished places of his boyhood and tell her about the years in Spain that had so utterly changed his concept of men and life. He told her how tortured with jealousy he had been the night before the wedding, watching her dancing and laughing with Pelham Howell and how he had stood in church the next day wishing most passionately that he had stood in his brother's place with Eliza by his side. Eliza, her face pressed to the snowy ruffles of his shirt and folds of his cravat, heard him with rapture.

'I had no conception that falling in love could come upon one like a thunderbolt. I could not help but think you utterly captivating, you know, glowering at poor Richard and teasing your aunt, but when I opened that stable door and saw you, wrapped in my cloak and crouching in a manger, I felt a sudden huge desire to tell you all I am telling you now. I meant to tell you again, you know, among the beeches of Selborne, and it all went to pieces in my hands – '

'You mean,' said Eliza, disengaging her cheek to gaze at him, 'that you did not mean to chastise me about Richard?'

'No,' he said shamefacedly, 'but I suddenly found I had not the courage to tell you that I loved you. I thought you would not believe me since I had known you but three days. So I was a coward and nearly perished with regret subsequently.'

'It is easy to fall in love in but three days!' Eliza declared resolutely. 'I know it is!'

With a cry of delight, Francis tilted up her chin and kissed her then. When eventually he lifted his face from hers and saw her shining eyes, he said,

'How very, very lucky we are.'

'I know it.'

'Not only to have found each other in the first place, I mean, but to have found each other again. We might so easily have missed each other through pride – I do believe, my dearest girl, that you have almost as much stubborn pride as I do.'

'It has been very beaten about recently.'

He sat her down again on the seat in the circle of his arm.

'Were you very unhappy?'

'Oh!' Eliza turned upon him a gaze full of remembered tragedy, 'I did not know it was possible to be so unhappy. But I think,' she added truthfully, 'that it has improved me. Just a little. A very little.'

He laughed.

'I tried to picture you unhappy, I regret to say, as some small consolation to my own miserable condition, but I really only thought you would be cross. If it had not been for Pelham, I doubt I should ever have had the courage to brave such crossness and come back, however much I longed to.'

'Pelham?'

'I owe you to him. I am in his debt for ever. He gave me my chance with you. I knew he was coming back to you yesterday, and I thought I could not bear to see him win you, and that I would go home, but I found that it was more unbearable to go without knowing if he had succeeded. So I sat and fidgeted for half the day, and then he returned and told me that he had failed, but that you were disposed to receive me more kindly than I had dared to hope.'

'Suppose you had not waited!' Eliza said in horror.

Francis smiled. 'Can you not spare a thought for Pelham?'

'Oh yes, indeed yes, without him I should – we should, I mean, be – Oh, Francis, think how we should be now if it were not for him!'

'We must never forget it.'

'Never.' Eliza promised solemnly.

She thought fleetingly of how she would have been now, at this moment, if Pelham had not been so generous. The prospect of everything, her whole horizon, had been absolutely changed by one short hour. The depression of the early morning now seemed to her a mood she could scarcely even recall. She glanced at Francis' hand on her shoulder,

73

at her own two hands under his one on her lap, at the face which had seemed so dauntingly remote and which was now hers to gaze at as dotingly as she wished.

'This morning I thought nothing wonderful would ever happen again.'

'And has it?' he said teasingly.

'The most wonderful thing,' she said seriously.

'I do – dearest Eliza, I do have your heart, then, or at least the hope of it?'

'Francis!' she cried, with some impatience. 'Have you not heard a word I have been saying this past hour?'

He looked down, adoring.

'I want to be quite sure.'

'And have your vanity petted?'

'No. At least I do not think so. I rather think it is that I want to be sure of your heart before I dare ask for your hand.'

'Dare, indeed!' she said delightedly.

'Yes, dare. Do not tease me. I have never asked for anything I wanted so much.'

'You shall have it,' she said.

Mr Lambert, crossing the home meadow on his chestnut cob, saw them then. He reined in under the elms on the far side and gazed with a little surprise and considerable pleasure at the spectacle of his niece, and what was presumably to be his nephew-in-law, in each other's arms at the end of the ilex walk. So that had been the trouble with little Eliza, then, how obtuse of him not to consider it, but then with Julia behaving so ungirlishly about her own affair, he imagined he had not been in tune to romantic complications. Excellent choice, too, he thought approvingly. Francis Beaumont would ride her on quite a tight rein, just what she needed. Smiling benignly, he urged the cob forward through the dry whispering summer grasses, and approached the pair. They broke apart.

'Sir – ' said Francis, his arm around Eliza.

'I imagine,' Mr Lambert said helpfully, 'that you might wish to speak to me. Shall I save you the trouble and myself the time, by saying I consent with all my heart?'

'If only,' Francis said to Eliza later, 'my father was of the same character as your uncle, the path of our true love would run as smooth as silk.'

74

6

Francis permitted himself the luxury of one day of not concerning himself with the looming problem of his father. He found that to be in a state of confessed love was even more exhilarating than he had believed possible, to the extent that Eliza's presence added a sort of radiance to every room and every remark. He had always thought her pretty; now that she was his he found her irresistibly so. Her wit, too, and her gaiety had both gained a greater lustre now that they were promised to him. He wondered at one point if he seemed at all idiotic and decided in the same instant that he cared not a whit if he did. He did not mind what the world thought of him but, gazing across the table at a laughing Eliza, he would do to death any world that did not prize her. There was much he ought to tell her, both of his father and what it would mean to be a soldier's wife, but on this hallowed day, this first day, he was not going to intrude the smallest cloud on the horizon.

Mrs Lambert had been perfectly incredulous when told. Her husband, riding humming home to the stableyard, had found her fretting in the dairy over butter that inexplicably would not come. To separate Mrs Lambert from a domestic crisis was no mean feat, but she was steered out into the daylight, guided to the circular seat beneath the tulip tree, and informed that not only had Francis Beaumont declared himself to Eliza, but also that she had far from discouraged his attentions and furthermore that as he, Mr Lambert, had been passing, he had given them his blessing to save time and trouble. If it did not render Mrs Lambert speechless, it certainly left her inarticulate. That anyone should wish to marry Eliza was astonishment enough, but that any man of distinction should want her was beyond belief. Her feelings did, of course, upon reflection, account for Eliza's manageableness lately, and at the mention of that, it came upon her aunt with awful poignancy that Eliza's marriage would leave her quite alone. Her husband pointed out that he at the very least did not intend to leave. That was quite beside the point, he was told with lamentations, how could Eliza be so selfish as to wish to leave the home that had succoured her so lovingly.

'My dear Maria, it has been our dearest wish to see the girls happily married!'

'But not all at once! Not so young! Not without the smallest thought for the love I have lavished upon them!'

She wept and accused copiously, patiently comforted by her husband, until it dawned upon her that the joy of another wedding to manage with her unrivalled efficiency was to be repeated within a few months. The images of desolation and empty rooms which filled her brain were instantly replaced by visions of wedding dresses and wedding breakfasts once more, and with these latter uppermost, she sped down the ilex walk to give her blessing and approval.

Mr Lambert did after all draw Francis aside after dinner.

'I omitted to mention a small matter.'

Francis looked enquiring.

'I very much regret that Eliza was only left a very small portion in her father's will, and thus will not bring you much more than the price of a few good hunters.'

'I am very blessed,' Francis said. 'I am lucky enough to be able to marry for love.'

'In that case, my little niece is more fortunate than she knows.'

A letter was written and despatched to Julia instantly which, as Richard would clearly read it, contained a postscript begging that no mention be made of the matter to Sir Gerard before Francis himself had spoken to his father. There was no question that the interview with his father would be impossibly difficult and probably violent. Not only were Sir Gerard's particular and passionate feelings for his younger son likely to make any wife, however suitable, an unwelcome intruder, but there was also his misogyny.

There was no denying it either that Eliza, for all her charm and energy and courage, was not particularly suitable. Her father had been an impecunious and improvident army captain who had died ingloriously of a fever, leaving a widow and baby, and the widow, Mr Lambert's spirited younger sister for whom he had always had a particular affection, had been killed shortly afterwards in an overturned carriage in bad weather. The Lamberts, as a family, were originally yeoman farmers rising rapidly with their mounting prosperity, and Eliza's father had come from small gentry in Somerset. Francis knew Sir Gerard would not care for that, as a start. Her parents, furthermore, had had little money, and the little they had had been used foolishly. They had never owned a house or even maintained what Sir Gerard would regard a proper establishment. Their lives had been untidy and so had their deaths. Looking at their daughter, it was possible to see that they had been delightful people, but that kind of recommendation was nothing to Sir Gerard.

Francis knew he must prepare Eliza. She must realize that she would meet with a barrier of active dislike and disapproval which bore no relation whatever to her qualities as a human being. She would be resented on the one hand as Francis' wife and, on the other, as a woman. She must not hope that charm or softness would produce any effect but irritation, but she must be consoled that Francis' own desire to marry her was strong enough to face the disagreeableness to Sir Gerard's reaction. He was at least blessed enough not to be dependent upon his father for money. His mother had been married for her own wealth, some of which had passed straight to her sons by the good management of her father, who had understandably detested his son-in-law. Indeed, Francis could house and keep Eliza with little difficulty and quite enough comfort, and this he knew it was most important to do, as he had seen the misery caused by soldiers who left their wives improperly provided for when campaigns called them away from home.

And there were going to be separations, long separations, unless some miraculous calm settled upon Europe. Francis privately believed that Napoleon's confinement to Elba provided no more than a temporary lull. He was, he knew, only at home because of it, and the army had indeed been dispersed to America, Ireland and even out to the East, but he had a sensation that the disbanded forces would have to be rounded up again. It did not seem even likely, let alone possible, that a commander like Napoleon would dwindle away on an island and anyhow, even if he did, the English would find other grievances against the French. Wellington had declared that the English were no enemies of the French, only of one Frenchman, but Francis thought differently. With luck he might manage the coming winter at home, but he doubted there would be much more. There was an unease in Europe despite the relief over Napoleon. Some trouble spot, some confused country like Belgium, for instance, would need English military attention before a year was up. When that happened he would say good-bye to Eliza without being able to give her the reassurance of when, if ever, he would see her again. He supposed he should have said all this before he proposed, but none of it had seemed to assume any significance when he was so anxious to secure her love and promise.

He would allow himself a week at Marchants, he decided, to tell Eliza all she needed to know, and then he would brave Quihampton. He knew that he should say to Eliza that she was quite free to change her mind if the obstacles ahead looked too daunting to be borne, but he shrank from giving her the chance. When eventually, in the course of their rides and walks, he broached these two looming subjects of Sir Gerard and soldiering, he was reminded of the time he had paused while striding up Selborne beeches to apologize to Eliza for the steepness, and found she was moving up more agilely than he. Eliza appeared to be able to grasp the reality of the future far better than he had ever hoped, and what was more, to regard them as a challenge rather than as crushing blows. Her main reaction to the prospect of Sir Gerard's animosity was one of acute disappointment.

'I have such a warm relation with my uncle, you see, Francis. We are so very comfortable together, that clearly it would be my dearest wish that I could feel the same with your father. But if he will dislike me, he will dislike me, and after all, you know I am quite used to being disliked. I have

78

not troubled to make myself very pleasant for a long time, and although I do hope I am very much changed now, I do know what it feels like not to be liked.'

Francis privately thought even her courage might fail under his father's influence, but he did not say so.

'Would it be very wrong,' Eliza went on, 'if you know that he is going to oppose us, just to marry and say nothing?'

'If he could stop us from marrying, dearest girl, I would tell him nothing. But as he can, at worst, only make matters unpleasant and cannot prevent us, I feel a duty to tell him.'

'I suppose he cannot then, at the very least, accuse you of dishonest behaviour.'

'No, he cannot,' Francis said, 'and difficult though I know he is, I do have a loyalty to him, a sort of affection, really, though I would not expect anyone to else understand it.'

As to being a soldier's wife, Eliza seemed determined to reassure Francis that it was what she had always longed to be.

'You will be much alone,' he kept saying earnestly.

'Why cannot I come with you?'

'That would depend very much on where I go.'

'Then I shall hope very much for a nice, accessible campaign in Europe.'

'Eliza, please. I am serious. Even if you could be in the same country, we could be very little together. I am trying to tell you that if you are my wife, I shall in all probability be away from you a very great deal.'

'Then I must bear it.'

'I am sure you will bear it. But I want you to prepare your mind for bearing it.'

'I will try tomorrow. I cannot possibly today. Look at the light on that wheatfield, Francis, and stop being so serious. You have lectured me for three days on the dreadfulness of being your wife, and if I wasn't so determined to marry you at all costs, I should think you were regretting having asked me.'

'Never!' he said, pulling her to him.

'Then stop talking about all the gloomy things. If you really want to marry me. I am perfectly willing to take on your father *and* the whole of the British army. I consider,' she said, putting her hands either side of his face, 'that you are worth it.'

He kissed her.

'I pray to God that you continue to think that.'

'Oh, I shall. I never change my mind, you know.'

'What there is of it,' he said teasingly.

Shrieking with indignation, she pursued him through the cow-parsley. He was surprised at how swiftly she could run and had to feign that he had allowed himself to be captured when she brought him neatly down, full length among the molehills.

Three days later, Francis rode away to Gloucestershire. He went with the utmost reluctance, and was almost cross at the cheerfulness with which Eliza bade him good-bye. He rode away down the drive between the pastures, turning frequently for a last glimpse of her smiling and waving, but when he was out of sight, he did not see the gladness die out of her face and the sudden mantle of quietness that fell on her spirits. She was, in truth, subdued because he had gone and not because she dreaded her future father-in-law's reaction, but she had not let Francis see the fall of her gaiety. Julia, had after all, been quite a success at Quihampton, and if she, Eliza, was as quiet and unobtrusive as she knew how, surely she would get at least a tolerable reception. She said as much to her uncle. Mr Lambert, who was making fishing flies in his study, remembered the stiff, abrupt man who had declined to dance or talk or play cards, and almost to eat and drink, and shook his head.

'It will be a great test of you, my dear. He is not an easy man. Francis is, you know, the apple of his eye, and he will not take kindly to the notion of a wife.'

That does not signify at all!' she said boldly. 'He cannot prevent us marrying!'

'He might not prevent you, indeed, but he will make his disapproval felt. You may well protest that you do not care for his disapproval, but it will affect you more than you think, especially Francis. It will affect poor Francis very much indeed.'

'He says it is worth it for me,' Eliza declared proudly.

'Dear little girl, I do not doubt that for a second. But Sir Gerard will be a cross you both must bear, and you must be very patient and restrained or it will be intolerable for your Francis.'

'I will try to be patient and I will try to be restrained and I will also try to make Sir Gerard change his mind.'

Mr Lambert had a vivid recollection of his sister and her determination to marry Robert Stanhope. He hoped very much that Eliza's venture would be more successful.

'Then you may begin your patience and restraint at dinner, my dear. Your aunt has had to dismiss two of the kitchen servants for dishonesty, and the matter is very much on her mind. I shall look forward to seeing this new patience of yours.'

A most affectionate letter arrived from Francis, but it contained only words of love, and none of how matters stood with his father. Eliza took this to be a good sign, and read the letter until she knew every syllable of it by heart. She was in the highest spirits these days, with energy that matched them. It seemed to her that, in the emotional torment she had known, she had reached the depths of human experience, and thus any subsequent problem, such as Sir Gerard, could only be insignificant by comparison. Within four days Francis was back. Eliza was not at home, she was out with her uncle, and when she returned, and heard the news of his coming, she fled breathlessly and ecstatically to find him in the library.

In the doorway, she stopped for a second. Francis was standing with his back to the room, his face to the garden.

'Francis,' she said, her voice full of repressed excitement.

He turned. Eliza was quite dismayed. She did not run into the arms he held out, she was too distressed by his face. He looked pale and dejected and infinitely weary.

'Francis?'

'Come here,' he said.

'Was it – was it very dreadful?'

He nodded.

'Come here,' he said again.

She went gladly.

'Will you tell me of it? Or would you – ' she stopped, 'perhaps you would rather say nothing.'

He smiled gratefully.

'Of course I will tell you, but I would much rather I had none of it to tell. Shall we go outside? I am so restless I rode at a quite ridiculous speed here – Eliza, I am so utterly thankful to be here. To be with you, too. I think I shall get an extra collect written into our marriage vows that empower you to inflict terrible punishments on me, if ever I show signs of becoming in the smallest measure like my father.'

A sort of relief had settled upon Francis as soon as Eliza had come into the room. She might not be able to understand his particular dilemma of affections – he was not sure he did himself – or sympathize with his desolation at his father's rejection, but he knew beyond doubt when he saw her again that she was worth every blow of the battle. And it had been a battle. Seated on their favourite bench at the end of the ilex walk, Francis described in as civilized a way as he could Sir Gerard's reaction to the news of the impending marriage.

'He was furiously angry at first, he is very violent' – here Francis omitted the flying objects that had crashed about his head, and Sir Gerard's opinions of women in general and Eliza in particular – 'and he feels a soldier ought not to marry – '

'You mean that this soldier ought not to marry, and if he does marry he ought not to marry me.'

'He is not a reasonable man, Eliza. He exhausted himself with rage the first day, and then the second was almost worse. He begged and pleaded with me and made appeals to my affections – I never saw him so abject before. To be candid, I did not like it, it made me uncomfortable. And then, to compensate for this weakness, he became icily polite the third day and as unbending as I have ever seen him. That was yesterday.'

Eliza sat with newfound patience and waited. She said at last, 'What did he say? Did he say we might not marry with his blessing?'

'He said – ' Francis took her hands in his and fixed her with a troubled gaze, 'he said that if we were bent upon marriage, he could not stop us. But he would never agree to meet you, he would never speak of you and that our children would have no existence in his eyes.'

Eliza sat aghast.

'He is very hard.'

'All I can say is that none of that changes my feelings about marrying you in the smallest degree.'

'Why is he so hard? What have we done, what have I done, that he should be so hard?'

'It is not us, it is him. He is as he is.'

'Can you bear to have his – his curse like this?'

'Indeed, yes, if you will help me. I have never felt such anger and resentment as I feel against him towards anyone in my life, but he is still my father, we have some bond, I feel his insults more keenly than I should feel any other's – '

'Would he not see me even once?'

'Not even once.'

'So he hates even the idea of me.'

With an exclamation, Francis put his arms around her.

'I want you. I love you. I want you and need you enough to dispense with all other relations. I cannot bear that my father should not know what I possess in you, but it must be borne.'

That night in bed, Eliza lay awake. The idea of the indomitable will of Sir Gerard fascinated her. She had a very strong will of her own, but she knew that even it had its weaknesses, and she could not believe that Sir Gerard's did not have an equal Achilles heel. It was difficult to understand the absolute obstinacy of the man, too, in his utter refusal even to see her once. She was not a particularly conceited girl but she had a feeling that she might manage Sir Gerard just a little if she were given the chance.

She could not accept fully the idea that Sir Gerard could reject her utterly since they had their love for Francis in common with each other. Rather than seeing that Sir Gerard might guard his own love jealously, she thought that hers could only have a softening effect. Surely he could not wholly resist a girl who only wished to serve and please the adored Francis? And surely she could use her high spirits and gaiety to lighten his gloomy bachelor life a little?

Clearly she must find a way to see him, even if she could not gain Francis' consent to do so, and then how pleased and proud Francis would be when she would present him with the beauty of a reconciliation. If it was to be done, of course Julia was the only way, but she must be careful how she put the matter. No one must know exactly what Sir Gerard had said. Staunch in her conviction that no human being could behave so unreasonably cruelly, Eliza lay in bed and watched the moonlight move over the white wall and made plans. Julia could not be contacted yet, of course, as her wedding journey was to last for several weeks, but she was to go to Bath for a short while in August to gather strength for dumbfounding London for her first winter season. An invitation had been extended to Eliza for that brief spell in Bath before Julia left, and perhaps she should take it. Bath was not far from Quihampton, well, not far comparatively. Of course, Julia might no longer care for daring plans if her immediate pre-marriage behaviour was anything to go by, but she might well be a little bored by Richard already, and longing for adventure. Eliza got up and lit a candle. Perhaps she could not send the letter yet, but there was nothing to stop her writing it.

Dearest Julia,

Even though I am to be married soon, it is not for a few weeks yet, and I should dearly love to see you before I become the second Mrs Beaumont. I cannot but feel that I could buy prettier bonnets in Bath than I can in Hampshire! Could I then presume...?

7

Bath was a revelation to Eliza. The strange and dramatic situation of the city itself, the houses, the people, the clothes, the amazing, captivating clothes, the social life, the talk. Eliza was not sure she cared for the talk, it seemed for the most part quite pointless, but she was conscious that her own forthrightness was regarded as both charming and amusing. Julia and Richard had welcomed her warmly, she had ample opportunity, which she took, to be pleasant to Richard, and altogether she felt that life had taken on a new and unexpected delightfulness.

Francis had brought her to Bath, stayed a few days, and then left to search for some suitable house for the future. He would have liked to have hunted with his old hunt, but clearly that was not possible because Sir Gerard still hunted keenly, so some other neighbourhood must be chosen. Pelham Howell lived near Newbury, and Francis decided, after consulting Eliza, that his advice should be asked.

'I do not want to drag you around the countryside, dearest girl, until there is some definite objective to drag you to. I would be much happier to think of you comfortably here, and when I find something possible I shall carry you off there to give you the chance of saying that nothing in the world would induce you to live in it.'

'Any house that includes you will delight me.'

'You mean any house that includes me and good stabling.'

His timing was perfect. He was to be gone a week and Eliza would have Julia a great deal to herself, and even with luck, time to put her plan into practice. Everything could not look more promising. Julia seemed, for her, quite

85

animated by being married, and she was so delighted that Eliza was to be her sister-in-law as well as her cousin that she was most amenable. Francis was safely absent, Richard lamentably easy to handle. Eliza planned very carefully how she would explain the matter to both Julia and Richard, and waited patiently for several days for the perfect moment to begin. It came late one afternoon, before they bestirred themselves from the comfort of chairs by the open windows to the discomfort of dressing for an evening party. Richard had placed himself as usual so that he could gaze with absolute satisfaction at his wife, Julia was idly watching swifts tumbling from the summits of the Abbey, and Eliza was sitting between them wondering how best to start.

'Did you spend much of your childhood here?'

'Here? In Bath? Dear, no. Bath is no place for children. It is dead half the year anyway. Children,' said Richard, his devoted gaze never leaving Julia, 'should grow up in the countryside. A city childhood is an unhappy and restricted childhood.'

'Our children,' said Julia, her eyes still on the wheeling swifts, 'will grow up where they are put.'

Eliza was anxious that the drift of the conversation should not change.

'Oh, but I am sure Richard is right, I am sure children are happier in the countryside. After all, we were happy at Marchants, were we not? And I am sure that Richard and Francis were happy at – at Quihampton!'

Richard nodded but did not seem disposed to reply. Julia yawned slightly.

'It must be so lovely at Quihampton. Francis told me quite a lot of it, of the hills and the house and the gardens. It sounds so beautiful and so unlike anything I ever saw –'

She stopped.

'I should dearly like to see Quihampton.'

'Have you not?' Richard said in mild surprise.

'No, and I should love to.'

'Two daughters-in-law in one summer,' said Julia, 'has proved much too much for your father.'

'Surely,' Eliza said eagerly, 'he would not mind if we were just to look at the grounds, at the house, perhaps from a distance.'

'If we did it very invisibly,' said Julia, 'but it is hardly worth it. It is a tedious hilly drive. I will draw you an impression of it one day.'

'But I want to see it with my own eyes, I want to see where Francis grew up.'

'Why does he not take you himself?'

Eliza looked down. She had not allowed for this question.

'I have not asked him.'

'Then you should do so. It is only proper.'

'But Richard, you belong to Quihampton, too! It is as much your home as his! Why should not you take me as well as he?'

'I would have thought,' Julia said, 'that you would have preferred to go with Francis.'

Clearly the truth, or at least part of it, was going to be necessary.

'I think he does not much want to see Sir Gerard just at present.'

Richard fumbled with a delicate reply to this, but Julia had no such scruples.

'No, I imagine not. You can hardly be what he hoped for for Francis, now, can you? No parents and but a string of pearls for dowry. No doubt poor Francis,' she said languidly, 'had a terrible time of it.'

Eliza did not react, partly out of the new and beautiful security she felt in Francis' love, partly because she did not want the prize she was edging towards to slip from her grasp.

'So you see he cannot take me, Richard, and I so long to go. I would be very quiet, very discreet, I promise Sir Gerard would never know I was there, I only want a glimpse. Please, Richard, please.'

'Relent,' said Julia to her husband, 'be indulgent. You love indulging whims and the sillier the whim the better.'

'It is not a whim,' said Eliza indignantly, 'and it is not silly! You have seen Richard's birthplace in a perfectly orthodox way and as that way is denied to me, I think you might be more helpful.'

'I shall be,' said Julia, and yawned. 'You may have my carriage.'

Half an hour had scarcely passed, and the scheme was afoot. Two days hence was the chosen day, all three would go. Eliza was enchanted. She was so sure the scheme she had devised once she got to Quihampton would work, that she gave not a thought to the deceit she had practised on Julia and Richard. She was going to give Francis a most wonderful surprise, he would be so grateful and adoring. With such an idyllic prospect before her, Eliza danced up the stairs to dress.

Two days later they set out for Quihampton beneath a ripe August sun. Julia was all for staying behind, saying it would be too hot and dusty, and she hated hills, but she was prevailed upon. Eliza dressed most carefully, choosing white muslin and blue ribbons and not too many curls, on the principle that what pleased Francis might have the same benign effect upon his father. Richard, oppressed with heat beneath his waistcoat, strove to match her gaiety since he believed they were setting out upon a sentimental pilgrimage of which he absolutely approved.

The fields were dry and yellowed, dotted with haymakers, the odd farmyard already decorated with a neatly thatched rick. Eliza looked out upon the countryside with new appreciation. The fact that the road was deeply rutted with hardened mud, which caused the carriage to throw them about most wretchedly, almost passed her by. She heard Julia's faint complainings, but could feel none of them herself. The stone of the walls and cottages turned from yellow to grey, the roofs became steeply pitched and split tiles took the place of thatch, the numbers of sheep increased. Eliza noticed it all with pleasure. At the top of a particularly long and painful hill, just when Julia was beginning to say she would rather be put out upon the verge and collected later than endure another moment of the journey, Richard halted the carriage. The road clung to a hillside, the dry turf climbing steeply beside them on the left, but to the right, the land fell away with terrifying abruptness and plunged into a narrow wooded valley. Down among the trees a church spire was visible, a space of fields, and a cluster of sharply pitched roofs with the glitter of water to one side of them.

'Quihampton,' Richard said.

Eliza strained to see. The main house appeared to be E-shaped, made irregular by the addition of wings, a stableyard and some curious building like a loaf, which Richard said was a dovecote. The carriage moved on, and soon a smaller road branched off to the right, leading down towards the church spire, and Eliza began to see lawns, and dark, stiff, square hedges, and grey paving, and the glitter and water was a great ornamental pond, nearly a lake, with a willow weeping on an island in the centre. It was wonderful, she was so glad she had made them come. They dropped lower and lower, and Eliza could make out the heavy mullions and the great golden cushions of lichen on the roofs and the twining Elizabethan chimneys. Then the road sank below the tree-tops, and they were plunged into green gloom and could see no more.

They came out into the village of Quihampton, clinging to the last of the hillside with steep gardens running back up into the woods from the cottages. Eliza expected cottagers to run deferentially to the gates at the sight of Richard, why did they not, she asked?

Richard cleared his throat. 'My father is not always of predictable temper, and I am anxious that our visit is as inconspicuous as possible.'

He did not add that his father was hardly a benevolent landlord either, and that the sight of the Beaumont arms did not bring an eager crowd of grateful tenants to one's carriage door. He had deliberately chosen a vehicle today whose doors were not emblazoned. Under Sir Gerard's influence, the village had suffered a great deal in the Napoleonic wars; there were gaps in some families, and in others where the men had returned, many of them could not work again so mutilated had they been. Sir Gerard made little allowance for this in the employment he offered. Francis had tried to suggest a more liberal policy, a more paternal responsibility to those families whose lives were rooted deep in Quihampton, but to no avail. Eliza, driving between the quiet grey cottages, felt a sudden chill. She looked up the steep valley sides and saw the great bare curve of the hills which shut it in, and thought of winter there, the valley a funnel for winds, the roads out of it impassable.

The carriage took them past the great gate to the house with its lodges and stone griffons, and plunged into a leafy lane that ran round the edge of the park. It was undeniably lovely, the trees had been beautifully planted. At a point where the house was hidden from view, a smaller gate broke the wall, a double iron gate still, but with no lodge and a thickly mossed track leading away into the trees. They passed through silently on the velveted floor, the sunlight hardly filtering through the leaves, the light thick and green. It was almost unpleasantly quiet. Nothing grew under these beeches, there was no life among the tree trunks. After a few hundred yards, the carriage was halted at a point where the open parkland came up to the edge of the trees, and a path led away to the left, still under cover of the trees, but clearly in the direction of the house.

With enormous complainings, Julia was helped down from the carriage. She could not conceive what had induced her to spend a day in such monumental discomfort, and she vowed she would stir no further. Eliza, on the other hand, all anticipation, was poised to speed along the intriguing path as if she had not spent all morning being shaken like dice in a box. Richard was in a quandary.

'Dearest Julia, I have promised Eliza a glimpse of the house.'

'Take her to obtain one, then, it is no concern of mine, but I will not move another step.'

'But dearest, I would not like to leave you on your own.'

'I am not on my own. I have Roberts and Perry and two most obliging horses, and they shall look after me until you return.'

Cushions and refreshments were brought from the carriage and Julia was supplied assiduously with both. Richard looked unhappy still.

'Perhaps,' Eliza said, 'you could take me to a point where I might have a view of the house, and just leave me there long enough to sketch it.'

'At the rate you sketch,' Julia said, 'that will not be above five minutes.'

Richard said worriedly, 'I hardly think it is proper to leave you there.'

'Of course it is!' Eliza said. 'Why, it is your own park, what harm could possibly come to me? I would hardly be mistaken for a poacher, and in any case, I can scream very loud.'

'She can,' said Julia.

Reluctantly, he agreed. They set out together along the inviting path, and Eliza was pleased to see that Julia was soon lost to view. A few more turns, a pretty bridge, and the house was plainly visible from the seclusion of the trees. After a catalogue of injunctions, and a great deal of time spent in finding Eliza a seat that was neither hard nor damp, Richard left her. She sat very still for a while, looking at the house and its narrow windows and steep roofs and air of silvery mouldiness. She could see the lawns and the box hedges and the walnut tree with Francis' hammock still slung below it, but not in any of the windows was there the smallest sign of life. She drew an impression of it all, quickly and badly for she was a poor artist, because she felt she had to have some cover for her escapade. Then she put paper and pencils down among the beech mast, weighted them with a stone, and began to walk quickly towards the house. The beech trees were most helpful and covered her movements to within a dozen yards of the door. When she reached the end of their shade, she paused to adjust her bonnet and smooth her skirt, then took a deep breath and stepped out into the full sunlight.

Her footsteps seemed to crunch alarmingly on the carriage sweep, but the house appeared quite asleep in the torpid August afternoon. The choice of door was difficult. She could see a small secluded one in the house wall facing the park, but she would have to pass several windows to reach it, and in any case, Julia and Richard might possibly see her. It would have to be the great door, oaken and grey and massively studded but standing mercifully slightly ajar. She thought of dogs. Surely Sir Gerard would have dogs? But none had come out at the sound of her feet, so perhaps they were chained somewhere. She climbed the steps and stood on the top one to look about, but all was hot and silent and empty, so she stepped quickly inside.

The blackness after the brightness was quite blinding for a moment. Then she made out the outlines of a great hall, the great medieval hall usually found at the centre of houses, but at Quihampton forming a grand overture to the later house beyond. Galleried and beamed, furnished with black Jacobean chairs, ugly and old-fashioned to Eliza's eyes, it loomed above her, lit only by high slits in the massive walls. Sunbeams, furred with dust, fell across the dimness. Eliza looked up, to the crown posts and the blackened beams. After Bath, it seemed a goblin place. But still there was no sign of any inhabitant, goblin or otherwise, so gathering courage, Eliza crept across the huge flagstones of the floor to a small linenfold door in the opposite wall. It opened easily, and gave on to a long Elizabethan gallery, windowed on one side, tapestried on the other. Here Quihampton was odd again, for the gallery was on the ground floor. The room had a stiff lifeless look. A few dark pictures hung obscured against the tapestries, vast curtains shrouded the windows, the glass in the latter was dim and greenish and full of imperfections. Eliza looked at the distance she must travel to the door at the far end, stiffened her spine, and began to walk.

Impassive Tudor eyes watched her from the walls as she walked in and out of light and shade all down the length of that cheerless room. She glanced back once to make sure the door she had entered by was still open, as a kind of talisman, but she did not pause or falter. The door at the far end was younger than the linenfold one, but opened with the same smoothness and offered Eliza a library within, a taller, newer-looking room, but furnished with the same lack of sympathy as the hall and gallery. There were great chairs, a gun case or two, pipe racks, dim rows of books, nothing charming or elegant or attractive to the eye. But the view was wonderful, the windows for the first time being of modern glass and admitting the full and lovely spectacle of the Elizabethan garden, the park, the walnut tree, the beech-clad slope of the valley. Instinctively Eliza went to the window, but no, she could not see Julia and Richard, so she was equally, and safely, invisible to them. Perhaps Francis had stood at this window as a boy, and wondered what would become of him when he grew up. Perhaps he had even wondered whom he might marry. Perhaps he had put his palms down as she did on the broad sill, warm from the sun, and leant forward, as she did, to gaze at the maze of little hedges, as complex and tidy as marquetry.

'I shoot intruders.'

Eliza had never felt such panic. A sort of blow of blackness

seemed to smite her brain and heart and eyes at once. She
reeled a little against the nearest heavy chair, staggered,
found her balance and struggled to turn round. Sir Gerard
was standing at an inner doorway, the door itself being a
section of shelves of books. It was so dark where he stood
and she had her back to the light that she could not make
out his expression, but she had never been spoken to with
such absolute hostility in her life.

'Who are you, pray?'

She simply could not speak. Her tongue and throat were
dry and constricted with guilt and terror.

'I repeat, who are you? Why are you prowling about my
house as if it were your own? What is your business?'

'To – to see you, sir.'

'See me? Why?'

'I thought we should – we should be acquainted.'

'You did?'

She nodded, dumbly.

'Why? I have no taste for silly girls in white muslin.'

A spark of anger at this loosened Eliza's tongue a little.

'My name is Eliza Stanhope. I thought we should at least
know each other since I am to – am to – '

She broke off. The interview was going in direct opposition
to plan.

'You are what?'

There was silence.

'Answer me!'

She could not. She wished she had never come. She felt
herself indeed to be a silly girl in white muslin. The dark
outline in the doorway there, tall and hard, seemed the most
menacing and dreadful thing she had ever seen, and all she
wanted to do was run. But the very terror that made her
long to flee also kept her rooted to the polished oak beneath
her feet.

'Answer me!'

He stepped forward a pace until he was beside a marble
head on a black pedestal, and the two relentless faces bore
down upon Eliza.

'You feeble woman, you feather-brained fool of a girl.
Why will you not answer me? Because you are weak and
silly like all your sex. There is no need to answer me. I know

the answer. You have dreams befitting the empty interior of your head, dreams of marrying my son. In doing so you will be the architect of every evil, every misery on earth to my son. You came here cherishing stupid woman's hopes of wheedling me, you cherish stupid woman's hopes about my son. You will fail. Why? Because I curse you. I curse you with every atom of my being. You, your marriage and your children are as doomed as if you lay dead already – '

'Stop!' Eliza screamed, white with fury, her clenched fists pounding on the chair back. 'Stop, stop, stop!'

A silence full of echoes fell for a moment.

'You are right, I was a fool to come, but I was not a fool about my own motives but about ignorance. I did not know I was to deal with a monster, a jealous, dangerous monster! Your curses can't touch me, I am safe, safe, safe, and why am I safe? Because it is me that Francis loves, not you! Me he has chosen, not you! You are absolutely powerless to touch us, there is nothing you can do!'

As she finished there was a sudden commotion at the back of the room, the marble head seemed to be swaying, Sir Gerard's face was contorted and working. Some simple animal instinct propelled Eliza like an arrow to the door, and as she burst through it, the marble head came lethally through the dusty air behind her and crashed through the window into the garden beyond. Gasping but never stopping, Eliza fled through the gallery and hall, down the steps, sobbing and stumbling across the gravel and into the shelter of the trees and the shadowed path. Speed was not necessary, though. After the last fragments of glass had tinkled from the shattered hole, there was no sound at all from the library, no movement, only the disturbed air settling back into its customary placidity.

Eliza had wept for many reasons in her short lifetime before, out of rage or despair or jealousy or frustration, but never out of fright. Now she lay, shuddering deeply on the ground, her eyes fixed and wide, whilst tears coursed down into the undergrowth and great sobs seemed ready to tear her apart. She had no consciousness of anything except that she had been more terrified by Francis' father than she had known it possible to be. As the minutes wore on, and she realized she was not pursued, the shaking was subdued a

94

little and as she became calmer, she grew aware of what she had done and the consequences to herself, to Francis, even to Julia and Richard. She had never felt so full of contempt and self-loathing. She wanted to run away madly and hide and punish herself with deprivation and unhappiness, but that would be evading the issue. She got up at last, and, making no attempt to calm her face or hair or clothes, stumbled back along the path, crushing her drawing under foot as she went, dry sobs and gasps still catching her breath.

Even Julia was roused at the sight of her. Richard, with a diplomacy and delicacy Eliza ever remembered gratefully, got up from where he lay reading aloud to his wife, and came wordlessly forward to Eliza and took her hand and drew her down to be consoled by Julia. Of course, she sobbed afresh, she tried to explain, but her voice was too torn with tears to be understood. Julia soothed and wiped and stroked and Richard knelt by them and waited.

At last, Eliza lifted her ravaged face and whispered with difficulty to Richard, 'I wanted to know him.'

A flash of understanding went between husband and wife. Julia gently disengaged herself and climbed into the carriage. Richard helped Eliza to her feet, assisted her in so that she might lie against her cousin and gave orders for everything to be packed away. Then, as the afternoon sun began to mellow, they left the scene of Eliza's failure with the mournful quietness of a funeral procession. Two days later the head gamekeeper found Eliza's crumpled drawing among the leaves and took it home, much puzzled by its appearance, to his wife.

8

Francis was initially extremely angry. Julia had suggested to Eliza that there were many ways of presenting the story to him when he returned to Bath, which he would find less disturbing than the unvarnished truth, but of course Eliza would have none of that. She greeted her lover with a face of deepest misery and flung the whole story at him in every detail before he had been in the house one half-hour. She had not been truthful over the expedition to Quihampton, and that had proved disastrous, and thus she was not going to risk any more catastrophes by omitting or twisting any detail of her story.

One fact, however, she did completely omit, she did not tell Francis about the marble bust. She was so intent upon purging herself of the guilt and shame she felt that she forgot Sir Gerard had behaved in an equally reprehensible way. It was also such a frightening episode that she did not find it easy to recall; her memory seemed, of its own accord, to slip past those few seconds. Francis watched her while she poured out her history of the afternoon, his face hardening, and she knew she was in for punishment. When he did speak, he sounded not like a lover at all, but like a very much displeased man ten years her senior in age, experience, worldliness and rationality. She was very shaken. When he had finished, he took her hand and begged her to promise that never again would she take some impetuous step in matters too subtle and complex for her comprehension. She promised.

He got up and left her then, on Julia's drawing-room sofa, and went to seek his sister-in-law.

'You look as if you have just finished making yourself most unpleasant,' she observed.

'I hardly enjoyed it.'

'I hope you were at least a little consoling.'

'Consoling!' he said in amazement. 'Console her for estranging us from my father for ever!'

Julia said firmly, 'Do not be melodramatic. Your father was estranged already. I think it would be most uncomfortable if he were any closer, in truth. But you should have been consoling.'

'And why, pray?'

Julia yawned. 'Well,' she said slowly and carelessly, 'he did almost kill her.'

'Kill her!'

Julia turned wide, amazed eyes upon him. 'Indeed he did. He threw a marble bust at her. I believe he broke a window. Did she say nothing of it?'

'Not a word! The angel, not a word!'

'Reflect upon that, then,' said Julia and picked up her embroidery. 'What a cross family you are, to be sure. How lucky you are,' she added with satisfaction, 'to find yourselves brides of such calibre.'

'Amen to that,' Francis cried, and was gone. Seconds later, with Eliza in his arms, he was begging for reassurance that she had not been in the least hurt and praising her for her reticence. She was still too humiliated to respond with all her characteristic enthusiasm, but she felt a warm wave of relief at the confirmation of her belief that nothing and no one could come between them.

Francis, on the other hand took no comfort in anything beyond the fact that she was alive. The depths of his father's nature that the incident revealed were awful abysses indeed. He had never dreamed that his father would stop at nothing, literally nothing, to fulfil the bigotries and violent selfishness of his nature. The love his father bore him did not resemble in any way the generosity of true feeling that Francis had always hoped he felt but rather some vicious extension of Sir Gerard's own self-love, and Francis shuddered at the thought of being the recipient of such animal instincts. He looked down at Eliza's head which he was holding against him with a force that must almost have hurt her. He slackened his pressure and tilted her face up.

'If you can bear to think of it,' he said gently, 'I should dearly like to know what you thought of Quihampton.'

'Oh, it was lovely,' she said quickly, 'lovely and unloved. So stiff and comfortless, but only on the surface. Do you – do you love it very much?'

'I did. I used to feel quite passionately about it as a boy. It is such a strange, old, unfashionable house, and it meant a very great deal to me. But it is very much changed without my mother, she was a very home-loving woman, she made the house very comfortable, very easy. You are right, it is stiff now. You might have loved my mother, I think.'

'I should have liked the chance. I haven't much experience of mothers.'

He took her hands tightly.

'I hate to be angry with you.'

'I would have hated it if I hadn't earned it.'

'There can be few women who would bear such chiding.'

'And few who behave with such folly.'

'I adore you. And I think I have found you a house.'

She was delighted. It was proof the future was real. His friends the Howells knew of a house not far from them, vacant at least this coming winter, and possibly longer. It had good grounds, a south aspect, stables in excellent repair and was within very easy reach of Newbury. Mrs Howell, Pelham's mother, had asked that Eliza might visit her for a few days so that they might look at the house together and Eliza could learn something of the neighbourhood. It was all very pleasurable, even if tinged with a slight anxiety at the prospect of seeing Pelham again.

Within a few days, the house in Bath had been shut up, Julia and Richard setting out for London, with enough trunks to hold wardrobes for the whole of fashionable society that winter, and Francis and Eliza for Newbury. Eliza had thought of going back briefly to Marchants, but a letter from her uncle indicating genially the ferment of pre-nuptial activity going on there, made her change her mind.

'But I do not want a large wedding!' she said to Francis

'I should really just like us both in a meadow somewhere, I could not bear all the nonsense that Julia had – '

'A meadow in the rain, perhaps?'

She wrote privately to her uncle explaining her feelings and begging him to put a brake upon the proceedings as far as he was able, and under the same cover a letter was dispatched to her aunt telling her of the plans for the house near Newbury. Then she packed up her few belongings and joined Francis. He said approvingly that he had never seen a woman who could travel with so few possessions.

'That accounts for the dreadful monotony of my wardrobe.'

They had the warmest of welcomes from the Howell household. Pelham was the first to their carriage, holding out his arms to Eliza, with a face so full of pleasure that she felt tears rising to see it.

'Capital, capital! There are no two people on earth whom I am more eager to see. You thrive on each other I see from your looks, positively thrive. Mother, here is Miss Stanhope whom I knew I did not deserve. Is not Francis a lucky dog indeed?'

There was no tremor in his tone. The moment of meeting was over, and thanks to him, over without any awkwardness. Francis had warned her that Pelham would not like any reference made to the past, so she put her hand into Pelham's and said, matching his tone as well as she could:

'Oh, Captain Howell, he is far from lucky! Such improvements are needed in me that he has a taxing future ahead of him.'

'May I join in that delightful task, Francis?'

'Within reason.'

'Grudging fellow! Never mind, I shall bide my time and when Francis falls in the gallant defence of his country, I shall take on his matchless widow and thus never have the interminable task of choosing a wife for myself.'

'But he won't fall in battle,' Eliza declared staunchly.

'I almost believe any remark made with such force.'

'I find it very comforting,' said Francis. 'If I were Fate I should think twice before crossing swords with such a will as hers!'

'Fate would not stand a chance.'

Mrs Howell, a charming and forceful woman, took Eliza alone to see her future house. She would not allow the young men to accompany them, she claimed they would only be a distraction. The rooms must be measured and appropriated to their various uses, and men were worse than useless in such matters.

Nashbourn Court lay some five miles from the Howells' over a most dramatic downland road. It proved to be a small, handsome house, some twenty or thirty years old, built of stone in a beautifully secluded position with a view falling away to the south towards Newbury. Mrs Howell propelled Eliza briskly around it, pointing out the excellent proportions of the drawing room, the small but impressive staircase, the imagination with which the shrubbery had been planted, the airy spaciousness of the whole atmosphere. Eliza needed no persuading. The only house she knew was Marchants and this seemed to her the perfect précis of it. Mrs Howell said she would arrange for servants since she knew the area so well, and what special requirements did Eliza have? Eliza, who knew only the barest rudiments of housekeeping since her aunt had hated to delegate even the smallest item of administration, laughed openly and delightedly at this. Her idea of marriage had been such a grand scheme up to now that she had not troubled to imagine herself ordering Francis' dinner and overseeing the dairy.

'I shall need a deal of instruction,' she said to Mrs Howell.

'Then you have come to quite the right person. I love to give it. Shall we return and say that you agree?'

Mrs Lambert, on hearing the wedding was to be small and quiet, was most upset, instantly feeling Eliza's choice to be an insult to her organizational talents. However, when Eliza informed her that her future address was to be Nashbourn Court, near Newbury, Mrs Lambert was much mollified.

'Does it not sound well?' she exclaimed to her husband, having tried the sound of it out upon him at least a dozen times.

'Very well, my dear.'

'Is she not a most fortunate girl to be living in a house that sounds so well?'

'Most fortunate but even more so, I think, in marrying Francis Beaumont in the first place.'

'Such a pity she cannot have the title, too!'

'I believe she would rather have the man than the title.'

The choice of guests proved a delightful problem for Mrs Lambert since some of the same guests who had attended Julia's wedding must clearly be asked again, but how to appease the great majority who would not be invited a second time and who would quite indignantly and understandably wonder why? Eliza, back at Marchants, was unable to see the difficulty. It was her wedding, after all, so what did the small social injuries of people she did not care for matter? At the end of September, she and Francis were to be made man and wife and she did not much mind in the presence of whom, as long as they were not too many. Mr Lambert settled the matter, to Eliza's delight, by saying that he could afford only a very small wedding in any case, since he intended to make his niece a very handsome wedding present.

'I prefer, my dear, to spend the money on a niece I am particularly fond of, and not on half the county whom I scarcely know or care for.'

Francis, seeing Mrs Lambert's undisguised disappointment suggested she might like to oversee arrangements and improvements at Nashbourn Court.

'After all, I scarcely know what I am about in a house, and I do not think Eliza is set upon doing it alone.'

It was a brilliant suggestion. Mrs Lambert may have lacked any kind of intellectual discernment, but her eye for line and colour was astonishingly faultless. A week before the wedding, the house was ready for them, pale, elegant and comfortable in the same admirable proportion that distinguished the rooms at Marchants. Servants selected by Mrs Howell were at work already, the gardens were being put in order, the stables made ready for their new inmates.

'There is nothing for me to do!' Eliza wailed.

'Except marry me.'

Three days before her twentieth birthday she did marry Francis in the church where, but two months before, she had stood behind Julia, wishing to marry hin.

It was as unlike Julia's wedding, to Mrs Lambert's distress, as it could be. Eliza chose to be married in the gown she had worn as Julia's wedding attendant, because not only was it worn but once, but also it delighted her imagination to realize that she was now living out in reality the fantasy she had indulged in when clad in it before. She carried a small bunch of flowers gathered for her by the servants in the kitchen at Marchants and only condescended to a veil at all because Mrs Lambert had kept the one worn by her mother. The guests were very few; Julia and Richard, the former handsome and glossy and already looking as if she had never had anything to do with Marchants; Pelham, who gallantly did duty as best man; Eliza's aunt and uncle; and the few friends round about who had known Eliza since childhood. Francis was as unwilling to include any other members of his regiment as Eliza was to include friends of more distant acquaintance.

'It is very quiet,' Julia observed, looking round the church and its sparsely filled pews, 'really, we need scarcely have bothered ourselves.'

'Hush, dearest,' Richard said in gentle reproof. 'Surely you would not have wished to miss your own cousin's wedding?'

Julia yawned.

'Dining with Lady Russell would have been a deal more amusing. I cannot say that I would travel sixty miles to see Mrs Knight-Knox and the Leslie girls for pleasure.'

'Are you fatigued, dearest?'

'No more than I commonly am when bored.'

Simple or no, Mrs Lambert contrived to weep quite as copiously at this wedding as she had done at Julia's more lavish one. Beside her Mr Lambert thought uneasily of the evening ahead. The mere dozen in the church were to dine with them after the ceremony, but Eliza had been insistent that dinner was to be nothing out of the ordinary, and that she did not want champagne. That part of the day Mr Lambert looked forward to, with its prospect of familiar food at a familiar time, consumed in the company of familiar faces. It was the space of day that remained after their departure that dismayed him somewhat. How was he to deflect Mrs Lambert from the most melancholy reflections on her bereft state, alone and daughterless? He watched Francis slide Eliza's wedding ring down her finger, and something in the sight of his tall frame bent protectively over Eliza's slight one, gave him inspiration. A small smile lit his plump face. Of course! He would divert his wife with the prospect of grandchildren, direct ones as well as great-nephews and great-nieces. His smile broadened. Come to think of it, it was a very pleasant prospect indeed, very pleasant.

'Come, my dear,' he said, bending towards his sniffing wife, 'this is a time for smiles, not tears.'

'So affecting! So very affecting! Quite as moving as dearest Julia's, quite as moving. Oh, how shall I go on without a single daughter to lean upon?'

As Francis and Eliza moved down the aisle, Julia watched them idly.

'I do believe that is the dress Papa gave her for my wedding. What a contrary creature she is, to be sure.'

She drifted slowly out of her pew and sailed down the aisle in the place of honour behind the bridal pair, watched in doting awe by her mother and some anxiety by her father. Outside the church she offered a flawless cheek for Eliza's kiss, saying:

'You are truly most fortunate, Eliza. It is you I should congratulate, I think, on your good fortune, rather than Captain Beaumont as is customary.'

Eliza, used to Julia's gentle malice, and secure in the day's perfect happiness, only laughed.

Pelham said, 'I am not accustomed to contradict one as fair as you, Mrs Beaumont, but I fear you are wrong. You may congratulate them both if you will, but the one who really merits congratulation is myself.'

Julia smiled but was not going to put herself to the trouble of asking him to explain himself. She allowed her mother to exclaim rapturously over her dress, and then was handed to her carriage. Francis watched her sleek form settle itself comfortably and then looked at Eliza.

'I know which is the lucky Beaumont,' he said fondly.

Eliza said fiercely, 'You are quite wrong. Richard is truly blessed to have such a wife. I insist he is, Francis, and that you are wrong.'

Francis pressed her arm. 'And you are the most unsatisfactory creature to pay compliments to that I ever encountered.'

'Maybe. But I wish you would stop not paying them on that account.'

'It is most unlikely that I shall ever be able to help myself.'

Dinner was a tolerable success, dominated largely by Mr Lambert's anecdotes. Delighted by the day's business, at ease in his own house among family and friends, he was happy and expansive. Julia took little trouble to suppress her yawns, Fanny Leslie glanced often at Francis in covert disappointment, Pelham applauded his host, Mrs Lambert fussed, and Francis and Eliza wished very much that it might soon be over. Once their healths had been copiously drunk, it seemed possible that they might leave. Eliza to her aunt's annoyance and cousin's mild surprise, did not wish to change her dress. A cloak would suffice, she insisted, the night was warm. Francis, amazed and delighted that she could behave with such unconventional simplicity, staunchly supported her. They must be gone as soon as they could, he claimed, and was rewarded with knowing laughter from Henry Leslie and Pelham.

Eliza kissed her aunt and uncle quickly.

'I cannot linger over saying good-bye, I hope you do not think me unfeeling but in truth I feel too much to say all I would say to you.'

Mr Lambert said, 'Say nothing, my dear, but that you will take care of yourself, and that we shall soon be seeing you again.'

Tears were coursing down Mrs Lambert's cheeks once more.

'Think of me, my dear Eliza, quite alone I shall be, quite alone. Do spare a thought for me, will you not? I shall be sadly lonely, indeed I shall.'

Mr Lambert drew his wife's hand within his arm.

'It is a thousand pities, Maria, that you regard my company as of so little consequence,' he said mildly, and motioned to Francis that they should be on their way.

Once in the carriage, Eliza leant out and looked at the group upon the steps, and felt herself supremely lucky and improbably happy. She waved once more and then sat back against the cushions.

'I shall not look back again,' she said resolutely.

They did not go away for a wedding journey, though Francis gallantly offered to do so, since Eliza sensed in him, for all his gaiety, an enormous desire to settle as master into his own house and direct its life to his own desire. He had, in fact, been trying to rest for four months, and managed scarcely a moment. There was, too – and even Eliza in her moments of most buoyant optimism saw it – a great deal of mutual acquainting to do. Eliza was woefully ignorant, Francis well read and cultivated, and thus she must strive to familiarize herself with all the things he took for granted, and he must not assume too much from her. These thoughts struck her with astonishment that first wedded night, looking about the house scattered with books and objects of his, possessions that spoke of whole areas of his mind and character that she did not yet know.

In the midst of her happiness, she said falteringly, 'I hope you will not find me very dull.'

He was standing before the fire, gazing with satisfaction at his domain.

'Dull?' he said in genuine surprise.

'I have read so little, I always fidgeted so, I wish now I had paid more attention. I think I will be rather – limited company.'

'Come here.'

He held her hands in his against his chest.

'Do you know the story of Pygmalion?'

'No.'

He told her, briefly.

'Shall I do that to you? Make good potential into my perfect woman?'

She broke away.

'No, indeed!' she said indignantly, 'I shall do it for myself! You may indicate,' she went on graciously, 'what you think I should begin on. Why are you laughing?'

'I am so glad I married you. I do not think I should care if you could not even read or write. My darling, we have a great future together.'

Later, much later, Eliza was to look back on that first winter together as an idyll. The house suited them perfectly, she even found herself capable of running it, and the situation was a joy. They rode as much as they could, often to the

Howells who became the second family to Eliza they had so long been to Francis.

It was evident that Mrs Howell regarded her as just the daughter she would have wished if she had been offered any alternative to her five sons. Mrs Howell was an excellent horsewoman herself, and it delighted her to see Eliza accept every challenge the Howell brothers threw her while out riding.

'Now boys, I insist you do not overstretch Eliza. She is very precious to us all – '

'Notably to me,' Francis said.

'And notably to Francis, and if there are any reports of rash and headstrong behaviour from any of you, I shall not permit you the pleasure of riding with her. It strikes me as most unjust that she should have to bear the tedium of all of you practising your gallantry upon her, without the added discomfort of being tossed into ditches and impaled upon branches.'

This sort of minor lecture was performed every time a group of them was assembled to ride. Everyone listened gravely, blew kisses to their mother and then rode off at full gallop whooping and shouting as if she had uttered the words merely to please herself.

Francis was not only spellbound by Eliza and her popularity in this most beloved of families, but was astonished at her sheer physical courage. He could not say that she was foolhardy, for if challenged to any dangerous feat, she would laugh and look at Francis and say, 'What – and follow a wedding by a funeral?' and the Howell boys would toss their hats in the air and cheer. But she jumped hedges that Francis himself regarded with caution, she would ride downhill as fast as any of them, and she had an endurance in rain or wind or cold that struck him forcibly. He never heard her complain. And when the wild, carefree day was done, they would dine with the Howells and then set off home in the frosty twilight, cherishing the prospect of their own solitude up at Nashbourn as much as they had relished the happy energy of the day. Warm and full of Mrs Howell's excellent dinner, they would ride out briskly and Francis would insist she rode with one hand so that he could hold the other, and the hooves would strike out in unison on

the flinty roads, an echo of their own perfect contentment.

Back at Nashbourn, the fires of fruit wood cut from dead
trees in the orchard burned encouragingly, and there was an
unspeakable satisfaction in walking in to them, and watching
their light play on the books and pictures and objects that
constituted this beautiful privacy.

Francis often read aloud to Eliza and tea would be served,
and then Eliza would say, 'Do you realize that I am under
no obligation whatever to embroider or card wools? I can
just sit here, and listen to you, and have absolutely empty
hands – '

'To conform to your absolutely empty head?'

'No, indeed!' she said indignantly. 'If you would only
let me finish, I was going to say that the contrast is wonderful,
because I have empty hands and a full head, and that
before the reverse used to be true.'

'I do not think I want you altered in any way.'

She looked at him solemnly.

'I must become a more civilized wife for you.'

Francis lips twitched.

'Dearest Eliza, I do not want one. Listen to me read if
you will, but please do not feel you have to stuff your head
with civilization as you call it. If I had wanted that sort of
wife, do you not think I might have chosen one?'

'I often feel that I was a sort of accident in your life,' Eliza
confessed. 'That I was not what you had in mind.'

'I had nothing in my mind except that once I had seen
you, I had nothing *but* you in my mind.'

Eliza revelled in these conversations but all the same was
mindful of her promise to Francis that they should never
forget their debt to Pelham. Accordingly, after a deafening
Christmas spent at the Howells, Pelham was persuaded to
climb the hill to Nashbourn and stay with them.

'Shall I not be horribly *de trop*? I am not good at playing
second fiddle.'

'You will not even need to try,' Eliza declared, 'since you
are first fiddle to both of us. Besides each other,' she added
truthfully, and Pelham laughed.

'I think if you had married anyone but Francis, I could
not have borne it.'

'When you speak so generously, I find it very difficult to reply.'

'In that case, as actions speak louder than words, I shall look forward to being ruinously cosseted at Nashbourn.'

Nashbourn was well designed for the winter. The garden dropped in terraces above a sweeping downland view, with well-planted walks and sheltering groups of trees, and then opened on to the downs themselves to give ample opportunity for dryshod walks should it prove too slippery to ride. They were all too energetic to remain housebound for more than the end of the day and would descend the garden to gain the freedom of the downs in the cold light air. Pelham, much taken by Eliza's notions of self-improvement, constituted lectures for her during these high, windswept walks, he and Francis often having to shout above the weather. Eliza bore this light-hearted instruction with a certain good grace which would abruptly finish in a defiant,

'Enough, enough! I will not hear another word. In any case, I begin to feel you do it as much for each other's amusement as my instruction!'

Politics somewhat naturally featured fairly prominently in these walks. Eliza, who had cherished a romantic view of Napoleon, born mainly out of admiration for his achievements despite lack of natural advantages such as birth or wealth, began to feel somewhat differently. One thing that puzzled her, when she heard Pelham and Francis talk of this dangerous genius, was how preoccupied they both seemed to be with him still.

'I do not understand you both. Uncle said we were at peace now that he is a prisoner in Elba. He said Napoleon cannot escape, and he said that much of our army has been disbanded or sent abroad because we do not need to fear any more.'

'Without implying disrespect to your reverend uncle – ' Pelham began.

'Which means you are about to be disrespectful.'

'Exactly. To continue. Napoleon may well be a prisoner, but he is not the sort of commander to accept imprisonment quietly.'

Francis slashed with his cane among some bramble clumps.

'I would not wonder if he were not plotting an escape while we talk.'

'But what would happen then?' Eliza asked. 'Would there be war?'

'How beautifully direct your wife is, Francis! Would there be war? Well, it would depend upon his ability to raise another army.'

Eliza, remembering the effect Napoleon's charisma had had on her, hundreds of miles away in her secluded life, said stoutly, 'Of course he could raise an army!'

'He would love to know of your faith in him, dearest.'

'Do not patronize me, Francis.'

'I would not dare.'

'Have you heard rumours, Francis?'

Francis shook his head and slipped his hand to cover hers inside her muff.

'Do not worry.'

'I am not worrying. I merely like to know.'

Pelham, gazing ahead of him into the vague grey day and watching his breath cloud before him, thought of recent conversations with his father. General Howell chafed when at peace and longed always to be campaigning, and Pelham knew that this must be taken into account when lending weight to his father's views.

'I think Francis may be right.'

'About what?'

'About Napoleon trying to escape.'

'I am pleased to be right, but displeased at the reason for being right! What have you heard?'

'I have heard nothing, but my father claims an escape is plotted for the spring, and that groundwork is going on for the levying of a new force loyal to Napoleon. You must remember that that is the kind of rumour my father longs to hear.'

Eliza looked about her at the bleached winter hillside and the grey clumps of dwellings in the valley, and thought how impossible it was that she could look upon this frozen tranquillity while, at the same moment, Napoleon was perhaps plotting an escape. What was he doing at this very moment? Was he writing, or thinking, or dining? Did he have a dog for company, or books? Was he allowed to walk abroad? Was he permitted to sleep alone? The men had continued to talk the while, and she came out of her reverie to hear Francis say:

'I do not actually want to be interrupted at this moment.'

'I should like to interrupt you and beg you to turn for home,' she said.

They returned to the comfort of the house. Much as she loved exercise, Eliza was not sure she did not relish still more this return to warmth and familiarity, when the curtains could be drawn upon the three of them, and Francis and Pelham would read, and then parody Shakespeare for her.

'That is not fit education for me!'

'It is the best you will get from us after such very good wine, dearest, and I am sure it is what Shakespeare himself would have wished you to hear.'

'May I read some myself? I am capable of reading aloud, you know!'

'Pelham, would she not make an admirable Rosalind?'

'Perfect! Very well – this sofa shall be the palace, and those chairs yonder the forest of Arden. I suppose I shall not be permitted to be Orlando?'

'Certainly not. It would be most unseemly. Dearest, you will have to dress as a boy for a portion of it.'

Eliza was delighted.

'A boy? Oh, I should dearly love to dress as a boy!'

'If I may not be Orlando, I insist upon being Oliver and the duke and all his courtiers especially the melancholy Jacques. Do you not think me most suitable for him?'

'Quite the reverse, Pelham,' Eliza said happily. 'You are more of our court-jester, and we shall miss you sadly when you go.'

'I shall go, though,' he said, smiling, 'before I become unfit for any other way of life. But I shall return for dinner with the regularity of a rising sun.'

He left them at the end of January, sliding perilously down to the valley on a road opaque with ice. They watched him as far as they could, and then Francis turned and took Eliza's face between his hands. He looked at her steadily for some time, then kissed her, and led her back into the house and to the comfortable and delightful ritual of their lives together.

In February Eliza found snowdrops in the garden and a few weeks later a sprinkling of white crocuses. She could not wait for spring up here at Nashbourn, nor summer, in order to complete for herself this first perfect year of her life when she could honestly say to herself that she had found a companion who suited her every need. They began to be a little more sociable, after their womb-like retreat of deep winter.

Julia and Richard came for a few weeks, and they exchanged guilty glances of relief when those few weeks were up. They were not easy guests, or perhaps it was simply that there was little that the four of them had in common any longer. Eliza was dismayed to find she was no longer in tune with her cousin, whose sleepy wit seemed to have deepened into something much more dangerous.

'When I saw their carriage coming up the hill three weeks ago,' she confided to Francis, 'I was longing to show Julia things, and tell her of our doings, and take her on our favourite walks and rides. I used to lie awake at night thinking of what she would most like to eat or amuse herself with, and somehow the moment she got down from the carriage in that positive cocoon of furs, I lost faith in everything that I had planned.'

Julia had indeed swept into the house, wearing an air of slight disdain, and not wholly kind amusement that would have daunted the most optimistic hostess. She stood in the hall and surveyed the effect that Eliza's energetic personality had superimposed on the elegance Mrs Lambert had left behind.

'Very snug,' she said. 'Quite a little nest. I imagine you have reserved the truly good pieces for the stable?'

Francis came quickly to Eliza's rescue. 'In the sense that the horses cost a good deal more than anything we possess in the house, yes.'

'Julia has faultless taste,' Richard said fatuously.

It was on the tip of Eliza's angry tongue to say, 'Except in husbands,' but she remembered that they must all spend twenty days together, and reluctantly bit it back.

It seemed a long twenty days. Time and again Eliza would proffer a scheme to have it taunted at and brushed aside.

'Would you ride with us this morning, Julia? There is a

point not three miles away with a most beautiful and endless view where you feel as if you were on the roof of the world –'

'If you mean the world you now inhabit, Eliza, the view cannot be very extensive. In any case, I do not choose to be blown to pieces for the sake of straining my eyes. I am sure Francis will stay and bear me company, and Richard will escort you to save your being entirely blown away.'

'I decline,' Francis said with a bow, 'because she rides so recklessly that I cannot resist going out with her, and I fear that no one will watch over her as well as I.'

Julia's face clouded briefly, then she shrugged and said, 'Then I must resign myself to counting stitches in the carpet until you deign to return.'

Eliza was most miserable during the subsequent ride.

'I do so wish to please her, and she staunchly refuses to let me. I always feel that I am in the wrong, I am the selfish one. I feel that I cannot reach her.'

Francis, who had read the undercurrent of messages in Julia's newly urbanized manners, declared with conviction that perhaps it was no bad thing that the cousins were no longer as close as they had been.

'Oh, you are wrong!' Eliza cried vehemently. 'Of course we should be close! What is there that separates us now?'

Julia's boredom, a cloud that loomed over the quartet from dawn till dusk, became a positively monumental thing as the visit drew to a close. That she missed London society was painfully evident, and that she considered visiting the Howells every few days a laughably inadequate substitute was unmistakable. In the last week Eliza did not even suggest their usual visit to the family, nor even that Pelham should come to them.

'He seems to bear her such dislike, I cannot think why. And she is too fine for them now I fear. Last Tuesday she must have yawned more than twenty times a minute, I could hardly bear to watch her.'

On the morning of their departure, Julia showed the first animation she had displayed since her arrival. In fact, she seemed almost like her old self, and kissed Eliza with something approaching warmth.

'You must come to us soon, indeed you must, and before that habit becomes an inseparable part of your person.'

'I take it off at night!' Eliza declared. 'But it is most practical for the life I lead.'

Julia looked her over, and smiled. 'That says it all, dear cousin. But when you are minded to try a broader and more amusing version of existence, I will be happy to show it to you.'

The moment the Beaumont carriage had jolted its way down the ruts and thankfully out of sight, Francis, noticing the slight dismay still lingering in Eliza's countenance, proposed that they should go down to the Howells as a diversion.

'Oh, yes! Oh, yes, I should be glad to go. I am thankful we can resume our life, Francis. Pelham added to it, but Julia and Richard seemed to interrupt it, and I hate myself for making that distinction.'

'Does it not prove,' said Francis teasingly, 'that Pelham's and my joint instruction has enabled you to perform such a division in your mind?'

'Not at all. I have never had any trouble in making distinctions. Reconciliation is my trouble, as you know.'

Francis took her hand with the intention of insinuating as delicately as he could some of his suspicions about Julia into Eliza's mind. But Eliza turned to him with such a brilliant smile at his gesture that he could not bring himself to do it. What was the point, in any case? All he wanted to do was to protect Eliza, and at the moment ignorance was her greatest protector anyway.

On the first day of March, Pelham came over to dinner. It was his usual weekly visit, and he came with a new novel and a bunch of wild daffodils, frilly and fragrant, for Eliza, and a bottle of port, with the General's compliments, for Francis. Francis thought he looked a little strained, but he was complimenting Eliza with his usual buoyancy, and she observed nothing.

'My dear Eliza, you are the perfect recipient of posies. I bring you daffodils – gathered by my own fair hand to the accompaniment of much creaking of knees – and you are wearing a dress of precisely that colour. You look like a spring blossom yourself. It fairly lifts the heart to see you.'

Eliza was laughing. 'Does your heart need lifting, Pelham?'

'Something does. I do have a feeling of dullness. I wonder if I am not getting to be like my father, perish the thought, and in need of a little military activity.'

'Can you not play at soldiers with your brothers?'

'Madam, can you insult me? Would you suggest that this battle-scarred veteran of the Peninsular wars could content himself with mere play after the heroics he has known?'

'And which you treated as play,' Francis said affectionately.

'Are you suggesting that I did not take service for my country seriously?'

'Not at all. Only the value of your own life.'

'I take the latter very seriously,' Eliza said.

Pelham groaned.

'Francis, will you exercise marital authority and forbid her to say things like that. They make my heart pound and my pulses race, and I cannot breathe for excitement.'

Eliza drew him towards the fire, seated him in the chair he preferred, and left them to find water for her flowers. The moment she had gone, Pelham turned towards Francis with the animation gone from his face and seemed about to speak, but Francis said quickly:

'Are you really impatient to be gone?'

'Only today. I have had a morning being domesticated by my mother. She insisted I should see the household accounts so that I should be aware of the cost of life. She claims soldiers have totally impractical and romantic notions of the value of money.'

'She should know, having been married to one for more than thirty years.'

'She does know. That is what made the morning so discouraging. Do you and Eliza discuss money?'

'Never. It would hardly be necessary. Eliza has not bought so much as a new ribbon since we married.'

'I am lulling you into a sense of deeply false security,' she said coming back into the room, 'Now, then – the pheasants are roasted, the sweetbreads creamed and the fire in the dining room has consented to burn for once, so will you come and eat?'

'The food here,' Pelham said later with his mouth full, 'is ambrosial.'

'All from your mother's instruction.'

'Then it must be the air and the company. In addition, of course, to my enormous appetite. Well, now, tell me what plans you have for the spring and summer that I may veto them.'

Francis twisted his wine glass in his fingers and looked down at the table at Eliza.

'I, selfishly, have no wish ever to move from Nashbourn. I am in a state of absolute contentment –'

'Which is quite disgusting to see.'

' – and from which I do not ever wish to be roused. But I think I shall take Eliza to London for a while and show her off, and then we may go to the coast for a few weeks, and perhaps we may toy with the idea of going abroad for a spell.'

At the mention of the last idea, Eliza saw a shadow flit briefly across Pelham's face.

'Abroad?' he said abruptly.

Francis said carelessly, 'Oh, nowhere too adventurous, Italy perhaps,' and reached for the decanter.

Pelham said with slightly forced jollity, 'Ah, the Grand Tour, I see. Nashbourn Court is not to be left out of the general swim of fashionable things. Shall you paint on your travels, Mrs Beaumont?'

'You know perfectly well,' said Eliza, fetching the port from the sideboard, 'that I cannot paint. I shall record scenes and events in my extremely efficient memory instead. I shall now leave you both, and beg you not to forget me entirely. Last week I was alone almost two hours.'

When the door had closed behind her, Pelham rose and filled Francis' glass carefully, then returned and poured port into his own. He stood for a moment and looked at the darkening room, firelight shining on polished wood and brass and silver, silent but for the comfortable crackle of burning logs and at Francis, his long length sprawled in his chair, contemplating the flames in utter tranquillity. Pelham seated himself again and leaned forward to put his elbows on the table. He cleared his throat.

'Francis.'

'Mm?'

'My dear fellow, I fear you lovebirds are going to have to change your tune.'

'I don't ever intend to.'

'It will not be up to you.'

'Oh?' Francis said idly, too replete to react vigorously.

'I have news for you. I realize information travels slowly to paradise up here.'

He paused.

'Go on.'

'Napoleon has escaped from Elba,' Pelham said.

9

The idyll was over. Not only for Eliza, but for a great deal of Europe, too, after a year of safely feeling Napoleon was no longer a threat. It quickly became known that Napoelon had arrived, applauded, in the south of France, and was travelling, acclaimed all the way, towards Paris. Europe was on its feet in an instant, recalling and reassembling its armies, and for a week or two everything seemed in a ferment of confusion. News travelled fast, but often inaccurately, and the further one was away from some major centre of communication, the more innaccurate might the report become, so Francis, within only a few days, departed with Pelham for London.

Eliza left at Nashbourn, found all her brave claims at the prospect of being a soldier's wife put to the test. She did not privately believe anything very dramatic could possibly happen too quickly, and in any case, Napoleon might be back but he had no army. Napoleon, who had been the hero of her girlhood, had become an enemy to her in a very personal sense. His actions now had a direct and wretched effect upon her own life. She thought about him venomously as she went about the tasks of the household with redoubled vigour – pointless vigour since Francis was not there to profit by the results – and vented her feelings upon Mrs Howell who came frequently to see her.

'There is not much point, my dear Eliza, in being so angry. It is quite wasted emotion, I do assure you.'

'I am angry, Mrs Howell, I am angry that the perfection of life should be spoiled by one man's ambition.'

'The perfection of your own life, maybe, my dear!'

'Yes, probably so. But on the other hand, I think Napoleon will not prove more than a major inconvenience to me.'

Mrs Howell burst into peals of laughter. 'What makes you so sublimely certain that he will be of no more than passing consequence?'

Eliza remembered the talks on the downs in those wild January days.

'Francis says,' she said, and blushed, 'that Wellington has an army in northern Belgium. Surely they could quell Napoleon should the need arise?'

Mrs Howell leaned forward and patted her hand.

'I am afraid it is only an army of sorts, my dear Eliza, not the kind of thing the General approves of at all, a very ragbag collection of mixed loyalties he says they are.' She rose and began to walk briskly about Eliza's drawing room. 'And we do not yet know how many men are rallying to Napoleon. The General says that it will be an enormous number, but of course we must remember that the General has no time for civilian life and cannot wait for the trumpets to sound.'

'Has the General gone to London?'

'Oh, days since. He was gone before Pelham. Now, do not look so distressed. Why should the General be any more accurate in his guessing than you? After all, you are both governed in your views by what you wish to hear. Now, shall I not help you to make something toothsome for Francis' return?'

He came back a week later, in early April, splashing up the streaming lane to Nashbourn in the dusk. Eliza met him eagerly at the door, taking his sodden cloak herself, and pushing him towards a bright fire of apple wood from dead trees in their orchard. He looked excited, but wary, as if he were in two wholly different minds about the news he had to impart. He had seen Julia in London, who was radiant and had said Eliza must come to her as soon as possible.

'Why?' said Eliza suspiciously.

'Because it wil be lonely for you here alone.'

'Where are you going?' she cried sharply.

He leaned forward in his chair and took her hands, and she noticed that his hair was curling with dampness and there were still raindrops on his cheek.

'We did discuss this eventuality,' he said.

'I know. Tell me, then.'

'I am to go to Belgium.'

'Then I have my wish!' she said with an attempt at gaiety. 'I did wish, you remember, for a convenient campaign. Belgium is very convenient.'

He smiled.

'Good girl,' he said. 'Good and dearest girl.'

'Tell me more.'

'Not many people in Europe believed Napoleon could do what he has done. He has been at liberty perhaps a month and has reassembled an army in that time, a considerable army, and they are all positioned in the north-east corner of France. So, you see, we must be in Belgium.'

'The English?'

'And the Prussians and Dutch and Belgians and Austrians and Germans and Russians. It must be Napoleon's worst and last defeat. It is all we can do, or Europe will be his.'

'So,' said Eliza simply, drawing her hands out of his and folding them in her lap, 'there is to be a battle.'

'We do not know. But we must be there, we cannot be taken by surprise. The Duke's orders, and, in my case, Lord Uxbridge's orders, are that we are to proceed to Belgium forthwith. Eliza – '

She had got up and was standing in front of him, her hands locked together.

'I will get you something to eat,' she said.

The pantries were empty. Eliza had not expected Francis, and thus most of the servants were not needed. It was as well, for Eliza was able to weep bitterly and privately in the dark coldness there, overcome with a sudden terror of what Francis was going to do. Of course there would be a battle; it was, to her mind, the only conclusive way to settle the matter. But he would be in it, and might not live through it, and she must stay here and worry and wait. It would be intolerable. She heard his tread on the flagstones of the passage.

'Eliza?'

He found her by the light of her single candle.

'Put that down, dearest. I cannot embrace a game pie.'

She flung herself against him, tears breaking out anew.

Francis' heart was wrung, both on his own account and for the pain he was inflicting.

'It will only be a short campaign,' he said, his voice not quite steady.

'But so dangerous!'

'So is hunting.'

'Oh,' said Eliza angrily, and stamped her foot, 'what an absurd comparison. And when you hunt, you take me, too.'

'I cannot do that, not to Belgium, even though I would give my right arm to be able to.'

'Why is it so impossible?'

'It is not proper or suitable or comfortable. It may well be dangerous, it will certainly be dull as I shall be much occupied – '

'I would promise to make no claims on you.'

'No, Eliza.'

She sighed.

'Do no other wives go?'

'I am not interested in other wives, only in my own.'

She looked up at his face in the shadowy candlelight and decided that, for the moment, acquiescence was necessary.

'Then I should rather be in London with Julia, than here.'

'That is what I hoped. It would give me more peace of mind.'

'I, on the contrary, shall have none of the latter until you are back.'

'Eliza,' he said gently, 'you knew this, I told you.'

'Yes,' she said, and picked up the pie again, 'you did. Now come and eat.'

Later that night Eliza lay wakefully, her left side heavily imprisoned by a sleeping Francis. He had flung a leaden arm across her which was hardly comfortable, and usually she would have pushed it away and retreated independently to her own side of the bed, but tonight she let it lie. A moon was peering fitfully from among shreds and rags of clouds, and she had tossed the bed hangings back so that she could see it. How enormously had her horizons widened since those days – days that seemed like the life of another being – of riding and reading and giggling and peaceful monotony at Marchants. Now she was a wife, and a wife in the same situation as thousands upon thousands of soldiers' wives whose happiness and security were threatened, too. Perhaps if she had been possessed of more imagination she might have been able to visualize more accurately what being married to a soldier must inevitably mean, but she had seen it in terms of activity and excitement and glory, not the certainty of danger and the probability of loss. Well, it must be borne. Francis had warned her, and it was not his fault that she had not grasped what he was trying to explain. If she weakened now, and kept weeping and reproaching him, it would hinder him in every way, and she could not bear to be responsible for his annoyance or unhappiness. Tears must be a thing of the past, she decided resolutely, in any case they were quite pointless and achieved nothing except despair at her own lack of self-control. She would abide by all Francis decided and not object in the smallest degree to any of those decisions. But, and here she made her own proviso to all her resolves, she would do everything in her power to be permitted to accompany him to Belgium.

They were up soon after dawn, on one of those clear, damp, pretty days that follow heavy rain in April, and while they ate an early breakfast, they were astonished to see Mrs Howell's carriage climbing the lane from the valley. She, being the wife of one soldier and mother to two more, bore the kind of parting now to be inflicted on Eliza for the first time with almost cheerfulness, and had come to see to the arrangements at Nashbourn so that Eliza might go to London with Francis immediately.

'How has she taken the news?' Mrs Howell enquired of Francis.

'Pretty well. There was a moment last evening – but only a moment. It is, you know,' he added, looking levelly at Mrs Howell, 'quite as bad for me. If not worse. I have never had the anxiety of leaving anyone so dear to me before.'

'Take her too, then!'

Francis stared.

'Do not gawp at me dear Francis, but take her with you! This is to be a most sociable campaign, if General Howell is at all to be relied upon. I gather most of fashionable society is planning to descend on Brussels to see the fun.'

Francis said stubbornly, 'I do not want to have Eliza mixed up with those sort of people.'

'If she don't meet them in Brussels, she will meet them in London with Julia and Richard. In any case, I think she will be an asset to you.'

'I don't doubt that.'

'Ah!' Mrs Howell said with significance, 'I'm sure you don't. But I have great expectations of your little Eliza. I should take her, too. She will surprise us all, and herself no doubt.'

Francis thought of the waiting around in Belgium that there would inevitably be whilst Europe watched for Napoleon to make a move, and what a joy it would be to have Eliza with him. And then he thought of the raffishness of military social life and the time she must occupy herself, and the reality of what he must do being so forcibly pressed upon her, and he remained firm in his original decision. Mrs Howell said nothing to Eliza except cheerfully as they parted:

'I have been trying to lose the General in the service of his country for these past thirty years, and he has not had so much as a scratch. You will probably have the same ill-luck with your Francis!'

Then she waved them away, and they saw her turn back into the house with the brisk step of impending efficiency. They set off for the last time down the precipitous lane, neither looking back, and made for Newbury where they were to collect Pelham. He had been trying to buy a horse, but decided that for a first-rate one, and surely the last blaze of the Napoleonic wars deserved a first-rate horse, he must go to Tattersall's. He was in the blithest spirits, and taught Eliza a mildly improper song as they swayed on towards London, a song whose impropriety, he said firmly, was sanctioned by the fact that it was four hundred years old. Eliza was very happy, and felt rewarded for her firmness with herself in the silent moonlight hours earlier. She was delighted to see the beginnings of the brown brick sprawl that was London creeping into the fields they passed, and she gazed eagerly from the windows. Hanover Square, when they reached it despite the ankle deep mud from the recent rains, entranced her, too, so stately and urbane, did it seem to her by comparison with everything she knew, even Bath. Julia's house was wonderfully elegant, even, Eliza thought privately, laughably so, especially if you contrasted it with the pretty comfortableness she had left behind at Nashbourn.

Francis, he disclosed that evening when they were alone at last, was to be gone within three days. Eliza made no demur. She slept determinedly well that night, and woke to find Francis still in his nightshirt, writing at the bureau by the window. He said he had not slept at all, but seemed buoyant in mood for all that. Eliza, having been in London less than twenty-four hours, said she must get outside today, she must have some exercise.

'Perhaps Pelham might ride with you in Hyde Park,' Francis said, his eyes not leaving his paper.

'Why not you?'

'I have Lord Uxbridge to see, dearest.'

'In that case,' Eliza said bravely, 'I will fling myself on Pelham's mercy and gallantry.'

Francis dropped a grateful kiss on her rumpled head and went to dress. He came back some twenty minutes later, looking unnaturally immaculate, and sat briefly on the edge of the bed. Eliza indicated their joint reflection in the looking-glass.

'Look at us!'

He saw himself, dark-clad and white-ruffled, like some precise silhouette, and beside him Eliza with her confusion of curls on the tossed pillows, shrouded in an inviting tangle of nightclothes and bedclothes. He caught his breath lightly.

'I cannot think of a better reason for being late – but I must not be late.'

She rose up in bed and put her arms around his newly laundered neck and kissed him with deliberate warmth.

'Are you always going to make it so difficult for me to leave you?'

'Yes,' she said.

Pelham was delighted to escort her to Hyde Park. To the astonishment of all, Julia, yawning, said she would accompany them. This proved an initial drawback because of the time it took Julia to dress, but Pelham gallantly beguiled the delay by teaching Eliza backgammon. She was very quick.

'I do believe,' he said with admiration, 'that you are more of a born gambler than Francis.'

Eliza said loyally, 'Only because I don't know any better.'

It was another lovely and gentle day, and Hyde Park was frosted with new pale greenness. They rode sedately abreast, Pelham between them, and Eliza was astonished to see how many passing horsemen raised their hats in greeting to Julia. Man after man went past with a smile, a bow, and a word or two. Eliza craned round Pelham to look with new interest at her cousin. Julia wore dark green, her skin was perfect and her expression unusually subtle.

'What are you thinking of?' demanded Eliza.

'Nothing,' Julia replied, and smiled.

At a sort of central *carrefour* they were halted by a party of four horsemen who hailed Pelham with loud familiarity.

'Brother officers,' he explained to Eliza, 'whose names I shall not trouble you with since all guards officers are identical.'

'I object!' a ringing voice cried from the back of the party.

Eliza turned to look. A remarkably handsome young man, probably not more than a year her senior, was looking at her – too boldly she thought – and smiling. There were cries of 'Hold your tongue, William!' from the others.

'My brother,' one of the others explained apologetically to Eliza. 'We regret to admit that he is a newly commissioned infantry officer – '

There was a roar of mock rage from the handsome William who rode his horse full tilt at his brother, scattering the party across the grass.

'A silly boy,' Pelham said sourly, retrieving his ladies.

'Who is he?' Julia said, smothering the small yawn she always gave when asking a question lest the audience should falsely suppose her in the least concerned with the reply.

'His name is William Cowper. He was thinking of the Law, I gather, but has unfortunately decided on the army,' said Pelham. 'He is an ensign with the 52nd Foot.'

William Cowper's brother came up to apologize, followed by the culprit, who looked not in the least chagrined.

'I must explain,' he said exclusively to Eliza, 'that it is infantry officers who do the real work in battle, for the cavalry are too careful in keeping their uniforms clean.'

'This information,' his brother said, 'comes from a man who has never been within a hundred miles of a battle in his life.'

William Cowper continued to bestow his frank and flattering stare on Eliza.

'Many a lady would have been unseated just now. You are clearly very skilled.'

She smiled. It was just what she liked to hear.

'May I know your name since you already have the advantage of knowing mine?'

'Eliza Beaumont,' and then she added with a coquettish glance she would have despised herself for a year ago, '*Mrs* Beaumont.'

'Mrs Beaumont!' he said in dismay. 'I do not think I can bear it!'

'You do not have to,' she said archly, and moved her horse away to a safe position on the far side of Pelham. William Cowper's fine eyes followed her as she went.

Pelham noticed his expression and Eliza's slightly heightened colour, and said to her, 'Was he impolite, or over polite?'

'Neither,' she said.

Pelham drew his own conclusions, rescued Julia from a trio of admirers and suggested that they should return. Eliza did not look again in the direction of Ensign Cowper, but she was thoroughly aware of being closely observed. If it had no other effect upon her, it inspired her riding, and she set off at a speed and with a suddenness whose only explanation was exhibitionism.

Upon their arrival home, Richard met them in the hall, fussing whether Julia might be dusty or fatigued or put out in any way. Brushing him aside, Julia sailed into her drawing room and cast herself upon the sofa.

'Whom did you see out riding, dearest? Did you pass many acquaintances?'

'Not one,' said Julia and yawned.

Eliza looked at her in startled amazement.

'But, Julia –'

'Not one,' said Julia with a shade of firmness. 'I very seldom see anyone I know.'

Eliza looked from her impassive face to Richard's complacent one.

'Julia –'

'You will oblige me,' Julia said with command, 'by not constantly interrupting. And you will both further oblige me by leaving me here to rest until dinner-time. I should be most grateful, Richard, if you were to step round to Lady Sidney and tell her how much too fatigued I am to attend her this evening. And, Eliza, I would be much obliged if you would write to Marchants for me. They long for news, and it troubles me to send it.'

In confusion and some indignation, Eliza consented. It was difficult to do otherwise while dependent upon Julia's hospitality. She saw her cousin settle herself upon the cushions with every semblance of intention to sleep, and as she left the room heard the great door close upon the obedient Richard. Upstairs, at the pretty French escritoire Julia had had placed in her bedroom, she sat down to describe in vigorous detail Julia's house, Julia's life, Julia's society and Julia's clothes. At the end of crossing the second sheet she heard the slam of a door and thought briefly that either Richard had been unnaturally quick about his errand, or that Lady Sidney had been away from home. One sheet and several exclamations later, Eliza gathered up pen and ink and paper and descended the stairs, intending most firmly to force Julia into adding at least one affectionate paragraph of her own. Sounds of laughter were coming from the drawing room, and Eliza felt a sudden lift of pleasure that Julia and Richard could, despite outward appearances, take some amusement from each other's company. Crossing the hall, Eliza failed to notice a strange hat and cane upon the chair by the door. If she had, she might not have flung open the drawing-room door with such unselfconsciousness, revealing Julia in the arms of a tall, tightly waisted officer with a plumy black moustache and boots as glossy as looking-glasses. Julia's hands were on his epauletted shoulders. His were around her body most possessively, Eliza thought furiously, and their mouths were but inches from each other. Eliza had no thought that she might be discreet.

'Julia!'

Julia's face flashed sideways, and the expression in her eyes changed from alarm to anger. The officer sprang back, wiping his mouth with the back of his hand as if Julia's last kiss were still visible there.

'How dare you!' Eliza shouted, forgetful of everything but her sense of outrage. 'How could you? How dare you!'

Julia spoke with awful control. 'And how dare *you* walk into my drawing room without announcing yourself? This is my house and my drawing room, and you may not roam them at will like the hoyden you are. Captain Lennox, may I most reluctantly present my country cousin, Mrs Beaumont!'

'I do not want to be presented!' Eliza cried as Captain Lennox did his best to advance with an easy smile. 'I could not bear to be presented to a man who – who – Oh, Julia, how could you act so?'

She turned abruptly and fled gack into the hall, dimly aware as she did so that Richard had entered the house again and was greeting Captain Lennox with hearty good humour. It was terrible, wicked, distasteful beyond anything Eliza had encountered before. Julia, her cousin Julia, was prepared to behave like that in her own house, almost without bothering to find any cover and entirely without bothering to offer any excuse. Was this what London life was like? Worse, was this what Julia was really like? Francis had known, of course, so had Pelham, she could see that now, looking back at their sympathy for Richard. In the light of the last distracting few minutes, even she could see it, recalling how Julia had flirted with Francis. The memory made Eliza feel sick. Francis! How near that danger had ever been she did not know, would never know. It was better perhaps not to know. She prayed that Francis might return and help her to compose herself. Perhaps she had made a mistake, it had all been so quick, perhaps they had only been talking. But no, grown people, married women, did not converse with officers in close embraces. And Julia had looked guilty for a fleeting second before she realized, Eliza thought with savagery, that being caught by Eliza was not much consequence. She could rely on Eliza's loyalty, after all. She always had. Eliza might be wild and impolite and awkward to have in one's drawing room, but she was fiercely loyal. There was no need to worry on that account. Well, Eliza decided, not this time. She would tell Richard. Why should Julia escape blamelessly from her wickedness, and why should poor Richard be kept in darkness? She would tell him after dinner. She went to the glass and smoothed her hair, preparing gentle speeches in her mind.

Halfway through dinner she saw the task was impossible. Captain Lennox came up in conversation, blandly talked of by Julia, and treated by Richard with the same complacent possessiveness he had for everything in his world.

'Lennox! Ah, yes. A capital fellow, capital. Always takes my advice, you know, most grateful to me for the greys I sold him, and quite rightly.'

'It is not the greys he is grateful for!' Eliza burst out. 'It is Julia!'

Richard laughed kindly.

'Indeed it is. He cannot do without her, he says. He was in the drawing room with her but half an hour ago when I came in, and professed himself vastly amused by the tale I had to tell him of the wranglings I had with my tailor. Said the story would be the toast of the regiment. Did he entertain you well, my love?'

'Vastly so,' said Julia indifferently.

'I would not have him bore you, dearest, indeed I would not. I am loth to forbid him the house since he relies so upon my counsel and has such admiration for you, but I will do so should you wish.'

'No, do not do that,' Julia said without urgency. 'He is very pleasant. It is a pity Eliza was so rude to him.'

Eliza spellbound with shock, could hardly reply coherently.

'Indeed I was rude, I had every reason to be rude, he was embracing – '

Julia flung back her head with laughter and Richard held up his large hand for silence.

'I would beg of you, Eliza, to control your temper while under our roof.'

'You do not understand me!' she cried, 'I am trying to tell you that Captain Lennox and Julia – '

Richard was shaking his head from side to side, eyes closed, thoughts quite self-absorbed.

'I want no information I cannot get from my beloved wife. I am delighted to have you, as my brother's wife, a guest in this house, but I beg you will behave with more courtesy and circumspection than my brother seems to expect from you.'

Eliza flung her napkin upon the table and hurried from the room. Francis must come home soon, he must, she could not bear the hypocrisy and blindness any more. She went back upstairs to her bedroom, and paced and paced, running to the door every time a step sounded in case it might be he. Her violent feelings were now directed at both Richard and Julia, and she was in a turmoil of disgust. If he were so self-satisfied, so egotistical, he deserved to be duped, but on the other hand, how could Julia bear to act out her deceit knowing Eliza knew the truth? It was hideous. She wanted to go away, now, back to Nashbourn, and never, never, come to London again.

Francis did not return until evening, and found Eliza sitting without candles in a state of considerable distress. She told him everything in a cascade of words immediately, her arms around his neck and her eyes still brilliant with indignation.

'Why did you not tell me, Francis? You knew, did you not, that Julia would deceive him. You knew more of her than I did! Oh, I cannot bear I should be so wrong – I mean, I do not mind being in error, but I cannot bear to be wrong for such a reason.'

Francis pulled her dishevelled head towards him until it lay comfortably beneath his chin.

'Yes, I knew, and I suppose I realized that some day you must know. But you were so staunch to Julia I could not bring myself to tell you, and now I wish I had. I wish you had not had to bear this afternoon on your own.'

Eliza said, her voice muffled by his coat, 'Is it very – very ordinary to behave as Julia does?'

Francis tightened his arms about her.

'In marriages made for money, I suppose it may be. But, not,' he added firmly, 'in those made for love.'

Eliza shuddered slightly.

'I could not bear to be jealous.'

'You will never have cause to be.'

'And nor shall you,' she declared fervently. 'Never, never. If you were to see me standing in a whole circle of officers, and they were all kneeling to me and offering me their hearts on the points of their swords, I should be thinking only of you, and you would know that my thoughts were only of you.'

'Do you mean that I have married the only woman on earth who will not flirt?'

'I do not know how,' Eliza said truthfully. 'But every man I talk to I am comparing unfavourably with you.'

'No wonder you are such diverting company.'

'You must not tease me about so serious a subject.'

'I am not teasing. I am devoutly, fervently grateful as well as being the most fortunate fellow on earth. Now come with me, and we will find Pelham and amuse ourselves.'

'I do not want to see Julia. I do not know how to behave before Julia. I cannot feel what I used to feel.'

'Nor can you make a scene every time you meet. Do you not think I do not feel guilty every time I see Richard and feel his ignorance? Or perhaps he is not ignorant. How can we know? He is a grown man, and if he needs help, he will ask for it. We cannot interfere, however dearly we burn to.'

Eliza swallowed, and nodded.

'I will try.'

'I love you,' Francis said.

There were two days left, and on the penultimate evening there was to be a reception whose importance was fully and repeatedly stressed to Eliza. It was to be attended by many of the commanders of the British army, and was to be the first taste Eliza was to have of the sort of social occasion that provided cover for decisions upon tactics and strategy. Francis' own commander, Lord Uxbridge, was to be there, it was even rumoured that the great Duke himself might attend. Julia was almost envious, but relented sufficiently to lend Eliza the set of pearls and diamonds Richard had given her as a wedding present. Eliza, unused to magnificent jewellery and reluctant to accept any favour from Julia, felt them to be an onerous responsibility.

'I shall have to sit down before half an hour is up, they are so heavy.'

Richard lent them his carriage. Eliza felt most apprehensive, especially when their arrival meant she must withdraw her hand from Francis' comforting grasp. Up the great staircase they moved, her cloak was taken from her, chandeliers blazing like galaxies above their heads. Francis, his hand beneath her elbow, propelled her gently forward into the crush of people, nodding here and there and seeming, to Eliza's amazement, perfectly comfortable. Lord Uxbridge, with curling hair and moustaches, was briefly gracious, but it was clear that he, like the other men in this great series of glittering rooms, wished to talk soldiering and not trivialities. Eliza could not blame him, she only wished she knew more of what they were talking. She looked about her, at the chatter and the colour and the animation, and thought almost with longing of the assembly rooms and provincial parties in Hampshire. She was brought champagne, an ice, asked if she cared for cards, questioned when Francis was going, complimented and stared at. It was unbearably hot, unbearable because the heat came from the press of humanity. Eliza shot a smile at Francis to show she was perfectly content and began to weave her way through the crowd to the windows. There was a small balcony outside which looked inviting, but clearly April in England was no month for languishing on balconies. So she opened the huge casement with difficulty, just a fraction, and let the cold air brush deliciously across her burning cheeks.

'I beg you will not catch cold, Mrs Beaumont.'

William Cowper was standing behind her, very close, and resplendent in his mess uniform. He was extremely handsome perhaps one of the most handsome men she had ever seen. In the confined space he had left between himself and the window, she turned round to face him.

'I feel I should love to catch cold at this moment, Mr Cowper.'

'And break my heart twice in one day? It was agony to learn that you are married, but I shall be entirely desolated if you are bent on self-destruction also.'

'I think this heat is more likely to destroy me.'

'Then come with me,' he said eagerly, and indicated a dim annexe at the end of the gallery which led to the card room. Eliza looked for Francis with quick apprehension.

'There is nothing to fear,' William Cowper said close to her ear. 'I am, after all, your slave already, and thus utterly obedient.'

Francis was not to be seen. It seemed to Eliza so complicated to resist this innocent invitation to find somewhere cooler and more comfortable. In any case, was she not a married woman and thus unassailable? As she had told Francis two nights before, the attentions of any man but himself left her entirely unmoved. William Cowper was nothing to her, nothing out of the ordinary, and it was better to be diverted briefly by him than to endure the tedium of knowing nobody in this press of people.

Without waiting for a verbal assent, William Cowper drew her hand through his braided arm, and propelled her skilfully to his goal, a small sofa in a shadowed corner where heavy curtains provided at least a measure of privacy.

'You are very sudden, you know,' Eliza said.

'Does that displease you?'

'No, but I distrust it.'

'You distrust the fact that we have exchanged but a handful of sentences, and yet that there is no other woman in the room whose company I seek?'

'Something of that order.'

'Does it not simply mean that you have never encountered such feelings as mine before?'

'If you have such feelings,' said Eliza, 'I do not believe in them.'

William Cowper leaned back for a moment, passed his hand over his eyes and said, 'You must believe, you know. I have never felt so, suddenly, as you put it, before.'

Eliza began to feel a distaste for the tone of the conversation.

She said, 'Why did you give up the Law for the army?'

He did not reply, he seemed sunk in reverie.

'I do believe,' she pursued, 'that it was for the sake of that romantic uniform.'

He gave her a wide and charming smile.

'If I had chosen the Law, I should not have been riding in Hyde Park yesterday morning, and I should not have seen you.'

Eliza snorted slightly.

'When do you go to Belgium?' she said.

'In four days. Shall you accompany your – your husband?'

Eliza looked down at her lap and sighed a very little.

'No,' she said in a low tone.

'Why not?' he cried indignantly.

'He does not think it – proper. Or right.'

'Should not you like to go?'

'Oh?' she exclaimed with impatience. 'Of course I should, but I cannot do what is – is not thought fit.'

'I should take you!' he declared gallantly. 'I cannot conceive of choosing any way of life that separated me from you. If I had you.'

'Well, you haven't,' Eliza said crossly, aware of the poor light this exchange was shedding on Francis. 'And I may not go, and I beg you not to talk of it further.'

'You are so lovely when you are angry.'

'I am not angry.'

'No,' he said in a tone of understanding, 'but you are very, very hurt that he, that your husband, does not want to take you to Belgium.'

'He does want to! He just does not think it is the best thing to do. He is thinking of me.'

'So am I,' said William Cowper.

He leaned forward and picked up her gloved hand. Very gently he unbuttoned the wrist and kissed the little pulsing space of skin within. Eliza watched as if mesmerized.

'I shall think of you always,' he said.

With a sudden shock, Eliza saw herself as if from far away, seated on a sofa in the half light with a young man kissing her wrist. She had been so absorbed in the implications of his remarks about Francis' refusal to take her to Belgium, and so unthinking of her own possible coquettishness, that not until this moment had she seen the picture she must present to anyone who cared to look her way. Colour rushed into her face, and in shame and confusion, she pulled her wrist from William Cowper's grasp.

'Please do not do that, do not touch me, indeed, you are most insulting – let me go –'

'Oh, you are lovely when you are angry,' he said again, 'but you now are angrier and thus lovelier. May I whisper one more thing to you, one for your ear only?'

'No!' Eliza cried, struggling to rise, and finding her dress firmly pinned down was forced to fall back into a corner of the sofa. 'No, you may not! I will not hear another word! You are despicable, despicable!'

'Only desperate,' William Cowper said smoothly. 'Desperate for a little of what your husband has in such abundance.'

'You are an obnoxious boy,' Eliza said emphatically. 'Nothing but an obnoxious boy.'

Across the rom Pelham, turning in search of Francis and craning his neck above the crowd, had caught a brief and chilling glimpse of William Cowper's lips pressed to Eliza's wrist. Averting his gaze as quickly, he saw that he had not been the only one to notice. Three people away from him, Francis himself stood transfixed, his height meaning he had no difficulty in seeing over the gathering to the annexe.

It was as if Eliza had never promised him her utter fidelity anew two days before. Somehow, in that heated room full of light and warmth and decorated women and gilded men and the seductive glitter of their lives, Francis forgot that he could rely upon her. The raffish atmosphere of the evening was stronger than any other impression and seemed more dangerous than it had ever struck him before. He seemed surrounded by curls and bare shoulders, whispers and flattery, a gaiety that seemed suddenly furtive. For a few moments he watched as William Cowper's faultless features came perilously close to Eliza's bent coppery head. He was clearly pleading, but it was not possible to distinguish her replies from her manner. Pelham slid to Francis' elbow.

'Shall I break it up?'

'No.'

Across the room, Eliza drew away as far as the limits of the sofa would allow, and a look of dismay crossed William Cowper's face. She looked now as if she was speaking sharply, but she did not rise and leave him.

'To think that if I leave her here,' Francis said between clenched teeth, 'I leave her exposed to this.'

Part Two

10

The Channel crossing was hideous. Eliza could not remember having even seen the sea before, let alone travelled on it, and the grey swelling of it looked most ominous from the quay at Dover. She stood wrapped in her cloak by her own trunks and watched with interest and excitement as blindfolded horses were led aboard, followed by crates and boxes, wheeled guns, and more soldiers, than it seemed possible the ship could hold. It was a damp and drizzling day and there was no horizon, for sea and sky merged in the grey dimness out there. Somewhere out there too was Ostend. They had originally been going all the way round to Antwerp, since it was so much nearer the capital, but Francis, knowing from miserable experience that he was no sort of sailor, had decided on the shortest possible sea route. Soldiers tramping past Eliza under their loads of ammunition and blankets looked at her keenly. Officers' wives were accustomed to travel in the shelter of each other's protection, but after the incident with William Cowper, Francis had decided, for the moment at least, to trust her to no protection but his own.

Eliza was allotted the officer's cabin on the upper gun-deck, and was uncomfortably aware of the crowding of men and animals everywhere else on the ship. Francis said he would try to join her, but that the sea made him an unfit companion for any but the grave. Eliza said he would be glad to nurse him. Francis smiled weakly.

'I would not have you do it. Seasickness is the most degrading of conditions, and I would rather you knew nothing of it.'

She did know nothing of it herself, but despite the closed door of her cabin, she was painfully conscious that she must be the only person on the heaving ship who was not praying for a speedy death. The sea proved treacherously choppy, and the ship tossed and plunged among the swelling waves. Francis, ashen and groaning, had left her half an hour after their departure from Dover, and after three hours of his absence, and being heartily tired of her swaying solitude, she ventured to leave the cabin and find him. The deck was appalling, slippery and horrible, the stench nauseating, the guns at the closed gun-ports draped with suffering forms. Eliza could see through the dimness the companionway, a sort of rope net, which led into the air of the upper deck, but she doubted, even could she brave the sickening smell and sliding bodies, that she could make her way across those foul and slimy boards. She retreated into her cabin, closed the door and breathed with relief the relatively pure air within. Being in the stern of the ship, she could see nothing of interest, England had gone, Belgium was hours away.

Some interminable time later, lifting her head from a game of patience she had no real interest in, she saw a gleam of steely sunlight through the mist. It was as good as it promised, and soon a pale soft glow was stealing over the sky and smoothing the sea as it went. Francis was brought to her later, supported by two sailors, and left in an armchair at her side, hollow-cheeked with misery, his eyes closed.

'Those men,' he said faintly, indicating the departing sailors, 'told me how glad they were to see us all setting out to give Napoleon a final thrashing. They said every man in our navy hates Napoleon. I told them that no hatred on earth equals that which I feel for the English Channel.'

She sponged him with eau-de-Cologne and made him drink a little brandy. He said, 'You may see worse than this you know.'

She thought of the deck outside and some part of her quailed a little at the prospect – but she would not admit to it. Francis slept then, and she sat and watched him while a faint colour returned to his cheeks and the westering sun streamed in upon them.

After southern England, Belgium seemed a discouraging spectacle, flat and featureless with reluctant inhabitants.

Eliza, after a fruitless tussle for hot water with the landlady at an inn in Ostend, complained of this national grudgingness to Francis. He was lying in bed, trying to prevent the room from seeming to undulate sickeningly about him by sheer will-power.

'You cannot blame the Belgians. Last year most of them were Frenchmen and now they are obliged to be Englishmen. It is difficult to be genial if you are thus confused.'

'I do not see that a simple request for hot water has anything to do with politics.'

Francis opened his eyes wide since he seemed better able to control the room's movements that way. 'Perhaps everything is politics to a Belgian.'

Eliza left him and went in search of Fanny. Mrs Howell had been most positive on that last morning at Nashbourn that Fanny would prove the most resourceful girl to take as a maid to London (and on to Belgium as Mrs Howell privately believed), but Eliza already had doubts. Fanny had been most reluctant to leave London, probably on account of Julia's second footman, and was now to be found leaning over the gallery rail of the inn and blowing kisses to the soldiers around the pump in the yard below.

Eliza said, 'Would you prefer to go down below among them?'

Fanny shrank back, and blushed. She was a fair girl with strong features and seemingly intelligent blue eyes which gave no indication, Eliza was beginning to feel, of the void that lay behind them.

'You will go, if you please, and see what sort of supper you can find us. Captain Beaumont is too much indisposed to need anything.'

Fanny was horrified. To go down to the kitchens whose whereabouts she did not know, among all these rough men, this foreign language, oh no, she could not, indeed, ma'am, she could not. Eliza, tired and hungry and unsettled herself, felt no pity.

'I am having to learn new ways, Fanny, and so must you.'

Fanny began to cry.

'I cannot, ma'am, I am afraid to, I cannot.'

Eliza reached out and shook her in exasperation. There was plainly nothing for it but to do it herself since if she had nothing to eat she felt she might weep, too. She left Fanny huddled in the dusk, and went down a maze of tortuous and poorly lit passages and staircases, following the odour of cooking. Her French was poor, but she did not mind how inaccurate she was as long as she got what she wanted. The kitchens looked dark and unwholesome and everyone in it rudely unaffected by her presence, but a little pot boy came to her aid, and with soup and bread and wine Eliza climbed back to her room for the first night of her life away from England.

There was a commotion on the narrow landing that led back to her room and the suffering Francis. An open door gave a glimpse of a lit room within and a tumbled bed and Eliza could hear sobbings and gaspings and a man's voice trying to soothe. She stopped, her tray in her hands, and waited. The man's voice at least was English.

'Louisa, I beg you, control yourself just a little. The nausea will soon pass, I do assure you. I did warn you that you might feel so, I did beg you to wait for a calmer day. Please, dearest, try to lie still, it will ease the pains.'

The gasping stopped long enough for some panted words Eliza could not grasp. She set down her tray upon the bare wooden floor and ventured to the open doorway. A girl with yellow curls and a crumpled green travelling dress was tossing backwards and forwards on the pillow, and over her bent a young man in uniform, a glass of water in his hand and a slightly desperate expression on his face. Eliza came forward into the room.

'May I help?'

The young man's head jerked up. He took in her voice, language and appearance and a flood of relief swept his face. He straightened.

'I do not know what to do for the best,' he said helplessly. 'She was so ill on the crossing and the pain will not leave her. I cannot persuade her to lie still.'

Eliza came to the bedside and looked down. She was a pretty girl, but greenish white at the moment, and her hair was damp with sweat. Eliza thought of Francis' stoicism at the end of the landing and her mouth tightened a little. She put her hand on the girl's brow. It was clammy but cool.

'She has no fever.'

'Oh, no – and she has not vomited for two hours or more, but she says the pain is still terrible.'

'It is! It is!' the girl shrieked suddenly, tossing restlessly back and forth.

Eliza bent over her.

'Nonsense,' she said firmly.

The girl's blue eyes flew open and her body halted in its twistings.

'Who are you?'

'My name is Eliza Beaumont. I crossed today, too, and my husband was terribly seasick as well. But he is lying still,' she added severely, 'and feels much the better for it.'

The girl sat up.

'I am Louisa Chetwood – and this is my husband Ned. Really, you have no conception of how ill I felt. Truly, I thought I would die, and I did not much mind if I did.'

'You are on dry land now,' Eliza said unsympathetically. 'You are in Belgium.'

Louisa Chetwood turned her blue gaze on the shabby room and shuddered.

'Will it all be as terrible as this?'

'No, indeed,' her husband said with fervour, animated by relief at the appearance of recovery, 'Brussels will be wonderful. Everyone will be there!'

'I smell soup,' Louisa said suddenly, and not without interest.

'It is mine,' said Eliza, remembering it cooling outside on the landing. 'My maid was afraid to fetch it.' She looked at Louisa and smiled mischievously. 'Would you care for some?'

Louisa looked briefly sheepish, but her appetite was too real. She nodded and blushed a little. Eliza brought her meagre supper into the room and set it beside Louisa on the bed. At the actual sight of the soup, greasy and full of nameless morsels, Louisa's recovery lapsed a little, but she was persuaded to take a little bread, and a glass of water and wine. Her poor husband, limp with relief at this miraculous turn of events, devoured the repulsive soup in seconds, gazing at Eliza over the bowl with eyes full of admiration and gratitude. Eliza, meanwhile, finished what bread was left and told herself that Fanny would simply have to go hungry, which perhaps might jog her courage on the next occasion that initiative was required. Louisa Chetwood, pushing back her tangled curls, became quite animated as the food encouraged her.

'You cannot conceive what a delight it is to see you! I thought Belgium promised to be a most savage place after that hideous crossing and this wretched inn! Do you ride? Do you care to dance? Oh, that is capital. We shall have such times together in Brussels. I begin to think it might be amusing after all!'

'I entirely agree that anything might be amusing after this, but I do not quite understand why the whole world is travelling to Brussels.'

'To see the fun, Mrs Beaumont!' Ned Chetwood said in surprise, 'It will be a wonderful time! And we may all tell our grandchildren how we saw Napoleon trounced.'

Louise clapped her hands together.

'Will that not be glorious?'

Eliza stood up, and brushed crumbs from her skirt.

'I must go to my husband. I hope you pass a peaceful night.'

'Shall we see you in Brussels? Oh, do say we may! You will find us in the Rue du Vieux Pont, number six, is it not, Ned? Should we miss you in the morning, come to us there, oh, say you will!'

Eliza looked down at her pretty, eager face and smiled.

'Oh, I should like to,' she said. 'We have no lodging yet but be assured I shall find you in yours. Good night!'

She closed the door carefully behind her, and with a lightened heart went softly down the passage to find Francis sleeping tranquilly on the dubiously laundered bolster of their bed.

Francis, worn out with nausea, slept profoundly and awoke demanding eggs and ham. He was told by the landlord via his servant that the army had eaten both. Francis produced francs and the innkeeper produced ham. Eliza, itching and unrefreshed after a restless night on a mattress which rustled independently of her own movements, tried with Fanny's help to wash, but it was not possible. The only pump was still surrounded by bellowing soldiers and Fanny clung to her refusal to go among them, even for a bowl of water. She had to content herself with a furious brushing of her hair, and the donning of clean linen, then she oversaw, with some exasperation, Fanny's repacking of her possessions, and went thankfully down to join Francis.

The day was grey and calm. A mist still hung over the sea and the flat coast and spread itself lightly over the level fields around. There was a journey of some seventy miles ahead of them to reach Brussels, and already Eliza felt that England and all she knew was a world away from her. She looked forward with some pleasure and excitement to Brussels and a wealth of people and entertainments she as yet knew nothing of. A closed carriage was brought, boxes stowed away, the door held for her.

She looked about for her friends of the night before, but they were nowhere to be seen. As they had assured lodgings, they were probably not under the same pressure to reach Brussels before dusk as the homeless Beaumonts were. It did not matter. Number six, Rue du Vieux Pont, Louisa Chetwood had said, and Eliza would certainly seek her out. She was not only the sole woman Eliza knew of in Brussels, but she promised also to be an entertaining companion. Eliza settled herself on the seat and considered that she was now more than the raw novice traveller she had been yesterday and had already managed several foreign situations without undue difficulty.

Francis paid the inn-keeper, who looked with sullen disbelief at the coins in his hand, and amidst a company of infantrymen also on their way south-east they left Ostend.

As the morning wore on and the mist lifted, it was possible to see further afield than the muddy edges of the rutted road. Francis had warned Eliza that the journey through Belgium might be both unpleasant and distressing since an army left a good deal of human debris in its wake, and thousands of men had already tramped towards Brussels. The first part only seemed unpleasant because of its monotony, as they jogged interminably through spreading fields of green and shuttered lifeless villages. There were soldiers everywhere, of course, company after company beating a path to Brussels, but these marching red-coated forms had quickly become a familiar sight to Eliza.

As they neared Ghent, she became conscious of other

human figures than soldiers in the landscape: the army's wives and children, the travelling merchants, groups of tailors and blacksmiths distinguishable by the tools of their trade strapped to their baggage. It was extremely fascinating, Eliza had had no idea that an army took such a vast and complicated life with it. Occasionally, in some patch of shelter, like a wall or a group of trees, there were signs of the toll an army took of its men and its followers in the handfuls of sick soldiers on the grass, the women, exhausted by the journey, sitting at the roadside. Numbers of expressionless and drained faces were raised to Eliza's as her carriage jolted by, blank-eyed in the face of the inevitability of their lot. She turned to speak to Francis, but he had a despatch box of papers open beside him, despite the lurching, and was oblivious to all else. She looked out again, fascinated and saddened. The tide of soldiery, that wave of red coats was like a sea sweeping relentlessly on, leaving the weak and the sick washed up in this foreign wilderness. Could it be preferable, Eliza wondered, to endure that crossing and then trudge wearily for anything up to a hundred miles, an infant in your arms, children at your skirts, rather than stay behind in England? Was it not better to be alone there than go entirely unconsidered and sorely tried here? She thought of those cheerless cottages at Quihampton suddenly, with their air of raw poverty, and saw that for some, at least, there was no worst or best to choose.

They stopped in Ghent to dine. Francis' servant, a stalwart man named Tom Bridman from remote Dorset, who had rightly decided Fanny was of no use to his master's wife, took charge of arrangements for both Eliza and Francis, despite his strong views on accompanying wives. They chose a small inn on the edge of Ghent which had an orchard and was not already a seething mass of soldiers, and were quickly provided with a small measure of privacy and a dish of stewed rabbit. The relief of being off the road was enormous. Eliza wondered how much further they had to go.

'About the same distance again.'

'But we shall not reach Brussels until after nightfall. And we have no lodging!'

'Then you are getting a taste of army life, dearest.'

'I am very stiff.'

'The alternative,' Francis said heartlessly, 'is to be saddle-sore.'

After dinner, Eliza found that Bridman had taken all her baggage in his own care with Francis'. Francis said he did not know what she had done to deserve such solicitude. Anxious not to appear to take this gesture for granted, she stopped on the way back to the carriage to thank Bridman, and found him rolling up a very small uniform into a manageable package.

'That is hardly for yourself, Bridman?'

'No, ma'am.'

'Then who is it for?'

'A boy, ma'am.'

'What boy, Bridman?'

'A dead boy, ma'am.'

'Dead?'

Bridman straightened up, the roll of white and scarlet cloth under his arm.

'A dead drummer boy, ma'am. Died in the barn there an hour back. Know his village, ma'am. Takin' his things back to his mother.'

Much moved, Eliza reached out her hands for the bundle of garments and spread them on the grass. White breeches that might have fitted her so narrow were they, a torn and grimy shirt and a uniform jacket, the side stiff with dried blood. She looked up questioningly at Bridman.

'They bled him, ma'am.'

In the pocket was a paper, folded round a lock of greying brown hair. It bore the boy's name and parish, written in an educated hand, probably the parson's. Eliza slipped her hand into the other pockets. There was a rosary of wooden beads and a chicken bone, picked clean. She touched the stuff of the breast of the coat.

'What did he die of?'

'Fever, ma'am.'

'How old was he?'

Bridman shrugged and knelt to fold the clothes again. Eliza watched him, A boy had breathed inside that cloth but an hour before, while she ate rabbit and laughed with Francis. Now the boy was under Belgian earth, buried by men who knew nothing about him and could do no more for him than see he was decently put away. Somewhere in southern England, a mother in a village did not know she no longer had a son.

'Will that be all, ma'am?'

Eliza abruptly recollected why she had come to speak to Bridman.

'I came to thank you for taking charge of my baggage.'

'Don't want it lost, ma'am.'

Eliza nodded and turned back slowly towards the carriage. All the soldiers milling about on the high road out there assumed a new significance, each one with as frail a life as the little drummer boy had had. Eliza climbed thoughtfully to her seat. In her own experience death had so far been something that came in the fullness of time, even her own parents' death had assumed the comforting remoteness of a legend. Old servants had died at Marchants, even one or two in childbirth, but they had died among friends and familiarity, not alone in a foreign barn, pillowed on straw and blanketed with inadequate clothing. The carriage moved off and Eliza gazed from the window at the stone barn until a clump of great elms hid it from view.

As they went on to Brussels, preparations for a similar journey were being made in England. Francis had had no communication with his father since the previous summer, but Richard had felt it incumbent upon him to inform Sir Gerard of Francis' movements. As soon as Eliza and Francis had left for Dover, Richard had written to his father to tell him of it, omitting to say that Francis had not been alone. Sir Gerard, solitary and bitter throughout a fierce winter at Quihampton, made his resolve immediately upon receiving Richard's letter. Orders were given to make arrangements for a journey of some months to Belgium, a brief note was despatched to his elder son, and Sir Gerard prepared to follow Francis silently, into battle if necessary.

11

Brussels was astonishing. Not a hundred miles away was
Napoleon's newly assembled army, and the capital was
rapidly filling with the Belgian, Dutch and German allied
soldiers that Wellington had professed himself so distrustful
of, yet an air of great gaiety prevailed as if victory was not
to be doubted. Eliza was entranced with her first view of
those springtime streets filled with uniforms and well-dressed
women and pervaded everywhere with an atmosphere of
holiday. By the end of two months, she was to find both the
uniforms and the atmosphere thoroughly wearisome, but
this first April glance was seductive in the extreme. They
found rooms as secluded as they could, after an uncomfortable first night cast upon Pelham's willing but cramped
hospitality, in the saffron-washed courtyard of an inn tucked
away behind the Rue Royale. The prices were exorbitant,
grossly inflated by the present demand for accommodation,
but worth it, Francis said romantically, since the inn was
named Les Deux Colombes and doves are after all notori-
ously faithful to each other. He was anxious Eliza should like
the rooms since he would have to spend any amount of time
away from her at Gramont, where the cavalry was stationed.

The apartments were tall and dim, with painted wooden
cupboards, a heavily curtained bed of rock-like hardness, and
high, shuttered windows that overlooked the cobbled space
of the inn's yard, filled with wooden buckets, geraniums and
a thin and filthy pig. Francis said he was sorry about the pig.

'After that ship,' Eliza said with distaste, 'any animal smell
is bearable. Pigs could not smell worse than people.'

Francis left for some official errand, and she stood for a

while and looked about her at the comfortless furniture and the locked trunks and the gloom and the foreignness. There was work to be done. Brooking no objection, no plea of fright, she sent a quaking Fanny for water and a scrubbing brush, tied her hair in a kerchief and opened the lid of every trunk so that she should be committed to unpacking it. When Francis returned he said he had no idea she was such a little home-maker. She made a face at him.

'It may hardly be on the scale of deciding the future of Europe with the Duke of Wellington, but it is what my uncle would call a commendable effort.'

In the weeks of waiting that followed, Eliza spent surprisingly little time in those tall, dark rooms at Les Deux Colombes. During late April, May and early June of 1815, the majority of the temporary population of Brussels were bent on pleasure, and they swept Eliza along with them. Among the flood of new faces there were several familiar ones: Pelham, almost daily; the Cowper brothers, William still claiming to suffer from his mastering passion; Henry Leslie from Hampshire. Scandal and Napoleon claimed equal shares in every conversation, balls and summer parties occupied the gentle evenings as spring turned into summer. Eliza found new friends among the officers' wives and would walk with them in the park on warm afternoons, whiling away the time until the men might be free to join them and amuse them again. At first, it was all pleasurable, all delightful, the novelty of people endlessly fascinating, but then the natural energy of her personality began to assert itself and she began to long for some role to play, some duty to perform.

'I envy you so!' she said to Francis one night. 'You have some allotted task to perform! Even Bridman does, burnishing your boots and polishing your buttons. But I have nothing to do, and I cannot see how I can be useful.'

'You are useful to me, just being here,' he said. 'I have a very small appetite for practical military talk, and it is an unspeakable relief to come back to you.'

He looked across at her, sitting on the edge of the sofa, twisting her curls in her fingers.

'Are you bored?'

'Not exactly. No – no, I am not bored. But I am not occupied with the right things. We have dined out every day this week and I have danced right through a pair of slippers and the time has passed very pleasantly, but I have not *used* the time, I have simply let it pass.'

'Did we use it any better at Nashbourn?'

'There was not the contrast then!' Eliza cried. She thought of that very morning when Francis had been called to Gramont early, and she had taken a full hour to dress and then walked with Louisa and dined with her later in a great company of new acquaintances. She had come back to Les Deux Colombes full of gaiety and gossip, and Francis and Pelham were there before her, engrossed in serious talk and strategy, and she had felt her mood to be trivial and frivolous by comparison with theirs.

'You have an occupation, a discipline!' she said.

Francis sighed.

'Would you prefer to go home?'

She was horrified. 'Oh, no, indeed no, I did not mean that! Oh, Francis I am very sorry to complain. I do not mean to worry you!'

'I am not worried, but I wish you to be happy.'

'I am happy,' she declared staunchly. 'I desired to come and I would be wretched if I had not. I am simply greedy for a taste of your world.'

'You would not like it, dearest, if you had it,' he said gently, 'and I am thankful that you are kept from it.'

Whatever Eliza's feelings, the days went slipping on without any of them being remarkable for anything other than the numbers of people thronging them.

She would still walk in the sunshine and dance in the evenings and play cards and eat ices, but she did it with less absolute delight than she had during the first weeks, and looked forward to seeing Francis not only for the delight of his company, but because she now loved to hear the army's plans. It was true he could tell her little, but she had enough information in her mind to satisfy her at least partially. When she could, she would sit unobtrusively listening to the men's conversation, and it always seemed to her extraordinary that there was all this endless talk about Napoleon and yet nobody seemed to do anything about him.

Some afternoons Francis was free to walk with her, and they would meet groups of fellow officers beneath the plane trees in the park. The parade of uniforms in the park always seemed particularly outrageous, theatrical affairs hardly suited to battle.

'Some foreign officers,' Pelham said with scorn, lounging on the grass at Eliza's feet, 'invent their own. It is a great help to Napoleon, of course, since it makes him more than able to infiltrate spies.'

William Cowper was inevitably hovering near, tolerated by Francis with a kind of repressed savagery, and largely ignored by Eliza.

'Worse than that,' William said, 'the French have managed to stop numbers of our spies. The post-chaises from Paris are constantly intercepted.'

Pelham and Francis looked away across the park elaborately unconcerned. William Cowper was not to be subdued by realizing that his information was hardly new. He continued:

'It is only a matter of time before Napoleon makes a mistake.'

Francis turned to Pelham. 'The Duke will wait to react to Napoleon.'

'He had better not wait too long,' Pelham said. 'Napoleon is determined to drive a wedge between our British and Prussian flanks, and if we loiter around Belgian villages much longer – what is the place?'

'Quatre Bras,' William Cowper said. He was ignored.

'Is the Prince of Orange to come?' Eliza asked.

William Cowper, delighted at a chance to answer her directly, spoke before Francis or Pelham had the chance.

'He is watching for the French. He is just my age – our age. Think, our age and in command of forty thousand men.'

'I pity that forty thousand,' Francis said over his shoulder. 'Let us hope the Prince confines himself to the simplest of orders. Twenty-two, is he? Scarce out of the cradle.'

'That means I am still in mine,' Eliza said.

Pelham said gallantly, 'I would prefer your command any day.'

'Are we a very bad army?' Eliza demanded.

'We are,' Francis said, smiling. 'Half the Belgians and

Dutch fought for Napoleon before Elba, and it is only changed frontiers that make them our luckless soldiers now.'

'Someone said,' Eliza ventured, for Francis was contemptuous of gossip, 'that Wellington has called the army infamous.'

Pelham threw back his head and laughed delightedly.

'How insulted Napoleon would be if he knew! To fight this disgruntled rabble for Europe at some undistinguished crossroads in this unremarkable country!'

'Then there will be battle?' Eliza asked quickly.

'My dear girl,' Pelham said, 'I do hope so, the trouble it's been to get here and the boredom of the last weeks.'

But whatever talk there was of battle, the air of calm and enjoyment never deserted Brussels, to the amazement of any Bonapartist sympathizers left in the capital. Eliza was taken, with indifference on her part, to what seemed an interminable series of cricket matches, for the husband of her closest new friend, Louisa Chetwood, was an enthusiastic player.

'Never did I see such a silly game,' she declared roundly to Louisa, as they sat in the shade of parasols on the boundary. 'Nothing ever seems to happen and I wonder they do not fall asleep where they stand.'

'Ned would not care to hear you say that,' Francis said smiling. 'He claims it is a game of outstanding subtlety.'

'He really likes to show off his calves in those breeches,' Louisa said, 'and he says that if I am watching him play cricket, I cannot be about any mischief for five or six hours together.'

'Do you not count me as mischief?' Pelham asked.

'No, indeed I do not. By the time I have sat here in the sun and not understood a single moment of the game for half a day, I am too worn out for mischief anyway.'

Eliza looked across at the white-clad officers dotted about on the shaven strip of green, and at the numbers of soldiers watching idly from the far side.

'May the men not play?'

Pelham threw his hands up in mock horror. 'Eliza, Eliza! It is an officers' game!'

'In that case, it clearly needs the common touch to liven it a little.'

'May I explain the principles of the game?'

'Again, Francis? No, you may not. When there seems no point to a game, the mention of principles seems quite preposterous.'

A faint burst of clapping came from the soldiers across the field.

'What happened?'

'Ned scored a run.'

Eliza looked amazed. 'But he did not run! He walked but a few steps, did he not, Louisa? I swear I did not see him run.'

'I doubt he can run,' Louisa said. 'He is so used to horseback I wonder his legs do not fail him utterly when he puts them to the ground.'

'I hope he does not realize what a deeply unsatisfactory audience he has,' Francis said.

'Oh, he does!' Eliza assured him. 'I asked him but yesterday why they do not perform on horseback! Think how vastly the game would be improved!'

Three times also, and with enthusiasm on those occasions, she was escorted out to Gramont for race-meetings, heavily patronized by all the cavalry commanders. At a cavalry review she had her first, and too generous, taste of pink champagne and a splitting headache to remember it by. As the days passed, tedium might be growing, but so was confidence. Eliza, no more than anyone else, could not imagine that the Duke did not know precisely what he meant to do, and therefore, could afford to idle away his time until the crucial moment, with Lady Francis Webster and Lady Georgiana Lennox leaning upon his arm. Eliza was fascinated by them both, the former because she was so evidently and heavily pregnant, the latter because she was so young, and would watch them covertly across ballrooms.

Louisa Chetwood would tease her. 'Hampshire is wholly removed from life, is it not, Eliza? Of course, you never did see society before, did you, Eliza?'

Eliza had to agree, but pointed out that surrounded by such looseness of character as she was in Brussels, her worldliness was improving fast.

'Not that I do not think Hampshire preferable for a lifetime.'

'How prim you are.'

'No,' said Eliza, 'practical.'

There were balls galore, some even given by Wellington himself, but most of the talk of balls was concentrated upon that to be given by the Duchess of Richmond on June 15. Stories were laughingly circulated of how, early in May, she had asked the Duke of Wellington if she might give her ball, and he had said that indeed she might as he had no anticipation of any activity before July. The Richmonds had rented a house in the Rue de la Blanchisserie, and by early June workmen were to be seen going in and out, engaged in their task of creating a setting of romantic magnificence for the ball.

Francis said one night, 'I gather from exhausted husbands all around me that the Richmond ball is the talk of Brussels.'

Eliza, with considerable self-consciousness said:

'I thought – I wonder – would it be a dreadful extravagance to have – ' She stopped.

'A new dress, dearest? Indeed you shall. And if the dresses being worn recently are anything to go by, it will hardly be an extravagance. There appears to be almost no material needed for the bodice at all.'

Francis was in a broad good humour. At dinner that day news had reached him that William Cowper, attempting to scale a wall while drunk in pursuit of some fair one who was encouraging him from a third-floor window, had fallen and broken his leg badly in two places. Not only did the accident keep him confined to his billet until the leg was set, but if Napoleon would only bestir himself, the 52nd Foot would be able to fight unhindered by the amateur advice of Ensign Cowper. Since hearing that Wellington was relying upon the infantry in any engagement to come, he had become impossibly cocksure, and a broken leg was a relief to almost all his acquaintances. Francis' reaction to the accident was almost boisterous. He did not doubt that Eliza's encounter with him had been wholly unintentional on her part, but all the same if William Cowper was laid up in his rooms with a broken leg and, it was reported, with several cases of claret, he was at least one pitfall the less for the Richmonds' ball.

On June 14, the day before the ball, Francis was summoned to Gramont. Eliza, thinking it of no more consequence than his other dashes to cavalry headquarters, went off with a light heart to her dressmaker's to collect her gown, pale green silk and infinitely becoming. It was low cut, lower cut than any dress she would have dared to wear at home, but there was no doubt that coppery hair, white skin in abundance and green silk were a seductive combination. She took it back to Les Deux Colombes in a state of great gratification. There was no sign of Francis. She dressed again and went to dine with the Chetwoods, staying to play cards, and when she was returning home in the evening, her carriage passed that of the Duke himself, presumably on his way to the Rue de la Blanchisserie. There were lighted windows everywhere and the sounds of voices and laughter in the soft, warm night. Eliza leant back drowsily on her cushions and looked up at the yellow summer moon, and idly wondered if Napoleon had grown tired of it all and gone home to Paris.

Their rooms were still empty, but Fanny had laid her night-clothes on the bed and lighted the candles. Eliza had scarcely laid down her shawl when there was a peremptory knock on the door and Bridman came in without waiting for an acknowledgement.

'Saw the carriage, ma'am.'

Eliza nodded.

'Bin waitin', ma'am. Rode from Gramont. Message from the Captain, ma'am.'

'Is anything the matter, Bridman?'

'Not as yet, ma'am,' he said ominously and held out a letter.

Francis had written:

Dearest, I am detained but there is nothing to cause you any anxiety. I will be back to take you to the ball tomorrow night. If by any chance I am further detained, I have notified Captain Chetwood that I entrust you to his care at the ball. Sweet dreams. Ever your F.

Army business again, always army business. Eliza tossed the note down, yawned and smiled sleepily at Bridman.

'Do you go back to Gramont now?'

'Yes, ma'am.'

152

'God speed then.'

'Any message for the Captain, ma'am?'

'Tell him,' Eliza said, 'that I will do as I am told.'

She summoned Fanny, an amenable Fanny now that Brussels had produced attractions even more glittering than London's, and was helped to bed in a mood of languorous contentment. It was, of course, a little melancholy to be without Francis but, really, Brussels felt very home-like now and secure, and tomorrow did promise enormous pleasures, and she did so look forward to dazzling Francis in that green gown. The pig below her window moved restlessly in its straw, the hens clucked comfortably together, while faint sounds of revelry drifted in on the June night and lulled Eliza to sleep.

12

By the time Eliza awoke, Napoleon was already several hours into Belgium. She awoke with deliberate slowness, savouring the summer morning and her own sense of being so thoroughly rested, and while she ate her breakfast the French Imperial Guard was driving the Prussians out of Charleroi, some thirty miles away from Brussels to the south. A note came from Louisa Chetwood to say they did hope Eliza could bear the monotony of dining with them on two consecutive days, but they had been allotted the duty of chaperoning her and intended to fulfil it conscientiously. Eliza sat at the open window of her bedroom and looked out at the blue sky and the red geraniums and the rosy tiles of the roof-tops. She wrote to Mrs Lambert, a letter that was no more than a catalogue of amusements, but which gratified her aunt more than any description of a more serious nature could have done.

'To think little Eliza is consorting with such people as the Duchess of Richmond and has actually seen the Duke of Wellington in person – it is quite beyond belief! Such a regret that Julia cannot share in it all, she looks so well in evening dress. What a shame to be confined to London when she would cause such admiration in Brussels.'

Just before three, Eliza summoned her carriage and was taken to the Chetwoods' to dine. As she moved at a leisurely pace through the sunny streets, a mud-covered Prussian officer was galloping into Brussels to inform Wellington of the fighting at Charleroi. Eliza was greeted with much warmth by the Chetwoods and a circle of friends already there, and several of the men endeavoured to persuade her to promise them dances nine hours later at the ball. The long windows of the Chetwoods' dining room were open, giving on to a long green garden, walled and sheltered, and thick with creamy roses. Eliza was offered pink champagne by the officer who had been responsible for plying her too lavishly at the review, and it was laughingly declined. There was a pineapple in the centre of a positive mountain of fruit on the sideboard, and enormous bets were laid as to how many leaves it had. Eliza was given the task of pulling and counting them, only to discover that her host was nearest, and then to be heartily accused of being in league with him. The pineapple was then handed to Captain Chetwood with a further wager that he could not hit the tree growing twenty yards away at the end of the garden. He stood upon his chair, shouting with effort, and hurled the tawny fruit into the hot garden, where it crashed into the grasses, feet short of its target. The noise was uproarious, and only after some while did Eliza notice a servant vainly gesturing to the Captain from the edge of the hubbub. She went quickly round the table and touched him on the shoulder.

'Ned, you are wanted.'

'By you, sweetest, I trust.'

Eliza indicated the servant. In a sudden silence, Captain Chetwood sprang off his chair and followed him.

'It will be the cook again,' Louisa Chetwood said. 'He is divinely skilled but when angry he likes to vent his rage by pouring hot soup over the kitchen servants.'

'Like this!' someone cried, emptying his champagne glass over his neighbour's head. This naturally called for instant retaliation, and with shrieks of delighted terror, the ladies retreated behind the window curtains and to obscure corners, fearful equally for their dresses and of missing anything. Eliza moved quickly to the door that led into the hall, and was soon rewarded by the door opening a crack, and Edward Chetwood begging her in a whisper to fetch Major Webster to him and to say nothing of it. Fortunately Webster was close at hand fending off a full decanter with a chair. Eliza held the door for him, feigned closing it, and stood, her ear pressed to the crack, pretending she was about to escape from the riot.

'Slender Billy's been through,' Chetwood said.

Major Webster, shaking wine from his ears and whiskers, looked bemused.

'Listen, Henry,' Chetwood said earnestly, 'my footman saw him.'

'Who?'

'The Prince of Orange, dolt, coming at a speed which means he must have news. He was making for Wellington's quarters.'

'Ah,' Webster said thickly, 'must go home and change. Can't fight in a wet shirt.'

Eliza went out into the hall.

'Is it begun?'

Ned Chetwood swung round.

'Maybe, Eliza, maybe. But I think Francis would be glad if your lips were sealed.' He gestured towards the dining-room door. 'In fact, I would be glad if you said nothing even to Louisa.'

Eliza nodded.

'Might I have my carriage?'

Ned Chetwood saw her to it.

'If Francis is not come home by eleven tonight, send for me. We shall not go earlier, I cannot abide being early.'

'I think I should not be able to dance if Francis is – is fighting.'

'He won't fight, sweet! The Duke has said so. This is to be a performance reserved for the infantry.'

'I can't believe that anything is truly happening.'

Ned Chetwood patted her hand. 'We do not know for certain that it is.'

There was no sign of Francis back at Les Deux Colombes. Eliza was thirsting to hear more of the tantalizing fragments she had heard at dinner but was powerless to do anything. Fanny, having been told she would not be needed until nine, was out on some doubtlessly amorous business. Eliza fidgeted and fiddled about the apartment, tried to read, tried to write, tried to embroider, failed in all, and ended by throwing herself on to the bed to toss restlessly and worry. Soon after six, Bridman came to her with a note.

Dearest, the cavalry are ordered to collect, but I will be with you before they do. Ever your F.

So it was true. She could not believe, looking out at Brussels in the golden summer evening, that the city could look so unaltered, so unruffled. Birds were wheeling in the translucent sky, the odd church bell was sounding, the pig and the hens were shuffling in the dust below, all as if no change at all had occurred, let alone such a momentous change. Well, if Brussels could and would remain indifferent, she would not. She found paper and ink, tossed an hour ago into a corner, and sat down to write to Julia, and to record events of that strange and momentous afternoon. Occasionally she glanced up, as if she expected to see black clouds gathering in the sky, and sometimes her gaze fell upon the green silk dress, which had now assumed the air of something infinitely trivial.

A little after nine, Fanny returned with an elated air. The sky outside was now deep, rich blue and Eliza kept the windows open, in spite of the menace of bats, for it seemed that to shut them was to cut herself off from anything that might happen. By eleven she was dressed, curled, perfumed and reluctantly on the point of sending a message to the Chetwoods when Francis returned. He was, to her amazement, in full evening dress.

'I thought you were under orders!'

'I am. But not until dawn. We ride to Quatre Bras at dawn.'

'And so,' she said, delighted at the dashingness of the scheme, 'you will dance till dawn?'

'If I get a chance I will dance with you till dawn. Looking as you do, I may not be so lucky.'

She smiled radiantly.

'Where is Napoleon?'

'Coming closer all the time. Moving north. He was thirty miles away, at Charleroi; he is now about fifteen.'

'At – at Quatre Bras?'

'We are going out to see what he is about in the morning.'

'Shall you be back – after the morning?'

Respectful of the green silk, Francis held her lightly by the shoulders.

'Probably not immediately.'

'And so I shall stay here and wait?'

'If you will.'

She swallowed.

'It is better than waiting in London.'

The carriage was called. Eliza did not see Bridman mount the box beside the driver carrying the valise containing Francis' uniform. The Richmonds' house could be identified streets away by the luminous halo that hung about it, and the sounds of music. The street was thronged, carriages struggling to deposit passengers at least somewhere near the entrance. There was a dazzle of warmth and light, jewels and gold braid. Eliza, quite forgetting how accustomed she had become to splendour in the last few months, fairly gasped as she went in, so improbable and wonderful did the ballroom look. It was draped and hung in crimson and gold, the walls covered with roses, the pillars with ribbons and leaves. The chandeliers were huge and glittering, hung over a floor already crowded with dancers. The Duke had not yet come, but he was expected.

Pelham found them quickly, followed by the Chetwoods.

Ned cried to Francis, 'You have deprived me of the greatest pleasure of my life in escorting Eliza here!'

Francis drew him aside to say a word in private, while Louisa chatted to Pelham, and Eliza watched the throng.

'He is come!' she said suddenly.

The Duke of Wellington was standing in the doorway, seeming entirely composed and talking to Lady Georgiana Lennox who had broken off dancing at his appearance. They spoke for a few moments, then Eliza saw Lady Georgiana turn away with a troubled expression, and it seemed that almost simultaneously the chatter in the ballroom had grown to an excited clamour. 'It is true, then, the rumours are true – we are off tomorrow.' Francis, she saw, was looking at her intently, so it was clearly no time to let panic affect her. But it was affecting plenty of others. A lady in a rose-coloured gown had fainted almost on to Eliza, and several more ladies were doing their utmost to follow her example. Officers with distant regiments to join were speeding about the room saying their good-byes, others seemed to be taking stirrup cups in the form of drinking straight from the champagne bottle.

In all this, Eliza was astonished to see that the ball did not immediately disintegrate, presumably because the focus of all attention was the Duke of Wellington, and he sat calmly upon a sofa with an air of serene well-being. His confident air, and the smiling manner with which he talked to those around him, made the hysteria and chatter in other parts of the room seem like an over-reaction. There was a great deal of movement suddenly, groups of people breaking up and re-forming, but it all seemed unnecessary as the Duke sat on, conversing easily and spreading about him a relaxed and unworried air.

'Dance with me,' Francis said beside her. They did not speak. Francis had always claimed that waltzing occupied all his powers of concentration, but that was not the reason he was silent now. They went round and round the great shining room, each trying not to think the final thoughts that pressed upon them, and to shut out the scenes of parting and hysteria that were everywhere about them.

'If Napoleon presses us back towards Brussels,' Francis said at last, 'I have made arrangements for you to go to Antwerp. You and Mrs Chetwood are to go back to Antwerp if Napoleon comes any nearer than Quatre Bras.'

She nodded.

'You will obey me, Eliza? It will put my mind at rest if at least I know that you are safe. Promise me that you will not stay in Brussels.'

This last promise she could make.

'I promise not to stay in Brussels.'

They went in to supper, instinctively choosing a crowded table as a distraction.

'Will you have another pineapple, Eliza?'

'I wager she could aim it a deal more true than Chetwood.'

'Champagne, Mrs Beaumont?'

'Ah, Francis, going to battle in dancing pumps, I see.'

'I cannot fight, Francis. I should never have danced so. I am quite knocked up.'

Between Pelham and Francis, Eliza left the supper room. Someone behind them said that Wellington had asked for a map and gone into the Duke of Richmond's study. Eliza turned her head to see who had spoken, and as she did so, she saw standing at the back of the supper room, spare and tall, a figure that recalled to her in a sudden gust of panic an afternoon nearly a year before at Quihampton.

It could not be him, it could not. What was he doing in Brussels? She strained her eyes to see through the crowd and the brilliant but wavering candlelight. It was Sir Gerard. He wore black but he was not, thankfully, looking their way. Spying, was he, Eliza thought furiously. She turned to warn Francis.

'Dearest, I do believe that your – '

Francis had gone. She looked wildly at Pelham, who was watching her with solemn concern.

'He left you this.'

Pelham drew a long and splendid string of pearls from his pocket and put them gently around her neck. Her eyes were smarting.

'For – me?' she said pointlessly.

'And this,' Pelham pushed a folded paper into her hand. 'The pearls would be easier to carry and conceal than gold.'

She clutched them. They were her purse, then. Francis had provided for her return journey in the terrible event of her having to go back without him. Tears were rising fast. She looked up at Pelham who was watching her with an intensity she could hardly bear. She looked away quickly, and her action seemed to release Pelham from some sort of spell.

'Eliza.' He touched her hand, the hand holding the pearls.

'Yes.'

'I think you're needed.'

He motioned to a sofa, just inside the doorway of the ballroom. Louisa Chetwood was stretched screaming on it, her desperate husband beside her.

'Ned must go,' Pelham said quietly. 'God bless you.'

She knew he was going, too. She said, '*Au revoir*,' in as convincing a tone as she could muster, thrust Francis' note down the bodice of her dress and went to Louisa.

'Go, Ned.'

Louisa was clinging, shrieking, to his arm, her eyes tightly shut, her face shining with tears. Eliza knelt on the floor and managed to transfer the hysterical grasp from his arm to hers, Louisa being far too immersed to notice the change.

'Bless you,' Ned Chetwood said unsteadily.

'Go!' she commanded.

He dropped a kiss on her free hand and vanished. Someone brought water, and sal volatile and brandy appeared.

Louisa was induced to sit up and drink and be smoothed and calmed a little. She went on crying, quietly and helplessly, her pretty face disfigured with tears, her hair disordered. Eliza continued to kneel, talking soothingly and constantly. For a few moments she was aware of a tall, dark shadow standing behind her, and froze in the realization of who it might be. But if the shadow had intended to speak, it changed its mind and moved away and Eliza resolutely did not look round. She called for Louisa's carriage, helped her to it amid the sudden rush of departing guests, and escorted her home as bugle calls began to echo through the city. She helped her to bed, sat with her until she slept, and left with a thankfulness she was ashamed of.

Later, she lay for the second night alone in the hard bed. She would leave Brussels, as she had promised, she would leave it tomorrow. But she would not go to Antwerp.

13

Eliza woke later to a sonorous thundering. Fighting through veils of sleep she thought at first that it was a storm, but gradually it came to her that a storm does not bellow and thunder out of a high, blue summer sky. It was guns, guns at last. There was a closer rattle, too, the rattle of wheels over cobbles, many of them, near at hand. The city was clearly on the move. Eliza threw back the covers, all recollection of the day before coming suddenly upon her with bewildering force. It seemed beyond belief that the dull thudding out there was what she knew it must be, and Francis perhaps in it. Not till later did she know that he had not been, and even if she had known such a comforting fact, she was quite sufficiently involved with military life by now to feel painfully affected by that distant boom of artillery.

Messages came from Louisa, from other friends. They all asked for news. It was undoubtedly to be a dreadful day, a day of waiting and speculating and worrying, the sort of day that Eliza's temperament was least fitted for. If she had been unable to concentrate on anything the afternoon before, today her inattention was hopelessly magnified. The choked streets, full of carriages and carts streaming northwards to Antwerp, did not help to calm the atmosphere. Louisa was frantic to go, Eliza equally desperate to stay lest there should be any news. Ragged rumours were abroad during the afternoon of the fighting at Quatre Bras, for Wellington sent messages back to the capital, but they were no help. Towards evening, Eliza could bear other wives and drawing rooms no longer, and took Fanny with her to go out upon the ramparts, and strain her eyes to the south.

There were huge crowds there already, and a general air of excited curiosity. Eliza moved slowly from group to group, hoping to glean here and there at least fragments of useful information. There was a great deal of animated speculation about the rumour that Wellington had almost been captured, but dramatic though that was, it did not mean as much to Eliza as hearing someone say, 'It is the Scottish regiments who have borne the brunt today, no cavalry at all.'

If that was to be believed, thank God for it. Francis might indeed be safe.

'Are we to go to Antwerp, ma'am?'

'Tomorrow, Fanny,' Eliza said absently.

Tomorrow she would take action or she would go mad. More than one day of this exhausting waiting would be more than she could bear. Her resolve was strengthened by feeling that if she stayed in Brussels she might come face to face with her father-in-law, and that was to be avoided at all costs. If she had no news to make her change her mind by morning, she decided, she would set about putting her own plans into action, plans that had only begun to form in her brain the night before as she danced with Francis. She had indeed promised him, long ago in Bath, that she would do nothing impetuous again, but surely that promise had been made for circumstances of ordinary life. Life was extraordinary now. Eliza looked once more into the dusk to the south, and heard those guns, and she felt afresh how powerless she was, a woman, and how it maddened her mind to be so.

Back in her rooms, Louisa was waiting, tearful again and full of awful apprehensions.

'The French are coming closer and closer, Eliza, I can hear them, every minute nearer, we shall be captured and taken back to France, I know we shall!'

Eliza looked at her with the same scornful impatience with which she had looked at Fanny two months ago in the inn at Ostend and wondered what it was that had seemed to make Louisa a desirable friend.

'They are not coming nearer. Those guns are ours as well as theirs. And if they do, they do not want women as prisoners, they want our soldiers.'

But clearly the vision of being dragged away to a remote

château by a debauched Frenchman with only one end in view had implanted itself too clearly in Louisa's imagination to be dislodged.

'I am so afraid to stay, Eliza, so afraid of what will happen when the French come, we shall all be made prisoner, perhaps we shall be made to walk to France, and Ned will never know what has become of me!'

Eliza demanded with some impatience, 'Do you wonder what has become of Ned?'

'Of course I do,' Louisa cried indignantly, 'But what can I do here about Ned? What good does it do Ned for me to stay? We must go to Antwerp tomorrow morning, I shall not stay a moment more.'

Eliza thought quickly.

'Dearest Louisa,' She knelt beside her on the wooden floor and looked imploringly into her pretty, dampened face. 'Dearest Louisa, please, please wait one more half day, just one more half day. I have one or two things to arrange, then I will come with you.'

'If we do not leave in the morning we shall be stranded somewhere in this horrible country by nightfall. No, I shall not stay, and nor shall you, for you promised Ned and Francis that you would come with me.'

'Then you must go ahead of me,' Eliza declared. 'I will get a horse and come after you.'

Louisa was horrified. 'Ride? Ride alone, in this country? Indeed, you cannot. And you cannot leave me to go ahead alone, you shall not leave me alone, Ned gave me his word that you should get me back to Antwerp, you know he did.'

'Then you must accept that we do not go until the afternoon,' Eliza said implacably.

Sobbing and petulant, Louisa was forced to agree. Ned had left her with a carriage and a very fast pair of bays he had extravagantly brought to Belgium for her use, and it was agreed that in this they should set out for Antwerp the following day, having dined early. Eliza said that she and Fanny would come to Louisa.

'But what is it that you must do that so delays you?'

'Pack,' Eliza said briefly, 'and – and arrange things.'

Later, in the blessed silence after Louisa's departure and the cessation of gunfire after darkness, Eliza lit a candle and sat down to write. She wrote a long and detailed letter to her cousin Julia, in which she described everything that had happened, and what she expected to happen in the next few days, and what she herself intended to do. She addressed it to Julia in London, then enclosed it in a further cover on which she wrote:

Mrs Edward Chetwood
    To be delivered to Mrs Richmond Beaumont of –

and Julia's address followed again. Then she summoned Fanny, was attended to bed, and slept with the sweet soundness that follows resolution.

Next morning, as she lay arranging her mind for the day ahead, a miracle happened in the shape of a message from Francis. He was unhurt, he loved her, and he begged her to waste no time in going back to Antwerp. It seemed, from what he could gather, that Wellington planned to abandon Quatre Bras and withdraw towards Brussels to a crossroads in cornfields, near a village called Waterloo. It was thought, wrote Francis, that Napoleon would be confronted there. At the bottom he had pencilled 'Destroy'.

Eliza, still in her nightclothes, found Francis' map of Belgium and spread it on the bed. Waterloo was marked only in small letters, perhaps ten miles almost due south of Brussels. The only obstacle between the capital and the village seemed to be a forest marked Soignes. It looked an undistinguished choice, there seemed to be nothing there except one small château, Hougoumont, and the crossroads. But at least it was not far, and that was a considerable advantage. She dressed, breakfasted, and called Fanny to pack. Everything they had brought with them to Belgium was strapped into trunks, and the trunks were labelled to Eliza, in Julia's care and at Julia's address. Eliza had few jewels besides her string of pearls, but what she had she pinned to her chemise under her gown, out of Fanny's sight. Towards the end of this operation, Eliza noticed that the sky, so cloudlessly blue for days, was blackening ominously. Within a few minutes, with the sinister and unnatural speed of summer storms, a heavy purple pall hung over the city and great drops began to thud down on the heated walls and roofs, turning quickly to an absolute downpour. Standing at their window in the sudden chill, Eliza and Fanny stared down at the inn's yard while the dust turned to a quagmire and the hens ran shrieking for shelter. Eliza looked at the sky speculatively. The confusion it would cause would help her, the wetness would not. She pulled Fanny back into the room, directed her to shut the final boxes, and for the last time sat down to write.

Dear Louisa,

I am quite safe, but unaccountably delayed. I beg that you will set off immediately upon receipt of this, with my baggage and Fanny, and I will join you as soon as I can. Fanny is provided with money.

À bientôt

Eliza

It would no doubt cause hysteria, but that could not be helped. Fear would overcome panic, and Louisa would certainly not delay, and if she did delay, it would be to no purpose, since Eliza would not be found. Fanny was given the note and instructions, and in the firm belief that her mistress would follow hot upon her heels, made no objection to taking carriage and boxes on her own to Mrs Chetwood. Eliza saw her maid and possessions jolt away among the sodden and mounting traffic in the streets and then returned, exulting and free at last, to her deserted rooms.

She stood for a while and looked about her. She now possessed the clothes she stood up in, a cloak, a string of pearls, two small diamond pins, a coral bracelet, a little gold, and her plan. The first part of the latter was to prove the easiest. It had occurred to her that to do what she wished she had to be inconspicuous, and a red-headed girl in white muslin and pearls was not inconspicuous. In fact, any kind of girl among soldiery was conspicuous, so she must abandon being a girl for the moment. If a man, what kind of màn? Obviously, Eliza thought to herself, a soldier. Slipping out of her room wrapped in her cloak, she went down the storm-darkened passages of the inn to find the small close cell behind the kitchen where Bridman had spent the nights he was not out at Gramont. So far, the storm had proved a blessing. Landlady and servant girls were all noisily in the

166

kitchen, sweeping frantically at a tide of muddy yellow bubbles seeping over the sill of the door from the yard outside. Safely past the doorway, Eliza found a pantry redolent of cheeses and garlic, an alcove crammed with logs – and beyond it, to her delight, a room no bigger than a closet with a truckle bed and a candlestick upon an upturned log. There was a rough dark blanket on the bed, but the pillow was familiar, gloriously familiar, a small hard bolster of white and scarlet cloth. Eliza darted forward and picked it up. It was, as she had hoped, the uniform of the drummer boy, who had died in a barn on the road from Ghent.

Her prize under her arm, Eliza sped upstairs, locking her door behind her. Stripping off her gown, Eliza fumbled her way into the torn and dirty garments. The breeches fitted as if made for her, the shirt would have to do, since the rent across the back made it broad enough, but the jacket was another matter. Tugging and straining, she tried to wrench her arms and shoulders into the stiff scarlet cloth, but it was hopeless. Dancing with frustration, Eliza gave a great thrust of her shoulders against the cloth and heard it tear ragggedly, the sleeve quite parted from the coat. Eliza, standing in shirt and breeches, stockings and slippers, was ready to weep with temper. What was she to do? Not even she would go off in only a shirt in a storm like this, especially a shirt so torn that her sex would be clearly apparent every time that the wind blew.

She cast herself down on the bed and beat her fists on the cover. Who could possibly help? Who was left behind who could possibly help? Only women, and no woman would countenance her plan. She needed a man to help her, but what man, what man she knew was not out there in that rain defying Napoleon. Suddenly, with a flash of inspiration as brilliant as the lightning darting outside, she remembered. William Cowper must still be nursing his broken leg, deprived of military adventure by carelessness in an amorous one. If there was a man she could exploit, William Cowper was the one. Quickly she took off the shirt and breeches, rolled them into a manageable bundle and donned her gown again. It seemed perhaps pointless to take trouble with her hair, on account of the rain between there and his lodgings, but no chances must be taken. She curled her hair as well as she could around her fingers, wound her pearls into a becoming collar high about her throat, tugged the neckline of her dress as low as she dared and plunged, cloaked, out into the downpour.

For the second day, William Cowper had dined morosely alone, listening with dull despair to the sounds of activity to the south that he was missing. His friends, for convenience, had sent the Belgian surgeon who lived two houses away to set his leg instead of troubling the regimental surgeon who wished to play cricket that day, and his leg had been curiously set, and was at times wickedly painful. He found the best antidote to the pain was brandy, and if that was not within his reach, claret. He had been more or less drunk now for nearly a week, and since early on Friday morning when everyone had gone, his drunkenness had been more, not less. On Saturday, he had been sobered a little by a roast chicken brought to him by his landlady, whose pragmatic heart was somewhat softened by his looks. Nevertheless, brandy glass in hand, he could hardly trust his eyes when the door of his room opened and Eliza stood there, coppery hair curling on her neck, muslin clinging damply to her limbs, panting slightly, her lips parted, her eyes brilliant. William Cowper dropped his glass.

In a flash, Eliza took it all in, the disorder, the dirt, the bottles, the uniform jacket flung on a chair, the flushed young man with an obvious fever. It was perfect.

'William!' she said, and let her cloak fall to the ground.

He forgot his leg, propped awkwardly on a chair beside him, and tried to rise, falling back immediately with a shriek.

'Don't try,' Eliza said, coming quickly forward, 'Dear William, do not try. See, I have come to make you comfortable.'

'I adore you,' he said unsteadily.

'You may tell me of that in a moment,' Eliza said, busy with the squalid bed. 'There now, hardly what you deserve, but better. Now, put your arm so – this will hurt a little, but it will soon be done – and lean against me, let me guide you – slowly – no William, not yet –' this uttered firmly under a clumsy attempt to kiss her, ' – there now, is that not a deal more comfortable?'

William found himself lying against his pillow, his throbbing leg before him.

'I knew you would come,' he said foolishly. 'I dreamed it.'

Still smiling, Eliza put the glass he had dropped into his hand and replenished it lavishly.

'Drink a toast to me!'

He raised the glass.

'To El-Eliza,' he said, 'and love.' He smiled lopsidedly and drank.

Eliza sat down beside him on the bed.

'Where is your servant, William?'

'Gone!' He waved the glass, and brandy splashed on to Eliza's gown, 'Gone to gain the glory I can-cannot gain.'

'I hope that he has not taken your horse,' said Eliza in sudden apprehension.

'It is no good to me, no good at all, I cannot r-ride it. Tell you what, lovely Eliza, you have my horse. P-present from me. You take it.'

She did not have to feign gratitude.

'Where is it, kind William? What a wonderful present!'

'Buy you diamonds one day. And castles. W-would you like a castle?'

'Not as much as a horse – where is it?'

'Down there. In – in the stable. Chestnut. You have him, take him.'

Even above the din of the rain, Eliza could hear the mounting rumble of traffic clearly fleeing Brussels. She left William's bedside for a moment and went to the window. It was perhaps five in the afternoon, still raining, gloomy and dark as if the month were November, not June, and the street below was packed with carts and carriages, all going northward, all with an air of panic and terror as they jostled and clattered together. Not for a moment did Eliza wish she were one of them, but it did occur to her to wonder what might become of poor, drunken, wounded William. She turned back to look at him slumped against his dirty pillow, the brandy glass held crookedly against his chest. She was sorry for him, and she would send help to him before she went, but she would not let him obstruct her in her objective. She went back to his bedside.

'C-come down here.'

He grasped her arm and pulled her down beside him. His eyes were glittering and his hand was hot and dry. He lifted it and pulled the muslin roughly off her shoulder, leaning awkwardly forward as he did so to bring his mouth nearer to the newly exposed creamy stretch of skin. With gentleness but irresistible firmness, Eliza put her hand over that exploring mouth and pushed William's head away, back to his pillow.

'Why, why – d'you do that?'

'Not now,' she said.

'Why not?'

'Because you are tired,' she said with emphasis, anxious not to anger him, 'and you are going to sleep now. When you wake, things will be different.'

'You stay? Eliza, you'll stay? Not leave me?'

'Do I look like it?' she said, and settled herself on the bed's edge, holding his unnaturally hot hand in hers.

'Sing to me,' he commanded.

'You will regret it.'

'N-never regret anything 'bout you.'

In her flat and monotonous voice, Eliza began to sing, instinctively choosing the lullabies and gentle rhythms she remembered from her childhood, and as she sang, William's lids slipped down and his handsome profile fell sideways on his pillow. Eliza let him sleep a good quarter of an hour before she tried to move, then she eased her hand from his grasp with infinite care, and stood up cautiously. There were several shirts strewn about the room and Eliza chose two of the cleanest, then used one as a cloth to wrap everything else in it, bundling up the silver buttoned uniform jacket, shako and belt. She noticed William's boots in a corner. He was tall, it was true, but very slender, and his hands were quite small, so perhaps his feet would be, too. She went over to them and slid her slippered foot inside one. Both foot and shoe fitted with ease inside the boot, and that was good enough. She added the boots and the breeches and shirt she had brought to her pile of plunder, tied up the bundle and slipped from the room.

The landlady met her on the stairs with a flood of French.

'Monsieur Cowper,' Eliza said with her execrable accent, *'a besoin d'un médecin. Vous allez tout de suite.'*

She extricated a gold piece from beneath her burden and her cloak.

'*Tout de suite,*' she said imperiously, and advanced down the staircase upon the woman, who backed before her until they were standing in the doorway to the wet street.

'*Où demeure le médecin?*' Eliza asked.

The woman indicated the house two doors away across the gleaming cobbles.

'*Vous allez,*' Eliza said again, '*tout de suite.*'

She pushed the woman out into the rain, and watched her dive among the carts to the doorway, knock, and be answered. She glanced up the housefront once more to the window behind which poor William, uniformless now, lay and sweated. Then, since the woman and a male figure were returning as best they could between the wheels that choked the street, Eliza darted down the alley beside her that led to the mews behind the house. Of course there was no chestnut there, she should have known there would not be, but there was an ill-kempt grey pony. Someone had taken William's chestnut, so she would take someone's pony. A felt saddle in poor repair hung on the wall, and a bridle mended with clumsy knots of twine, but even they were better than nothing. Eliza saddled him in the dimness and left him tied to his manger, morosely watching her as she climbed back into her breeches and her three shirts. Three shirts certainly padded the jacket a little, but it was still too large for her. She tried turning back the cuffs, but the braid and the buttons and the density of the cloth made it impossible, and the shoulders were laughably wide. She was glad that at least the light was dim, and also that she had no looking glass. The shako was a better fit, however, especially with her curls pushed up inside it, and as a final touch she thrust her feet, still slippered as before, into William's boots.

It suddenly came to her that she was hungry, standing there ludicrously clad in a hotchpotch of other people's uniforms, alone with a pony in a Belgian stable. She had been so bent upon this first stage of her plan, and so unused to having to think about food, that she had quite omitted to provide for hunger. It could not be helped. For the moment at least, she must bear it. Before morning, she thought, entirely forgetting the thousands of soldiers who had passed before her southwards, she would pass a farm or cottage and they would give her food. She climbed with difficulty on to the grey pony, and urged him out of his stall into the alley beyond. A woman was standing there, in the rain, her head shawled. She came up and laid a hand on the bridle.

'Come with me, soldier boy.'

Eliza was delighted.

'I fear not,' she said in as deep a tone as she could muster, 'We have work to do.'

'I'll give you something to remember Brussels by!' the woman called after her, but she urged the pony forwards, and once out in the street, set his nose southwards, against the traffic, and towards the village of Waterloo.

14

It rained all that night, ceaselessly and heavily. It rained upon Eliza jogging through the mud down the Waterloo road, past daunting wagonloads of wounded from Quatre Bras; and it rained upon Francis in his bivouac behind the infantry lines on the southern edge of the forest of Soignes, a comfortless bivouac without rations or water since the officers' baggage had not yet caught up with its owners. Eliza, wet through within a few hours of starting despite her cloak, allowed herself no regrets since she had, after all, set herself this task of following Francis, and Francis himself knew that, as a soldier under orders, regrets were irrelevant. The only sleep she got was an hour or so under a wagon, overturned by the ruts, and abandoned in the mud; the only rest he had was spent wrapped in his cloak in a soaking field of rye, watching while a fire Bridman and some others had managed to light was gradually extinguished by the persistence of the rain. They were both hungry.

If Eliza had learned anything from her terrifying experience at Quihampton, it was that you cannot depend upon events matching the pattern you have laid down for them in your imagination. She had decided, with her customary suddenness and certainty that she could not and would not endure to be left behind to worry and wait for news. She knew that several civilians, such as the Duke of Richmond and his son, were intending to watch whatever action there might be from as close quarters as possible, in the same spirit as they attended Newmarket racecourse and thus it was not unheard of to follow the army, at least at a discreet distance. Private soldiers' wives often had to follow, they had nowhere else to go. She also had a vaguely defined but powerfully felt notion that if Francis were wounded, she could help him. How this act of heroism was to be performed among the entire British army, she could not quite see, but she clung to the idea tenaciously. And quite apart from her adoration of Francis, there was in Eliza too a desire for action and excitement, a wish to know at first hand what Francis had known throughout the Peninsular wars. She did not like being like other women and she did like doing what was forbidden. Much of her character had been matured and sobered by marriage and an earnest wish to be the perfect wife for Francis, but still there lurked beneath it all the scapegrace and tomboy that had driven Mrs Lambert to distraction during a childhood at Marchants.

Marchants! Emerging from the forest in the grey dawn at the village of Mont St Jean, Eliza could see, from her muddy and weary pony, a wide shallow basin of land filled with standing crops that reminded her suddenly and poignantly of Hampshire. All her tiredness and stiffness and wetness, her sore and sleepless eyes, her uncomfortable and sodden uniform vanished from her consciousness as she looked about her. People and carts were still moving past her on the Brussels road, but not many were curious about a wet boy in the uniform of an ensign of the 52nd, certainly not curious enough to investigate beyond the first glance. The road ran straight on in front of Eliza, across the shallow valley ahead, and vanished over the brow by a building of some sort. A lane ran across the road just in front of her, with a deepish valley to her left, and to her right the land had divided into a mass of folds, and all over and around these Eliza could see troops stirring, smoke rising, and hear the murmur of voices. She must, she decided, find somebody to talk to, and ask what was going on. She looked to the left, considered it, then turned her pony's head and made off, stiffly and slowly down the lane to the right, leaving Francis, had she but known it, stirring in the cocoon of his cloak only a few hundred yards in the opposite direction.

At last the rain had stopped and there were glimmers of sun, and plumes of steam began to rise from the men and horses all over the valley. At that first touch of early morning warmth an enormous drowsiness assailed Eliza. She had after all not slept since the previous night, bar the hour or two under the cart, and had lived with high tension and effort throughout. She looked about her as she moved along and noticed a group of bushes away to the right of the lane which mercifully seemed to be nobody's shelter. She dismounted and dragged her reluctant pony up the bank behind her. The ground under the bushes was damp but not sodden. Eliza laid her cloak down, secured the pony, and cast herself down upon her unyielding bed. She was asleep in moments. The sun came out gradually behind a bright grey haze, and the pony, finding himself not securely tethered at all, pulled himself free with no difficulty and ambled off in the direction of the horse lines in the valley below.

For two hours Eliza slept as soundly as a child, her dreams undisturbed by the popping of muskets as soldiers all over the valley below her cleaned their guns. About nine that morning, when the baggage was ordered to the rear, and troops began to climb out of the valley northward to obey the order, two sergeants of the Foot Guards came upon a strange sight. The flash of scarlet first caught their eye, and upon investigation they found, beneath some thorn bushes, a figure in familiar uniform fast asleep, its shako rolled off, and a tumble of red curls obscuring its face. Sergeant Webster knelt and drew back the cuff of the jacket, disclosing a small and well-kept pale hand, wearing a wedding ring.

''Tis a lady, Tom.'

'What she'm doin' here?'

'Beats me.'

They crouched beside her under the bushes for a while, noticing she was as wet as they, and that the scarlet dye had run like bloodstains into her white belt which hung loosely enough about her to accommodate at least half another occupant. Their scrutiny was at last rewarded. Eliza stirred, turned her head, and was woken by the bright grey light filtering through the branches above her. Her eyes opened, took in the sky and the thorns, and came to rest gravely upon the watching soldiers.

'Is it all over?' she said.

Webster smiled.

''Tis not yet begun. 'Twill be this morning, ma'am,' he added as an afterthought.

'I want my husband. I – I came to find him. He's a dragoon. Captain Beaumont.'

'Can't have him now, ma'am. All under orders. Best go back to Brussels.'

Eliza struggled into a sitting position, her cloak warm and horribly damp beneath her.

'Certainly not.'

The two sergeants exchanged glances.

''Twon't be no sight for a lady, ma'am.'

Eliza remembered the ship.

'I am prepared for that,' she said proudly.

Sergeant Dixon shifted a little. It was not his job, not in his orders, to organize stray women found in uniform. If she wanted to stay, she might stay. She was no responsibility of his.

'You mun' keep back, ma'am. Keep with the baggage. No point getting hurt.'

'I'm not afraid.'

''Tisn't a question of fear, ma'am. If your Captain gets himself wounded, what use are you to him dead?'

Eliza nodded.

'Of course.'

'Come wi' us, then.'

Obediently, she crawled out of her hiding place behind them. The valley below had changed enormously in the two hours while she slept and was now a shifting mass of men, horses and weapons moving to their ordered positions. Sergeant Dixon pointed over to the right, with the glimmer of a smile.

'Your regiment, ma'am.'

'My –?'

He indicated her uniform. Eliza coloured slightly.

'Goin' to defend Hougoumont. Boney's expected there.'

Hougoumont, the little château on the map yesterday morning.

'Where are you taking me?'

'To safety, ma'am.'

She followed them clumsily in William Cowper's boots, stared at with a mixture of admiration and amusement by the soldiers around. The adventure, she thought, had indeed begun, but it did not seem to be what she had expected.

After several hundred yards of stumbling westwards along the ridge, away from Mont St Jean, the two Foot Guards stopped by a group of trees where a field hospital was being set up.

'Mr Johns, sir.'

The surgeon turned round, still holding the saw into which he was fitting a new blade.

'What have you brought me, Webster?'

For the second time the two sergeants exchanged glances.

'A lady, sir.'

With an uncomfortable sensation that she was being ridiculed, Eliza said clearly, 'My name is Eliza Beaumont, and my husband is a dragoon. I have come because it is intolerable to wait in Brussels.'

'Thank you,' the surgeon said. He finished slotting the blade into the handle, and then he said, 'Do the Light Bobs know you are masquerading as one of them?'

'The Light Bobs?'

'The 52nd.'

'No, they don't. I thought I would be less conspicuous' – here the surgeon glanced over her clothing and smiled – 'and I borrowed it from an ensign who – who doesn't need it.'

'A lady of enterprise, Mrs Beaumont.'

He turned away again to replace the saw in a formidable array of knives and scalpels that lay beside him in a plush-lined wooden box.

'Do you, Mrs Beaumont, count a strong stomach among your qualities?'

'I hope so.' The mention of stomach reminded her of her own agonizing hunger. It was no time to be ladylike now. 'I am extremely hungry.'

The surgeon laughed loudly. 'We might spare her a biscuit, eh, Dixon?' He turned to Eliza again. 'Well, if I give you a biscuit are you prepared to make yourself useful to me?'

Eliza, her thoughts entirely absorbed by the prospect of food seemed not quite to comprehend him.

'There is to be a battle today, and a great many newly wounded men will be brought to me, here, under the tree. I shall stitch wounds, take out musket balls and amputate.

177

I shall need all the help I can get. Do you think you are too gently born to give me any?'

'I have never seen a wound,' Eliza said, but added stoutly, 'but I will try.'

'Then the biscuit is yours. Off you two go,' he said to the two sergeants.

The biscuit, dry and tasteless but unbelievably welcome in her mouth, Eliza watched the two running down the valley to rejoin their company. They passed a group of the 52nd Foot hurrying to form up at Hougoumont.

'Didn't know you recruited women!' Dixon said.

'Women?'

'Just found one. Asleep under a bush. Ensign uniform. Given her to Surgeon Johns.'

'Who is she?'

'Dunno. Some lady. Wife of a dragoon.'

'A lady?'

'Hand as small as a child's.'

'A lady in the Light Bobs.'

They went on with the news among the Foot Guards.

'There's a lady ensign in the Light Bobs.'

'A lady!'

'Couldn' be worse'n the ones they've got!'

'A lady!'

'Tom, Tom, d'you hear? The 52nd have got a lady officer!'

The hum grew and buzzed down the lines. Necks craned and turned as if any moment a girl in full uniform should come dashing past them on horseback, issuing commands as she went. The 52nd themselves hoped she was a lady of distinction who had chosen their uniform deliberately. The Scottish regiments in Hougoumont laughed at them derisively.

The lady herself, quite unaware of the stir she had caused, was standing on a pile of baggage in order to have a better view across the valley.

'Take a look at the enemy,' Mr Johns had said, 'before there's too much smoke to see a pace in front of you.'

The enemy was worth looking at. Eliza's own feelings were now so confused and fragmented by the strangeness of her surroundings and her sudden involvement in events that she was glad to feel simple excitement as she stood on the loaded cart and looked at the glitter and flash of uniforms across the valley, the tiger-skins and great coloured plumes, the copper helmets, the gold and silver fringes and all the splendours of the French army. The surgeon pointed out to her the famous Imperial Guards in their long dark blue coats, and the carabiniers in white, all marching to their places to a riotous background of trumpets and drums.

'Take a good look,' Johns said. 'It won't look like that tonight.'

Eliza looked away from the French, back along the ridge, the way she had come in the dawn that morning. Behind the crest of the ridge was one long packed line of red coats, thousands and thousands of men, lying down as they had been trained to do, awaiting Napoleon's first move. One group only, in blue coats, seemed to be standing.

'Dutch–Belgians,' the surgeon said scornfully. 'Know no better.'

Beyond the Brussels road, Eliza could see cavalry. For a moment, she had a wild and frantic impulse to run along that length of prostrate scarlet forms and find Francis somehow among the cavalry, just to see him once more, one word more, in case – in case! It would not do. She must contain herself. At least the waiting here would be occupied. She looked down at the preparations made for the wounded under the trees, the terrible tools gleaming with linseed oil, the sponges and rolls of linen, the coated plasters and canteens of diluted spirits. She hoped she would not faint. She felt proud already of the sort of easy camaraderie she was treated with by Johns and his assistant surgeon. She did not want to spoil it by fainting.

The waiting was enlivened about eleven by the sight of the Duke of Wellington himself, in dazzling white breeches, riding along the ridge towards Hougoumont with his staff. Each company cheered him as he passed, but he waved to them in silence. Eliza watched him reverently.

Johns said, 'Perhaps we shall get some action now.'

The tension of waiting now palpably tautened the air all about them. The sun was coming through. It was Sunday, Eliza remembered. She leant against the tree and thought of childhood Sundays at Marchants, and delightful married Sundays at Nashbourn when she and Francis had occupied the Court pew, and sunny Sundays in Brussels where she had knelt in church gazing at the dresses between her fingers.

Suddenly the world burst apart. With a noise more sudden and deafening than anything she had ever heard, and clouds of dense and foul-smelling black smoke, the French cannon opened up in the direction of Hougoumont. Battle had begun.

15

From their positions along the ridge, many hundreds of
yards apart, Eliza and Francis heard the struggle for
Hougoumont, and saw at last flames and smoke rising as the
château burned. Another observer watched, too, from a
discreet distance on the edge of the forest. Sir Gerard
Beaumont, mounted on a splendid chestnut and severely
dressed in black, was surveying the scene in front of him
through a telescope. He had picked out Francis' regiment
when it came out of bivouac, and was keeping his sights
relentlessly trained upon it.

Francis was in high spirits. He and Pelham rode stirrup
to stirrup until they were under the shelter of the crest of the
ridge with the rest of the brigade, thus protected in some
measure from the French cannon shot coming bounding
thick and fast up the valley. The sound of the guns, the
sight of his regiment in their scarlet and gold with their
great black plumes all poised for dramatic action, was
exhilarating indeed, especially after the months of lounging
about in Brussels. He was thankful to think of Eliza now
safely in Antwerp, and eagerly looked forward to rejoining
her and telling her of all that had happened. He began to
hum.

'The infantry is coming,' Pelham said beside him.

Francis turned. A ripple of anticipation was running down
those magnificent lines. The French commander, d'Erlon,
had ordered the advance of his sixteen thousand infantry,
and they had begun their steady, remorseless march down
their side of the valley through the gunsmoke towards

Wellington's army. Rumour came that they had broken effortlessly through the first line of defence at the farm, lower in the valley, and were now falling upon the 95th Rifles and the Dutch–Belgian Light Brigade as they came steadily and terribly up the slope. Francis' whole body and mind were tense with an absolute concentration. He could see nothing, for the crest of the ridge ahead of him hid the advancing Frenchmen, but he could hear, in all its horror, the firing, the screams and cries, and the steady boom of the cannon, Napoleon's 'beautiful daughters'.

'Uxbridge,' Pelham hissed suddenly.

Lord Uxbridge had come thundering up from the right and gave an order, then wheeled abruptly and galloped back to the Household Brigade. His order was repeated to the dragoons, 'Prepare to attack.' Francis turned in his saddle and gripped Pelham's hand for an instant.

Pelham said, 'I will see you in Paris,' and smiled. Looking for the last time down those red and gold ranks, Francis saw each man, rigid with anticipation, leaning slightly forward in his saddle, oblivious of everything except the impending excitement. At last, after what seemed an interminable time, the ten bugle blasts for 'Charge!' came clearly over the roar of the artillery, and with shouts of exultation, the whole brigade of horses swept up over the crest of the ridge and down like a thunderbolt on the French infantry.

Francis had never known such speed in his life, smashing his way through those French lines as if they had been stalks of corn. He was conscious of the pounding of the horses beside him, a blur of mud and trampled clover and rye, and scores of French faces falling under his slicing sword and vanishing beneath those flying hoofs. On and on they thundered, pounding down the muddy slope, howling and cheering, sabres wheeling in an ecstasy of speed and slaughter. Francis felt he could conquer the world, riding on and on in this savage glory, his horse as ecstatic and dangerous as he, its great hoofs crushing and battering what he had failed to kill. He heard a shout of 'Charge the guns!' from the Scots Greys beside him as he thudded across the bottom of the valley, and he felt the whole brigade surge onward again, still whooping, to plunge deep into the French battery.

It was a mistake, clearly a mistake. With a sudden icy

sobriety that fell upon him as powerfully as the exultation of a moment before, Francis saw that they had gone too far. His comrades were still wheeling about, hacking and slashing at French gunners and drivers, but the French lancers and cuirassiers were coming to their help. The British cavalry would soon be overcome and isolated, their retreat cut off. Francis turned his blown horse abruptly and found a French lancer feet from him, his great weapon swinging lethally down towards Francis' right side. In a movement that was purely instinctive, Francis raised his sword, throwing the lance off to the side, and then plunged it, at the end of the same movement, outwards through the Frenchman's neck. A moment later, sword still flailing, he was out in the open, and with a dozen others, pounding down on the last line of lancers between them and their own army. The two lines met hideously. Francis saw a man he knew, on the ground, frantically trying to ward off the lances with his hands, and heard the crash of weapons and the screaming of horses. Then, by some miracle, he was through, and regaining the safety of the ridge.

He lay for some while on his steaming, panting horse's neck, his eyes shut, absolutely spent. His heart and lungs seemed ready to burst his body apart, his sword, hideous with what he had done, hung forgotten from his limp and mud-splashed hand. Gradually he opened his eyes and saw the shattered remnants of his squadron about him. 'They say we are half gone. The Greys are worse,' someone said. Sitting up slowly and gazing about him, Francis saw no sign of Pelham.

Perhaps he was further down the line, separated from Francis in the speed and chaos of their charge. Francis stood in his stirrups to look over the sorry fragments of his brother officers. Leslie he could see was still alive, as were Munro, Elliott, both Bryants. He urged his exhausted horse on a little among the heaving, blowing animals of his squadron.

'Howell. Where's Pelham? Who has seen him? Where is Howell?'

The younger Bryant, a boy fresh from England and already blackened with smoke, raised his dirty face to say, 'I saw him. He was before me as we went into the French lines. He shouted to me to follow him. He opened the way for me.'

'Did he turn? Did you see him come out? Who saw him come back?'

Young Bryant shook his head.

'I did not see him after that.'

Francis shouted, 'Who saw him? Who saw him after we charged the infantry? Did you notice nothing, Bryant, nothing at all?'

He shook his head. He was too tired to care. Howell had been good to him, friendly and helpful, but he did not know him well. He did not see the urgency. He himself was alive.

'Fool!' said Francis pointlessly and moved his horse out of the group. A soldier was leading a pair of great greys that had stampeded riderless back out of the mêlée to some shade beneath the trees. One of the pair had a blaze of white down its face.

'Stop!' Francis shouted.

The man halted.

'Whose – whose horse is that?'

'Dunno, sir. Came back of its own accord, sir. Might be needed later.'

Pelham had bought a grey at Tattersalls with a great blaze on its face. He had said it gave the animal a great look of intelligence and quite compensated for the disadvantage of the beast also possessing two white stockings. Francis' gaze dropped to the legs. Two grey, two white.

He said hoarsely, 'Where's Captain Howell?'

The soldier gestured down into the booming, smoke-filled valley.

'Yonder, sir, I shouldn't doubt.'

Yonder, under that deadly trampling and gunfire, in all that flattened corn and mud, perhaps crying out unheard in that murderous noise. Of course, Francis thought, shaking the fear away, there must be several horses with two white stockings in all the numbers of the Royal Brigade. But then not many dragoons had greys, it was the Scots Greys who did so, perhaps it was one of theirs, not Pelham's. The squadron was being urged back along the forest edge to await further orders and there was nothing, Pelham or no Pelham, that Francis could do but obey.

The exhilaration had gone, the glory faded, and in their places came the bitter truth of what had happened. Francis bowed his head, shielding his face with his arm, and wept bitterly.

Eliza, though so close, had no conception of what had happened. The first casualties had started arriving soon after the initial shelling of Hougoumont, and every energy she possessed, both physical and emotional, was now wholly absorbed. The first man she saw wounded had had his knee shattered by a cannon ball. He was young and squat and tough-looking, but he gazed with a look of stricken horror at the pulpy mass of scarlet on his leg, the fragments of bone and twists of sinew, all horribly enmeshed with the fabric of his breeches. Eliza had no desire to faint but an overwhelming one to vomit. She looked desperately about her, her stomach and throat heaving with revulsion.

Johns looked up long enough from his probing to say, 'Don't dither about!'

She did not. She was behind the trees in an instant, shuddering and clutched by nausea. When she came unsteadily back, her face candle-coloured, Johns said, without looking up:

'Take off that ridiculous jacket and come here.'

She hesitated, her head still swimming.

'In the army,' Johns shouted, 'it is imperative to obey orders! You cannot work trussed up in that jacket! Take it off!'

She did as she was told.

'It must come off,' Johns said to the soldier.

Eliza was astonished to see the soldier smile and nod.

'A wooden leg,' Johns said to her in explanation, 'is a badge of bravery.'

The man was stretched out, his arms held by a couple of comrades, and Eliza was told to fortify him at intervals from the canteen of spirits. She was also to pass what the surgeon called for. She knelt on the grass by his head, fearful of being overcome once more, and talked to him soothingly, as much to calm herself as him. He looked at her all the while, quite shocked enough by what was happening to him, not to be in the least surprised to be ministered to by a girl.

The hours wore on. Even though thousands of wounded lay still on the battlefield, and their numbers were ever mounting, the crowds waiting for treatment at the field hospitals grew and grew. There was no moment for nausea now, no moment for anything but doing as one was told, one's hands slippery with blood, one's nostrils filled with the stench of flesh. The amputations were terrifying, limb after limb lopped off as if it had been no more than a branch of a tree, and then the patients being helped to the shade and left there with their grisly stumps and a little opiate for consolation. Soon after two o'clock, the news came through that the Union Brigade had charged, become drunk with its own success and ridden on to its destruction. Johns, seeing from Eliza's face that she did not realize that the dragoons had been formed into the Brigade for the battle, saw no point in undeceiving her. He was struggling to extract a musket ball from a man's shoulder.

'Damnation that my hand's no smaller.'

Eliza come quickly forward.

'Let me try.'

She took the sticky forceps with no more distaste than if they had been a fan, and bent over the wound. It was a round musket ball wedged just under the shoulder blade.

'Whatever you do, sir,' the man said, hunched and tense, 'do it quick.'

'I am not a sir,' Eliza said.

The man straightened up suddenly in astonishment, just as Eliza slid the forceps round the ball, the bone ground down on it and ejected it like a cork from a bottle. Eliza picked it up from the grass. Johns had told her to give the men the foreign bodies she found, it heartened them. The man stared from the musket ball to her face, his mouth opening and shutting, wordlessly.

'Next,' Johns bellowed. Ointment was slapped on the torn shoulder, and the man was pushed to the side still gazing and gasping at Eliza.

'Keep those,' the surgeon said, indicating the forceps. 'You can do the probing.'

'I don't know how!' she wailed in horror.

Johns was unmoved. 'Nor do half the surgeons in the army. Get on with it.'

A space was cleared for her in the crowd and boards put on trestles for her patients. For a moment Eliza straightened her aching back and looked with longing at the free blue air above her, and then the needs of the wounded over-whelmed her and she bent to her task again.

Behind her, Johns said to the assistant surgeon, 'Bad news of the charge?'

'Yes, sir. Most of the Scots Greys gone.'

'What about the dragoons? Her husband is one.'

'Pretty bad too, sir.'

Johns pulled a face. 'Don't tell her of it. Game little girl.'

Never had Eliza worked as she worked that afternoon. The world shrank to a space of ghastly and gaping red flesh, ripped and torn by musket balls and grapeshot. She soon saw that grapeshot was much the worst, ragged pieces of metal, even horseshoe nails, clamped together in canvas bags or canisters, and exploding when fired to do hideous damage. Someone brought her brandy and water sometimes, and she acquired a devoted pack of soldiers hovering round her, equally desperate to help and to avoid being sent back to the field. Steadily she toiled on, man after man laid in front of her, while she dug, clumsily at first but with mount-ing skill, coins and bullets, scraps of leather and bone out of their mutilated bodies. Once she thought that perhaps someone else along the ridge was performing just the same service for Francis, but the thought made such frantic distress and despair rise in her whole being that she sup-pressed it with all the energy she could summon.

A man said to her, 'You'm an angel, lady.' Her eyes filled with tears. She brushed them away with her sleeve and saw how everything she wore was splashed with blood and mud. But that was not the worst of it, nor were the wounds the worst of it. By far and away the worst aspect of that after-noon for Eliza was the noise, the ceaseless dull booming of artillery, the screams of hurt horses, and the groans and cries and shrieks of pain from the soldiers. It was terrible to endure it, going on and on, and all the time it went on it meant more and more wounded men, each rattle of musket fire, each thud of cannon meant another swathe of broken men in dreadful pain.

Eliza's sight, as the hours went on, began to blur and swim with the effort of her concentration, especially as the latter was achieved on a stomach now unfed for thirty-six hours. Towards six o'clock in the evening, Surgeon Johns paused from his own gruesome task and came over to her.

'You must stop a little while, you're as green as a leaf.'

She straightened to look up at him, and as she did so, what she had feared would happen, happened, and the world blackened and swayed as she fell forward, fainting over the soldier she was trying to help. Twenty hands shot forward to catch her, and she was tenderly lifted and carried over the now foul and slippery grass to a less crowded spot behind the trees. They laid her down on the ground while someone went for brandy, someone else for some sort of food, any food, and others loosened the layers of shirting about her throat and fanned her with their caps. She opened her eyes and looked unseeingly into the circle of faces.

'I want Francis,' she said.

Francis did indeed have need of her just then. After the cavalry charge, he had spent fruitless time searching along the ridge for Pelham, until it was complained that he was an obstruction and he was sent back to the edge of the wood to rejoin his squadron. The men had all dismounted and were sitting or lying, smoking and talking, in moods that varied from the utterly disconsolate to the irrepressibly optimistic. Francis flung himself down on the edge of a group, gnawed with anxiety and sorrow over Pelham. He must just hope and hope that he was in a hospital somewhere around the field, carried there by some loyal men. Thank God, at least, Francis thought, rolling over and burying his face in his crossed arms, that his beloved Eliza was safe – safe, clean and far away from this senseless bloodbath. After perhaps an hour or so of lying in black despair, the order came to mount again. The centre of fighting had, it seemed, shifted back to where it had started at Hougoumont, and a great series of cavalry attacks had begun between the château and the farm of La Haye Sainte. With scorn it was reported that some of the Allied troops were showing strain and weakening, and the Union Brigade – or at least the sorry remnants of it – were required to provide stiffening. They rode down towards Hougoumont over a battlefield that bore no examination and were drawn up behind the wavering Allied infantry squares, and embarked on what Francis considered the most nerve-racking duty he had been yet called on to perform. Their duty was not to advance, but to encourage the infantry, and indeed to make it difficult for them to break up and flee, and thus they sat there, stationary for almost two hours, while enemy fire blazed into them. Men fell all around him, knocked to pieces as they sat steadfastly on their horses, and the only consolation Francis could see was that the French were gaining no ground. But he survived. Looking around him, he could not see how. Shot grazed his stirrup, but he survived.

At six o'clock, battered by tension and noise, his eyes smarting acutely from the smoke, he was almost in a trance when the order again came to charge. The charge had none of the impetus of the morning; Francis noticed how often he missed his aim as he thudded through the French infantry, and how his companions were falling all around him, too utterly exhausted to defend themselves. The remnants were ordered back and, in a daze of weariness, commanded to charge again, this time at some cuirassiers. The shock was not great as the two sides met. Francis saw French faces, as grimed and red-eyed and desolated with tiredness as his felt, go harmlessly by. There was a cry suddenly of, 'The Prussians!' and a great fresh brigade of Prussian cavalry swept in upon them all, and began to drive the enemy back. For a moment all was confusion, the French retreating, the Prussians pursuing, the British trying to get out of the way. A man behind Francis yelled out triumphantly, 'Boney's done for!' and Francis half turned in his saddle to smile in agreement. As he did so, a blistering pain shot down his side and leg, scorching and searing through cloth and flesh. He doubled up with an unheard cry, and in the mêlée of hoofs and slashing weapons, shouts and cries, slipped quietly and helplessly from his horse into the tangle of mud and men underneath.

16

It seemed no orders were given about the wounded that night. The moment the French began their frenzied retreat as darkness fell, Sir Gerard Beaumont at one end of the ridge and a weak and dazed Eliza at the other started their hopeless search for Francis. Neither had any certain knowledge that he had fallen, but then neither had any knowledge to the contrary. Sir Gerard found what few dragoons remained, but they were not in a position to be helpful. They were stupid with exhaustion and the darkness made it impossible for them, or anyone else, to tell precisely who was present. Sir Gerard was not to be put off. He had not seen Francis return from the great cavalry charge in the morning and could find no one who had seen him either since then, so he supposed that if he were hurt, then he would be lying either down in the valley, or further up, where the French artillery had been when charged by the British cavalry. With lanterns and two horrified servants whom he had brought with him from Gloucestershire, he began his descent down one of the most dreadful battlefields of history.

Between forty and fifty thousand dead and wounded men lay untended that night on the field of Waterloo. By the end of the night the numbers of dead had mounted, some dying because of their wounds, some quietly stabbed by the hordes of looters roaming the place by moonlight. Every articulate cry in that ghastly place was for water, and there was none to be had. Sir Gerard rode staunchly through it in search of his son. It was a hopeless search. The piles of corpses made moving difficult, the fitful light of the moon

and his lamps gave him a thousand illusions that every
scarlet coat, every curly dark head, was the coat and head
he sought. His will alone at first kept despair and weariness
at bay. He rode for several hours, stumbling, calling out,
peering fruitlessly among that awful carnage, and was
finally deserted by his servants. He followed them. That
morning he would never have contemplated such a thing,
but this dark field, its sinister business still going on, was
something even his unbending spirit could not withstand.
He rode back to Mont St Jean, resolving that he would not
go far, and would resume his search at daybreak. He found
the village overflowing with men, every cottage, every barn
a hospital, and bought, for an incredible sum in gold, a
place on some straw in a rickyard.

Eliza fared no better. In her case, however, it was not her
own will that made her give up the first fumblings of a hunt
for Francis, but the will of others. Surgeon Johns had been
roused from his mysogyny to open admiration for Eliza
during the day, and was also a practical man in the extreme.
He knew a battlefield after dark was still highly dangerous,
and the chances of finding anyone almost nil. So he commanded Eliza to stay where she was and placed two slightly
wounded comrades to guard her, and told her that if she
did not try to move all night, he would send men to help her
in the morning, but that if she tried to escape, she would
forfeit any assistance from him. Still bewildered after losing
consciousness, Eliza submitted and retired to her space of
ground attended by her two grinning guardians. Someone
brought her a blanket, still damp from the night before but
welcome. It was tucked competently round her, a spare
jacket was rolled loosely about her head, as much to muffle
the groans around her as to provide a pillow, and Eliza,
worn out to the last of all her resources, fell into a deep and
dreamless sleep.

And what of Francis? For six hours he lay, unconscious
or only partly conscious, in a tangle of pain and pressure, so
confused with other bodies that even if he had been conscious,
he would have found it difficult to locate his own limbs. At
times he drifted towards the surface of his mind, but then
the tearing pain would begin to claw at him again, and he
would subside into oblivion. He was dimly aware of a

hideous craving at times, a craving so absolute it was enough to make him faint anew. He was thirsty. He was groaning and sobbing like the thousands round him, and did not know what he was doing. Towards midnight the blessing of unconsciousness began to abate a little, and Francis, pinioned along almost his whole length by a French cuirassier whose weight could only mean he was dead, began to open his eyes for minutes at a time, while rags and tatters of recollection floated, maddeningly unrelated, about his head. He kept thinking about his horse, about Nashbourn, about a red-haired girl in a rage on a summer hillside, about an elderly man in a rage in a library somewhere – and above all about water. Water, water, water. He thought he had a canteen somewhere, but his frantically scrabbling right hand could find nothing but mud and cloth and a moustache. He tried to wrench his body sideways, but a blaze of pain shot down his side from rib to knee and he lost consciousness. When he struggled to the surface again, there were voices. He opened his eyes cautiously.

Above him, three figures, muttering together so indistinctly he could not even make out the language, were systematically stripping all the gold lace and braid off the corpse on top of him, pulling off his rings, turning his pockets inside out and wrenching at his buttons. This done, they moved to the heavily moustached figure beside Francis, who moaned faintly as he was moved. There was a flash of a blade in the moonlight and a quiet gasp, and a second Frenchman was denuded of anything of value he possessed. Francis felt his heart was pounding visibly enough to be seen through his uniform, and he closed his eyes and feigned death. To his relief, the corpse that was crushing him was abruptly heaved off, and then to his inexpressible horror, rough hands began to plunge crulley about his person. The robbers were Belgian, he could tell that now, from their dialect. Half fainting, half icily awake, he felt his pockets being emptied, the gold lace torn from his tunic front, and then suddenly, as a hand that gave more pain than it knew thrust under the tunic against his wounded side, he heard an English oath, and hand and Belgian were gone.

Private Peters gave the Belgian a final kick and knelt down

by Francis. He was not a man of many principles, his pockets were crammed with French booty, but even he would not tolerate the sight of a Belgian peasant robbing an English officer. In their flight they had dropped some of what they had stolen, and Peters picked up an oval gold locket and slipped it into his pocket.

'Water,' Francis croaked from parched lips.

'Sorry, sir, none to be 'ad,' Peters said, a full canteen on his back. 'You bad, sir?'

Francis' lids slid down. Peters glanced down him and saw the dark spread of blood.

'Won't – die,' Francis said.

'No, sir, 'course you won't, sir.'

'Wife,' Francis said, 'wife – ' he began to fumble across his chest with his right arm. 'wife – hair – '

Peters pulled the locket out of his pocket.

'Lookin' for this, sir?'

Francis gazed stupidly at the swinging golden oval. Peters opened it. There was a picture, and a curl of hair, both obscured by the darkness. At the glimpse of the curl, Francis suddenly had a flash of coherence.

'Most precious,' he said firmly. 'Most precious – to me – but yours if you stay – you stay till daylight – '

'And a word to my sergeant, sir?' Peters said hopefully. The locket wasn't worth much, but he had a pocketful of gold napoleons already, and a good deed might atone in his sergeant's eyes for his misdemeanours of the past three months in Belgium. Francis gave the faintest of nods, and slid down into a morass of nightmares and violence, while Peters settled himself comfortably among the limbs around, laid his gun at the ready and took long pulls from his canteen of a mixture of gin and water.

He stayed there, as good as his word to his own surprise, till morning. As dawn broke, and daylight began to creep over the field, he took out the locket again in an attempt to learn if the dragoon he was guarding was a dragoon worth guarding. It was little help. There was a miniature of a pretty girl, the engraved letters 'E.B. to F.E.B. – September 1814', and a copper-coloured curl. He fingered the curl. Seen that colour somewhere before recently, not a common colour, not a colour you'd forget easy. 'Course! The Light Bob's lady! He'd feigned a wound to help someone up to the field hospital just to have a look at her the afternoon before, and she'd been working away like a demon, those curls as uncombed as any servant girl's. Wonder if –? He glanced down at Francis' blanched face. No, course not. His wife would be sitting in Antwerp in silks with a pet dog and a lady's maid, like as not. Peters snapped the locket shut and looked up, squinting against the growing strength of the sun. A group of men in British uniforms, thank God, were coming uncertainly among the chaos, one of them seeming to be supported by the others and peering frantically about as he came. Peters stood up and shouted. The others looked up. They seemed to be, more or less, in the uniform of the 52nd, and there were a couple of grey-hooded stretcher-bearers with them.

'Over 'ere!' Peters shouted.

The small man in the middle seemed to be protesting. He tried to pull his arms away and gestured with his head in another direction, but the men either side pulled him for-wards, and they all came stumbling on together. Peters could distinguish little about them as they were silhouetted against the sun, but he could hear the two bigger men talking in tones of encouragement. Once the small one sank on its knees beside the red-clad body of a dragoon and tried to turn it over, and then Peters saw with a leap of surprise that the little figure had red hair.

'Oy!' he shouted imperiously. 'Quick! Over 'ere!'

The small figure was dragged onwards, and with every step, Peters became more certain of who it was. The lady of the Light Bobs, God damnit! It was, he was sure it was. Surprise never lingered long with Peters.

'Got summink for you, madam,' he shouted impudently.

Eliza hardly heard him; she felt desperate among all these red coats, each one of which might be Francis. She had woken before dawn and found Johns to be as good as his word. Her two sergeants were to go with her in her gruesome search, and what was more, two stretcher-bearers had been spared, and a blanket to serve as a stretcher. Johns, grey and haggard in the early light of dawn, had given her two final pieces of instruction. The first he said was that she was to be back at the field hospital before dusk, since the army was mostly moving on in pursuit of the French, and it would be perilous for her to remain alone on the field. If she did not return then, he would guarantee her no further protection. The second instruction was a miracle.

'I have news for you, too.'

Eliza held her breath.

'I sent a boy out last night, down to the dragoon lines to see if they could help at all. They had some information you could use, I think. Your husband was seen yesterday after-noon after the Union Brigade Charge, several men testified seeing him alive. The dragoons waited and rested for a few hours, and then were sent to back up the infantry lines down near Hougoumont. Two men saw your husband ride down there. No one my boy could find saw him ride back. If you want what's left of your captain, that's where you'll find him.'

Eliza opened her mouth, dread and hope boiling equally within her.

'Don't thank me,' Johns commanded.

'Good-bye, then,' Eliza said unsteadily.

Johns looked as if he would say something, but changed his mind, grunted only, and turned back to his never-ending task. Eliza, firmly escorted, set off in search of Francis.

They seemed to crawl on for hours. She was so absorbed in her search for a certain shape that her absorption made her in part blind to the terrible scene she was stumbling through. She thought she found Francis a hundred times, and the patient sergeants would pull her to her feet and propel her onward through the carnage. When they heard Peters' call, they went towards him not so much because he might be of any interest, but because he did at least make a diversion in their sickening quest. Eliza, eyes on the ground, had really no idea of what they were doing, much less that a private was calling to her across this confusion of men and horses. She let herself be pulled onwards, tearing her arms from theirs every so often to fall upon yet another red coat that did not belong to Francis. When they eventually reached Peters, she raised her pale and dirty face to him and wondered who on earth he was. He, for his part, wondered if this bundle of filthy and bloodstained clothing topped with a haunted and equally filthy face and a mop of dishevelled curls could really be a girl at all, and perhaps he had made a mistake. Eliza straightened and looked at him with sudden haughtiness. For all her distress, she did not like to be leered at by unshaven men with blackened teeth who stank of gin.

'What do you want?' she demanded.

'Summink – I've summink might interest you – ma'am,' Peters said, and then could not remember why his near-dead dragoon could possibly interest her, or anybody.

'Oh?' she continued to regard him imperiously.

Without quite knowing why he did it, but acting out of some blind instinct, Peters pulled the locket out of his pocket and swung it before her eyes. The effect was instantaneous. Her expression of disdainful pride was swept aside, and a look of absolute passion took its place. He found himself deluged in a flood of questions, screamed questions, and the locket was wrenched from his hand.

''Ere – give that back. It's mine – 'e gave it to me!'

'Who? Who gave it to you? Where is he? Where did he give it to you – ?'

Sullenly, Peters jerked his head towards the ground behind him. Eliza, in a state so wild she could hardly trust her eyes, saw Francis lying there, ashen, his eyes closed, his side blackened with blood. She fell on him, weeping with relief, stroking his hair, begging him to open his eyes, covering his face with kisses. He did not stir. They pulled her off him, and Peters, not without a certain pleasure, held her firmly while Francis was rolled as tenderly as possible on to the blanket, and lifted, swaying, into the air, a man grasping each corner.

'Ready to go, ma'am?'

Eliza wrenched herself from Peters' hold.

'Is he alive? Oh, is he alive? Should you move him? Oh, tell me, is he alive?'

One of the stretcher-bearers turned his grey hood towards her. 'He's alive, but he won't be so much longer, not if we don't hasten.'

Eliza plunged forward, the locket still in her hand. Peters, outraged at having no tribute paid to him for his major role in the drama, bellowed for justice.

'Wot about me, then? Where's me locket? 'E promised me that locket – I stood by 'im all night like I promised! 'E'd be dead if it weren't for me!'

Eliza paused. If it hadn't been for this man, she might still be stumbling about the field, vainly searching. She turned round.

'I stood by 'im all night, I tell you! I kicked robbers off 'im – you look at 'is tunic, all torn it is, they ripped the lace off and they'd have killed 'im if it weren't for me! 'E come to and said the locket were mine if I stood by 'im till mornin'. 'E promised me, lady! 'E said 'e'd put in a good word with my sergeant an' all. You wouldn't 'ave 'im now if it weren't for me!'

'Turn your back,' Eliza commanded. Peters stared. 'Turn your back! I shall not give you the locket because it is worth more to me than it ever could be to you, but I shall give your something you could sell for much more, if, – ' she said with rising emphasis, 'you turn your back!'

Reluctantly, Peters turned.

Fumbling through the layers of her disgusting clothing, Eliza came eventually to her chemise, startlingly white and alien by comparison with her swathes of shirting. Carefully, she unpinned one of her diamond brooches. It was a crescent, not particularly large in itself, but it had three or four excellent stones in it. Mr Lambert had given it to her as a wedding present, saying, 'A little something, my dear, that you can sell *in extremis*.' It seemed to Eliza that life could never be more extreme than now, and Francis' survival was laughably cheap at the price of a diamond brooch. She turned and held it out to Peters, its facets catching the morning sun with brilliance. He took it in his palm and looked at it for a long time, then he raised his eyes and regarded Eliza with admiration.

'You're a real lady then, aren't you, ma'am?'

'Good-bye,' Eliza said. She felt she should have said some words of gratitude but the thing to be thanked for was so enormous it beggared words. In any case, this man's manner was so hideous that thanks would be misconstrued. Quickly she turned away and began to follow the little stretcher party, lurching and stumbling and slipping in William Cowper's boots, her locket in her hand.

17

Eliza's rejoicing was short-lived. They toiled up the side of the valley through the battlefield already humming with flies and heat, only to find the field hospital three-quarters dismantled and the wounded being loaded into carts to take back to Brussels. Eliza was aghast.

'Where is Mr Johns?'

A soldier looked up from some baggage he was strapping.

'Gone to Paris,' he said shortly.

'But he said that if I was back before dusk, he could help me!' Eliza cried desperately.

'Didn't have his orders then, did he? Moved off an hour back. Whole regiment's to follow the French.'

Eliza went back to her waiting stretcher palely. Her face told them everything. The two sergeants shifted anxiously, as perturbed as she by the news, if for different reasons.

'You cannot abandon me now,' she pleaded. 'Just take him to the village for me, I beg you. Please do not leave us here. Please!'

One of them said, 'We should be followin'.'

'You shall!' she cried. 'Take him only to Mont St Jean for me! Please, I beg you. This last help –' Her voice broke a little.

The sergeants sighed and muttered together a while. Then, to Eliza's inexpressible relief took a new and firmer grasp of their corners of the blanket, and turned back towards the lane.

They found Mont St Jean hopelessly crowded, every cottage, barn and pigsty already packed with wounded, every well invisible beneath a swarm of thirst-crazed men. The sun rose higher, and Eliza had a brief and stunning thought of how it must feel to lie out there on the battlefield, wounded and helpless to shield oneself from its pitiless glare. They jostled their way through the village, asking at every door for a place to shelter, but short of the village street, there seemed not an inch. One woman did proffer a beaker of water which Francis drank at a gulp, but she could give no further help. Francis had a high fever now and was sweating in his makeshift stretcher, and Eliza, peering at his damaged side, saw with her newly experienced eye that he must have help soon.

'There must be somewhere!' she begged the woman who had given water.

'Not in the village.'

'Somewhere near then!'

'Well . . .' she was doubtful, 'it is a distance to the east, but my brother has a farm, a good half-hour – '

'Where?'

The woman pointed and gave brief directions.

'Will you bear him on a little more?' Eliza begged the men. They exchanged glances and one sergeant said, 'Yes, ma'am,' and in the midday glare, they left the village and trudged on through fields of rye along the border of the forest. The heat was dazing, the rye seemed to quiver and shimmer, and along the road crept other wrecks and relics of the previous day. The men said nothing, and Eliza bent her head and followed the steady beat of their boots in the dust.

It proved to be a small farm, the barns already requisitioned by some allied wounded, but the farmer, a sullen and taciturn man, allowed Francis to be laid in a great wooden manger in a cow-byre. It seemed paradise to Eliza. A high partition divided the manger and its stall from the rest of the barn, there was straw to lie upon, and a blessed coolness and dimness after the glare outside. The four men laid their burden down, covered him with the blanket and, turned to go.

'Must go back to the comp'ny, ma'am. Moving on to Paris.'

Eliza knew that now she was to be absolutely alone, and

that without their steady and patient help she could never have achieved what had so far been done.

'Turn your backs,' she said, for the second time that day. It was perhaps foolish to give them so much of what she had left, but she was so unutterably thankful to them. She pulled out her small store of gold, pinned in a handkerchief to her chemise, her other diamond pin and her bracelet. Then she went to the door again.

'You may turn round.'

She offered the trinkets and coins in her outstretched hands.

'You deserve far more, but I have nothing more to give you.'

They all looked uncomfortable.

'Take them. I do not want them. You need them. Only,' she added, 'do not quarrel over them.'

They looked at each other and licked their lips.

'Then I shall leave them in the mud.'

With a superb gesture, Eliza let the jewels and gold fall to the ground and turned away into the byre. There was a slight scuffle behind her, and when she looked again, men and money and trinkets were gone.

She was by now tired, hungry and thirsty, but there was no time to think of any of those needs. Francis lay sweating and moaning behind her, and if she did not attend to him immediately, all the effort and endurance of the last three days would be set at naught. Pulling the door as wide as she could to admit light, Eliza set about examining his side and leg. It was, as she had feared, a grapeshot wound. Small and jagged pieces of metal had torn through, or become embedded in the flesh of his side from his heart to above his knee. Like the first wound she had seen yesterday, the cloth of his clothing was horribly embedded. Yesterday she had had superior advice, forceps, ointments, plasters, spirits and opiates. Today she had her clothing and her fingers. Yesterday, however, she had wanted to help because there was no alternative, but today, her own happiness, her own reason for living, lay bleeding and wholly helpless in a manger.

In the dimness, Eliza stripped off all her upper clothing, selected her chemise, and the cleanest parts of the innermost shirt, and tore them into strips. Then, clad in her breeches

and William Cowper's shirts she went out into the yard for
water. The pump was surrounded. Jeers and shouts broke out
as she went forward, and she saw that there would be a
struggle to get even a cupful. The house was not far. Chin
high, Eliza walked round the group of men and pushed open
the farmhouse door. The farmer, his wife and sons and two
labourers were sitting around a table. The farmer waved and
shouted angrily.

'I need water.'

'Out there!' the wife screeched. 'Out there is water.'

'I cannot get enough. I need it for my husband.'

Six faces turned to her.

'I am a woman,' Eliza said awkwardly.

The wife turned and said something to her husband, but
he shook his head.

'The well is out there!' he said again. 'Water for you is
there!'

'Where do you draw your water?'

The wife again spoke quickly to the farmer. He said, 'If
we give you water they will all want it.'

'I will buy it.'

One of the sons laughed.

'I will buy it,' Eliza said again. She reached in among her
shirts and pulled out the string of pearls, 'I will give you one
pearl for a bucket of clean water. I will give you one pearl
for a jug of wine and one pearl for bread.'

Muttering and exclamations broke out round the table.
The laughing son was guffawing helplessly now, his huge
red mouth full of bread. The farmer got up eventually and
came to Eliza.

'Two pearls each for water and wine and bread.'

'One for wine and one for bread. Two for water.'

The farmer looked at his wife. She nodded. One of the sons
went through an inner door, and Eliza saw a small dim room,
just like the airy well-room at Nashbourn, and heard the
welcome and beautiful sound of water being drawn from a
depth. He came back with a great wooden bucket. Eliza held
out her hands for the bread and wine.

'Pearls,' the farmer said. He picked up a knife from the
table and held it out. The thread of the necklace was
knotted between each pearl, and carefully Eliza counted

four, and cut them from the remainder of the string. Then she knotted it around her neck.

'Will you help me?' she asked the son carrying the bucket. The boy nodded.

The farmer said, 'Not by the yard.'

He opened the well-room door again, and the son indicated that Eliza should follow. He led her down a dark passage, and out into a small herb garden behind the house, whence it was possible to slip around the outside of the barns to the byre on the further side without crossing the soldier-strewn yard.

A mouthful of bread and wine, water for Francis, and Eliza set to work. All that afternoon she toiled on, probing and extracting, wiping and washing, terrified at the quantities of fresh blood that gushed out whenever she touched him, and at his clammy pallor and quick, shallow breathing. He had not opened his eyes since she had found him, not even to drink. The pile of metal pieces grew, the mound of blood-soaked shreds of cloth stained the straw, and though the wound looked cleaner, it was brutally jagged, and Eliza knew that Surgeon Johns would have stitched it. She was especially worried by the part of the wound by the knee, where splinters of thigh bone showed that something much heavier had struck him there. If the missile was still in his flesh, Eliza could not find it.

As the light began to fail, Eliza started to wad some strips of her chemise, sprinkled with wine and water, against the wound, and then, with strips knotted together, to bind these wads tightly against him by swathing his chest with make-shift bandages. It was horribly difficult. He was a dead weight, and the bandages had to be inserted somehow between his body and his jacket. Even if she could have removed his jacket, she would have been afraid to do so because he was sweating so, and if she bound the strips outside his jacket they would not press firmly enough on the wound to close the edges of it together. Wrestling and panting, she strove to accomplish it, while the dusk crept on and the air dampened. The one blessed aspect of the afternoon was that she had not been mobbed and disturbed. Perhaps the soldiers in the yard supposed her to be still inside the farmhouse.

Eliza tied the last inadequate band of linen round Francis' thigh and bent in the near-darkness to feel his face. It was wet, not with the sticky moisture of sweat, but slippery with tears. With a shocked exclamation, she bent closer and saw the shine of his eyes, open at last, and felt his right hand come up and press her head against his face.

'Eliza. A miracle. Eliza, Eliza.'

She was weeping too now, her cheek against his, her body arched over his chest to avoid pressing on his wound. He was murmuring incoherent, broken words, mostly her name, over and over.

'Eliza. Dearest, beloved. Eliza. Beloved Eliza. Eliza.'

They clung together in the darkness, and Eliza knew that if morning never came, if this was the last moment, it had all been worth it; he knew her, she had seen him again, they had been together. She never asked him about the pain, he never asked her how she was there, or even where he was, they just clung and murmured. Then he asked for water in a voice so normal, she was suddenly delirious with joy. She gave him water, and he drank it and then lay back and took her hand, and slipped quickly into sleep. Eliza gently disengaged her hand and then rose to shut the door and place a bar against it which would wake her if it fell. She crept back to Francis' side and made herself a passable bed on the floor below his manger, feeling her way in the darkness to pile straw for a pillow. There were comforting sounds from the other side of the partition, sounds of animals grunting and settling themselves. Eliza pulled her jacket on again, its feel and cumbersomeness familiar now, then she lay down, her hand on the knotted pearls about her neck, and slept.

For three days she nursed him. Every morning and evening she would steal along the secret path behind the barn and bargain with her dwindling necklace for soup and wine, water and bread. She had a sensation she should leave him long enough to find a surgeon, but she could not bring herself to, and had she but known it, a surgeon in those first days might not have helped him. She had seen Johns bleed men with leeches and blisters, but she was afraid to bleed Francis, and thus, unknowingly, she saved his strength. She washed his wounds every day, and washed her makeshift bandages, and bound him up anew with the tattered strips of linen. He still had a fever at nights, sometimes muttering, always tossing, but in the day he was conscious, watching her always, wanting her to talk to him.

It seemed to her that she told him of her adventures at least ten times a day. She would laugh and say, 'I told you of that!' and he would press to hear it again, and then would say, 'You are a miracle, truly a miracle.' He made her put on her tunic again and again, to give him some sense of what she had actually done, and where she had actually been the Sunday before.

On the morning of the third day, Eliza went as usual to the farmhouse. The farmer's wife had become almost benign and welcomed her with a perfect pantomime of winks and nods. Eliza was puzzled. She made her usual purchases, and then found herself pushed, in a flurry of gestures, back into the well-room. The reason was soon clear. From a cupboard in the wall, the wife produced a bundle which she thrust into Eliza's arms, and then, finger to lips and her eyebrows working in a frenzied injunction to secrecy, pushed Eliza out into the yard again. Back in the byre, the bundle revealed itself to be a gown of coarse cloth, a rough shirt, several pieces of linen, and a comb. To Eliza, rolls of silk and purses of jewels could not have been more welcome. She had been nearly six days in breeches now, six days without the sensation of petticoats, six days with nothing to smooth her hair with but her fingers. She was in high spirits. She washed herself and donned the gown, and pirouetted for Francis around the stall, snapping her fingers and laughing. The dress fitted her about as snugly as a flour sack about a broom handle, and Francis laughed as heartily as his side would allow. Then she flew to wash him and bind him up, so that she could dress him in the clean shirt.

However, when she looked at what was left in the bucket, she saw that she had not brought enough water with her that day. She had been burdened with the bundle of clothing and thus had only had one hand free for water, and the task of cleaning Francis and his bandages would take more water than that if she were to accomplish it with the zeal she felt fired with. No matter, she would go back for some, and what is more, she felt buoyant and brave enough this morning to take the short cut to the well in the yard among its jesting, swearing inmates.

'I shall not be long!' she said picking up her bucket. 'A few minutes, not more,' and went humming out into the sunshine.

A cheer from the stragglers lying about in the sun greeted her as she came. It was a ragged cheer because most of the men were in a clump about the well-head, the ones on the outside of the group trying to see some object of attention in the centre of it. Eliza faltered. It was not going to be easy to draw a bucketful of water as quickly and unobtrusively as she had optimistically hoped. As she slowed her steps, several men on the outside of the group saw her come, and shouted to the others, and they began to move away, and grin, showing blackened teeth in their stubbled filthy faces. Eliza gripped her bucket handle and waited. Perhaps she should go back. Now they had noticed her, they would follow her and the tranquillity of the past forty-eight hours, so necessary to Francis' recovery, would be shattered. She turned to go, but several men shouted at her, in a language she did not understand, but in a tone which had something of a request in it, and not a rough request at that. She looked back. Three or four soldiers were coming forward, and one of them was holding something in his hand, a piece of paper, buff-coloured, closely packed with lines of black printing. The man holding it asked her his question again, but Eliza shook her head.

'I do not understand you.'

The man tried again, gesturing to the others that they might help. One of them said, in barely discernible French:

'*Anglaise?*'

'*Anglaise?* Oh – yes, yes, English. Yes, I am. I speak English.'

The soldier with the piece of paper stepped forward, still speaking unintelligibly, and pressed it into Eliza's free hand. She looked up at the gathering ring of men around her and smiled.

'Thank you,' she said.

Chatter broke out around her, they were all pressing round her, unwilling to go away, pointing at the paper and questioning her. She set down her bucket and took the paper in both hands. It was crudely and roughly printed in ink that smudged as she touched it, and across the top in uneven capitals it said 'PROVISIONAL CASUALTY LIST – CAVALRY'.

Eliza's throat went dry. Her thoughts had all been for Francis, only for Francis, she had forgotten everything and everyone but him. Her eye went dodging desperately down the list, the packed names, hundreds of them there must be, none of them she knew. Oh, thank God, she thought, there's no one here, he isn't here, he is safe somewhere, how could I forget him – Howell, Pelham, Capt., she read towards the bottom of the second side, Royal Dragoons. The letter 'd' was after his name, not 'm' as some had. What was 'd'? What did 'd' stand for? The small print at the foot of the sheet helped her. 'M' for missing it said, 'd' for dead. Howell Pelham, Capt., of the Royal Dragoons, dead.

Eliza screamed, again and again, gripping the paper with her eyes wide and dry and staring, and her mouth emitting these ragged, piercing sounds. Then abruptly she dropped the list, and casting herself in the dust among the soldiers' broken boots began to weep as if she would be torn apart by it. The men watched her in awe and bewilderment for a while, writhing and beating her fists down there, and one of them picked up the casualty list and tore it carefully into shreds as if he could thus prevent its doing further damage. Two middle-aged men eventually stooped and tried to lift Eliza, but their touch seemed to appal her. She began to struggle to her feet in her voluminous dress, sobbing and gasping, her face unrecognizable with dust and grief and her hair in knots.

Blindly she fought her way through the group, making for the open gate of the farmyard and the white road and standing corn beyond. She stumbled as she went, not caring now how she tore the garment that had so delighted her but half an hour before, and plunged across the road and into the field of grain beyond as if it had been the waves of the sea. The men in the yard stared after her as she crashed through the corn, and saw her trip and fall headlong, vanished from their sight and hidden by the quivering gold. Some tried to follow her, but they were held back.

Down there in the spiky dusty gloom among the corn stalks, Eliza ceased gradually to weep. Through the terribleness of grief came the unbearable thought that she deserved the shock that Pelham's death had been. She had promised Francis that she would never forget him, and that they owed each other to him – and she had forgotten. She had never thought to look for Pelham once she had found Francis, and perhaps he had died from wounds she might have staunched. She had forgotten him because she was tired and busy and overwhelmed, and at a time when he most needed to be remembered. She owed him her happiness, and she had let him slip from her mind. How would Francis take it? How could she tell him? She could not tell him now, the shock would be too great. And the Howells? How could Mrs Howell survive the news of the death of this most adored of sons? How could any of them live without him, for so long part of the fabric of their lives, what would the days be like without his face and wit and kindness?

She sat up slowly and dusted grit and corn stalks from her hands. In her mind's eye rose the desolate picture of Pelham riding alone down the drive at Marchants after she had sent him away. She tried to recall other moments, better, happier moments, but nothing would come to her but that solitary figure jogging away, head bent, shoulders slightly stooped. She had not even said good-bye to him in Brussels as he would have wished. She had failed to hold his gaze so that he never said what he was minded to say. She was selfish, selfish, selfish. She could never have loved him as she loved Francis, but he had been to her as a most beloved brother, and she had always repressed in him any release he might have gained from opening his heart to her. And at the last she had forgotten him.

Eliza got up stiffly, and without smoothing her hair or straightening her dress, retraced her battered path through the grain, earth falling from the folds of her skirt as she went. The men in the farmyard parted silently to let her pass and she went through them unseeingly to the byre. Just before the door she halted, then seemed to search about for something. A boy in the nearest group darted forward and picked up her bucket, running to hand it to her. She looked at him blankly, then smiled faintly and took the bucket in one hand, smoothing her hair vaguely with the other. Then she turned for a moment and looked at them all, watching her, and walked on across the yard, and round the corner back to Francis.

She set the bucket down on the floor, keeping her face averted from his eyes.

'What has been happening, Eliza? You have been gone so long I was quite anxious. And someone screamed not long since, somewhere out in the yard. I knew it could not be you because that is not the path you take, but it sounded like a woman – '

'It was me,' she said.

He tried to raise himself but could get no purchase for his elbows in the straw.

'What has happened? Dearest, tell me, tell me, I can bear to know anything. It is ignorance that I cannot bear. Come here – come to me.'

She went to kneel by the manger, raising her tear-stained face to him.

'I went to the pump in the yard, to be quick, to get back to you. And – and the soldiers out there had a casualty list they could not read. It was in English. They gave it to me. It was a cavalry list – ' Her voice faltered. She bent her head, and a hot tear splashed on to Francis' hand that was gripping the edge of the manger.

'Pelham,' she whispered, and put her head down on the manger's edge.

'I – I knew,' Francis said unsteadily. He thrust his hand between her face and the wooden edge, and twisted himself to lay his cheek on her hair, 'Don't worry about telling me. I knew.'

Late that night, when she had made Francis as comfortable as she could, Eliza took up her usual position by him and abandoned herself to thoughts she could not resist. She thought Francis was asleep, so wept as silently as she could for fear of waking him, pressing the stiff cuff of her jacket against her mouth, and biting hard on the braid that encrusted it. Suppose Francis were not recovering, and that in her inexperience she only fancied that he was because she so desperately wanted him to? Suppose she were to lose everyone who was dear to her because she did not help them or because she did not give them the right sort of help?

'Eliza?'

She sat up immediately.

'Francis! I thought you asleep! Are you in pain?'

'No. No more than usual. It is not that – '

His voice sounded broken and strange. Eliza stood up, clad only in her soldier's shirt, and leant over him.

'What is it, Francis?'

He felt for her hand and put it to his mouth. He was shaking.

'Will you come to me?'

'Now? While you – oh, dearest one, it will hurt you so, it will tear the wound open again – '

'Please,' he said. He slipped his hand under the shirt and up her thigh and side. 'I do not mind the pain – the pain is nothing, it does not matter, not that pain – ' he choked. There was a small pause, and Eliza brought her face down until it was almost touching his.

Francis whispered, 'I need the comfort of you.'

Eliza woke at first light, horribly stiff, wedged between the byre wall and Francis. He slept, as he had to do, on his back, his hair littered with straw, and stubble darkening his chin. Eliza bent sideways and kissed his sleeping mouth. He smiled and muttered, but his eyes never opened. Carefully, she eased herself out of her cramped sleeping space, and climbed delicately over him to the floor. Memory flooded her as she dressed, and though the sunlight gathering strength outside seemed heartless by comparison, the night before had made Pelham's death less savagely painful to bear. She combed her hair, rubbed her face with the hem of her dress, and picked up her bucket for the morning errand for water.

When she got back Francis was awake, clear eyed and smiling. He reached for her as she came near and pulled her into his arms without a thought for his leg and side.

'No! No! I must wash you – I never cleaned your wound properly yesterday, and I shall not rest until I have done it.'

'It is only dawn,' Francis said comfortably, as if a day of pleasure stretched before him. 'You have all day to do it.'

'I wish to do it now. I was so distracted by – by yesterday, I forgot and I must do it at once.'

She knelt beside the manger, and began the difficult task of unravelling the damp and clotted bandages from his side. Once they were off, and dropped into water to soak, Eliza went to push the byre door wide so that the maximum amount of light might reach the corner where Francis lay. She stooped to inspect the wounds and noticed with a leap of pleasure that the gashes down his side were healing fast. They would clearly heal raggedly, not having been stitched, but the flesh looked clean and healthy. Below, his hip however, the story was different. Eliza was thankful Francis was too immobilized to twist himself to see. Most of the pieces of shot had lodged themselves at this lower end of the wound, and every day new pieces of metal and fragments of bone were working themselves to the surface. This was not in itself particularly worrying, but the flesh of Francis' thigh seemed to Eliza's anxious gaze to be darkening, and the wound itself was still suppurating horribly. With apparent cheerfulness that morning, Eliza set to work and washed and bound the upper wound. Then she took the bandages off Francis' thigh and suppressed a gasp. It was worse, much worse. It was dark and hideous, much more so than the previous day, and as Eliza bent forward a faint and dreadful gaseous stench rose from the torn flesh. For what seemed minutes she sat on the straw and looked at his leg and made herself realize that she had not the skill to deal with his suffering any longer.

'Is anything troubling you?' Francis said.

She said in as steady a tone as she could manage, 'I believe that the time has come for me to leave you a little while while I find a surgeon.'

A shadow fell over the doorway. Neither Francis nor Eliza looked up, both entirely preoccupied with the implication of what she had said. Then a clipped English voice, familiar to them both, spoke in the silence.

'Permit me to save you the trouble and fetch a surgeon to you myself.'

18

Francis' leg was amputated before nightfall. Sepsis had set in in the lower part, and the only way of saving him was this drastic operation. Sir Gerard had ridden back to Brussels at once, at a speed remarkable for a man in his sixties in the heat of August, and returned in the late afternoon, dishevelled but triumphant, with a surgeon who had been unable to resist the offered inducement to gallop ten miles on a blazing afternoon.

While they were gone, a stretcher was eagerly cobbled together by the soldiers in the farmyard. The farmer's wife, all compliance with Sir Gerard's gold chinking in her pocket, prepared a cool ground-floor room for Francis, and he was carried as tenderly as possible across the yard and laid on the first bedstead his body had known for a week. The movement was clearly agonizing for him. Eliza, grasping his hand and walking by his side, saw all trace of colour flee his face, and sweat break out on his cheeks and forehead. When he was settled, and the shutters were closed against the dusty glare, she sat by his bedside in the dim quietness, and stroked his forehead, and talked to him with gentle and soothing repetitiveness.

Once or twice he opened his eyes to look at her, and smile faintly, and once he said, 'My father –' in a troubled voice, and she said:

'Sh – sh – it is all right, do not think of it, do not worry.
He nodded gratefully and his lids slipped down again.
The surgeon was a competent little Belgian, a precise and

efficient man who spoke enough English to congratulate Eliza on her nursing of Francis.

'This bleeding, it is out of date. Only soldier surgeons perform it now. It weakens the system. You have done well not bleeding, madame. And the upper wound, it is clean, so clean. It will heal. I commend you, madame.'

He wanted her to leave while he performed the amputation, and half of her agreed with him. But the other half was determined to see through this last agony of an agonizing time, and to be near Francis should he want her. So she seated herself by the bedhead, and armed herself with brandy for Francis, and also the knowledge that she had seen it all before, albeit not performed on a man she loved. Sir Gerard stood on the far side of the bed and watched, his face unreadable.

When it was all over, Francis, who despite noble attempts to resist unconsciousness, had fainted once or twice, looked up at Eliza with a slight smile and said:

'What use will you find now for all my left boots?'

Eliza choked.

'Don't – '

'I shall get by very well with one leg. If you are with me, I cannot see that I need arms and legs in any case. I never knew a human being so infinitely brave or resourceful as you are.'

The surgeon came up to the bedhead, drying his hands on a piece of linen.

'You will do very well, monsieur, very well. I am sure madame will nurse you as well as she has already done. You must be very quiet for some days, and she must watch for a fever. But I think you will do well. I will return to see you in a week.'

He bowed and smiled, and Sir Gerard held the door for him.

'You should sleep now,' Eliza told Francis when the door was shut. 'I will stay with you until you sleep, and,' she added looking up at her father-in-law with some defiance, 'I will stay with you alone.'

Sir Gerard said nothing but left the room without another glance at Francis or his astonishing wife. When he had gone, Francis looked at her earnestly, and said:

'Do not go near him if you are afraid.'

'I am not afraid. He will not hurt me again. Now close your eyes and dream.'

When she left him some fifteen minutes later and went up to the small room the farmer's wife had vacated for them to use as a salon, she was disconcerted to find Sir Gerard there. He rose when she came in, bowed, but remained as silent as he had been since his first remark.

'Are we to live like this until Francis recovers?' she said boldly, looking up at him. 'Are you going to treat me as if I were invisible for as long as we are together? It is going to make life most tiresome for us all, and difficult for Francis.'

Still he said nothing. His gaze went right past her to some point on the wall behind her head.

'I am sorry that I trespassed at Quihampton,' Eliza went on, 'and I am naturally sorry that you bear me such open animosity, but if you cannot come to terms with these feelings, you must simply bear them. We are so much as one, Francis and I, that your scorn is nothing to us. I seem to have saved him, but I did not think of saving him for you. I saved him for myself, and it is for me that he is glad to be alive. You threatened to curse our children, and if that is still the case, we shall take care our children know nothing of you. If you wish to live in embittered solitude, you may. It is your choice –' She stopped.

Sir Gerard's gaze had moved suddenly from the wall to meet her own. She could not tell what he thought, his eyes gave nothing away except that whatever he thought his feelings were not savage and furious like those she had encountered before.

'I have an uncle I love dearly,' Eliza said. 'He is to me what a father might have been, so I know what a daughter's feelings could be. As you are the father of Francis, you may imagine what you might be to me. If you do not want those feelings, I must accept that, as you must accept our indifference to your hostility to our marriage. However, if we are to live together for a while, you must accept our terms. You are a trespasser in our lives, you came prying after us, you are the intruder this time. Until Francis is well, I must shape our lives, and if you are to be part of it, you must abide by our rules.'

She did not think she had ever made so long a speech in her life before. When she had come to the end, and Sir Gerard still neither moved nor spoke, but continued to gaze at her, she felt the calm she had enjoyed while speaking begin to slip from her. Quickly, before whatever effect she had had upon him was dissipated, she turned and went through the door and downstairs again to the sanctuary of Francis' room.

She did not see him at supper but ate alone in the dusk, and returned to sit by Francis until she was too weary to keep awake one moment more. A pallet had been laid for her on the floor, and she lay thankfully down on it and smelt the scent of herbs and grasses that filled her pillow. Above her Francis breathed deep and evenly, and out of the silent summer night a great yellow moon rose among the poplars.

A week went by with Francis daily growing more cheerful and well. Eliza knew Sir Gerard was still in the house, for his boots were left upon the landing, and food was carried in to him, but he did not appear before her once. She became quite used to the idea of his silent presence and was quite surprised one day to see from an upper window his stiff black-clad figure riding back along the road to Brussels. She flew downstairs to the kitchen.

'*Le monsieur Anglais, il est parti?*'

The farmer's wife was making pastry, and she went on rolling and shaping the great pale slab on the kitchen table. No, she said, he had not gone for ever, he had received a letter that morning and said that he must go to Brussels but that he would be back before nightfall.

'*Quel dommage,*' Eliza said fervently, and returned to Francis.

'What is your father about, do you suppose?'

Francis propped up in bed by pillows, was shaving himself precariously without the aid of a looking-glass.

'Is he bothering you?'

'Oh, no. We never see each other. I cannot think why he stays.'

'He will have a reason. As we are due to leave in a few days, he is bound to show his hand soon. How am I faring?' He held his chin up for Eliza to see.

'Unevenly. Let me help you. Francis, have you thought what will become of us?'

'Do you not wish to return to Nashbourn?'

'No!'

'Nor I.'

'It would be unbearable now. We must go to Mrs Howell briefly, but I could not stay – not yet.'

'Should you like to go to Julia? Or to your uncle?'

'Not to Julia,' Eliza said with emphasis, 'I could not go to London after – after this. I sent my things to her because I thought that if I did not return, she would accept the fact more calmly than my aunt, but I could not go to her now.'

'Marchants?'

Eliza shook her head. 'Not even for my uncle's sake. Can we not be somewhere alone together?'

Francis thought fleetingly of the paradise Quihampton might be without his father, and dismissed that impossible dream as quickly as it had come.

'We shall find another house.'

Eliza wiped the last fragment of lather from his jaw and leaned back to survey her handiwork.

'Very handsome. Yes, no doubt we shall. I do not much mind if we are gipsies as long as we are gipsies together.'

'I think that is hardly practical.'

'Why do we need to be practical?'

'Because, dearest love, we must live. We must have a house – and a family and a way of life. The last few months, and notably the last few weeks, have been some sort of fantasy, sometimes terrible, sometimes not. But it is over, and the business of living must go on.'

Eliza looked crestfallen. 'Why are you so serious suddenly? Is it not enough to be alive?'

'More than enough. But as you know, there is a difference between living and mere existence.'

'You mean that we should decide what we shall do when we return to England?'

'We must,' said Francis.

Sir Gerard returned at sunset. Eliza saw him ride in, and some moments later heard his tread across the tiles of the downstairs hall. He went to his room immediately, and the door closed behind him with finality. She left her listening position at the keyhole and returned to the bedside.

'Your father is back.'

Francis nodded. He had been deeply preoccupied since their conversation that morning, and appeared hardly to hear anything Eliza was saying.

'I wish he would go!' she burst out suddenly. 'I thought I did not mind him here, but I do not think I can bear him about the place much longer! Why does he not return? He knows you are well now, there is no reason for his staying – '

A knock sounded sharply on the door.

'*Entrez*,' Francis said absently.

The door opened and Sir Gerard came in, still in his black clothes, now dusty from riding. He made no apology for interrupting them, but crossed to Francis' bedside and seated himself, without invitation, on the chair Eliza customarily occupied. Eliza did not move from where she stood at the foot of the bed.

'I shall be gone by dawn,' Sir Gerard said peremptorily, his eyes on Francis, 'I have been in Brussels today, and a carriage will collect you and your belongings in a week from today, and take you to Antwerp where you may board the *Madalena* for England.'

'I presume,' Eliza said sharply from behind him, 'that I may accompany Francis on this journey home?'

Sir Gerard did not turn his head. With his eyes still fixed on Francis he said, 'A silk merchant and dressmaker will attend you in the morning, madam. They are under instructions to provide you with all you need for the journey home.'

Eliza went scarlet. She looked in confusion at Francis, but he was saying to his father, 'It was good of you to trouble yourself, sir, but I think we might have managed the arrangements for ourselves.'

'I did not do it for you in particular,' Sir Gerard said. 'I did it because I have business to attend to in England whose outcome affects you, as well as myself. You will oblige me by coming to Quihampton upon your return to England.'

After a swift and revealing glance at Eliza, Francis said, 'You must explain yourself a little, sir.'

'I cannot,' Sir Gerard said, rising from his chair.

'Then I fear we cannot come.'

There was a brief pause. Eliza thought how well Francis looked with heightened colour. Sir Gerard crossed to the door, then turned as he opened it to say:

'I have news from your brother. Mrs Beaumont has proved herself just the idle, foolish wife she promised to be and Richard finds himself in considerable difficulties. I have no sympathy for him. He would make his bed and now he must lie upon it. But it affects the plans – my plans. I may say no more, but you will comply with my wishes and come to Quihampton.'

'No, sir,' Francis said.

'Forgive me, Francis,' Eliza said quickly, 'but – but yes. Yes, we will come.'

For the first time since he had entered the room, Sir Gerard glanced at her. He looked at her for a full five seconds most searchingly, then bowed and was gone. The moment the door had closed behind him, Eliza flew to Francis.

'Oh, poor Richard! What can have happened? What has she done now?'

'More of the same thing, I would imagine. Why it should affect my father I cannot conceive, and nor can I think why you should suddenly agree to go to him.'

Eliza spread her hands helplessly. 'I do not know. I suddenly felt that we should, that it was right. Oh, Francis, I cannot bear to think of what Richard might be suffering!'

Francis thought of the intense animosity she once bore his brother, and looked up at her to see her face alight with sympathy.

'You would once have borne it very easily.'

'That is not fair! That was long ago, long before I knew – I knew anything.'

'I think,' Francis said, catching her hands in his, 'I think that you are the most remarkable being alive. You are, among a thousand good qualities, brave, loyal, gallant, true and beautiful. I do not know what I have done to deserve you.'

Eliza shook her head helplessly.

'I do not care about merit,' she said. 'You are what I want.'

They reached England on the first day of September. Eliza stepped on shore clad in green silk of Sir Gerard's purchase, followed by Francis swinging on crutches which he managed already with considerable nonchalance. No one was there to meet them. Eliza, despite all her protestations of wishing to be alone with Francis, had secretly hoped that perhaps her uncle and aunt at least might have come to Dover, but there appeared to be no one. They created a good deal of stir on the quayside since they had come home on an ancient troopship converted crudely into some sort of floating ambulance, and they looked very different to the rest of the passengers, who were huddled in blankets and swathed in dubiously clean bandages. The men stood aside as best they could to let them pass along the quay, and a group of fisherwomen stopped sorting the slippery contents of their baskets to watch them, Eliza, with her chin high to show she did not care that no one troubled to greet them, Francis still half a head taller than most men despite bending slightly for his crutches.

'Sir – excuse me, sir!'

Francis stopped. A man in familiar livery was pushing his way among the boxes and bundles and loitering people.

'Grimes!'

'Captain Francis, sir! I knew 't must be you, sir! And Mrs Beaumont, ma'am. I bin sent to bring you back, sir. I bin waitin' half the night. The carriage is this way, ma'am.'

The livery was her own, now. Sir Gerard had remembered them and had sent the carriage. Eliza put her hand on Francis' sleeve and said.

'Would you rather rest before travelling that far?'

'No,' he said. 'I am anxious to know what my father has summoned us for. I do not think I could rest until I know. We shall have to put up somewhere tonight as it is. Come, Grimes, and lead the way.'

Eliza had wondered if her second view of Quihampton would remind her very painfully of the first, but she decided, as the carriage wound downhill above those lichened roofs, that she felt nothing but an enormous curiosity. She glanced sideways at Francis, and saw him gazing from the carriage window wearing an expression of almost painful pleasure. She put her hand in his, and, without looking round, he tightened his grasp on her fingers. He loved the place, of course he did. Whatever his father was, Francis was a Beaumont, and had been born at Quihampton and grown up there, and it was natural that it should be part of the fabric of him. It was equally natural that he felt pain that his elder brother, who did not care for it as he did, should eventually possess it. Never mind, Eliza thought, she would manage, she would somehow make another house as dear to him.

A flurry of barking dogs poured down the steps as the carriage rolled over the gravel. The great door was open again, but with a less forbidding air than in the August before. A footman followed the dogs, swearing at them as he ran down the steps, and the door of the carriage was opened.

'Good afternoon, James,' Francis said.

'Sir,' he replied, his eyes upon Eliza in open admiration, 'your father's waiting, sir, and Mr Beaumont. In the south drawing room.'

Francis and Eliza exchanged glances.

'Richard!'

'And may I take the liberty of saying welcome home, sir. And to your lady.'

It took some moments for Francis to negotiate the steps.

'We shall have to find a house on a plateau, I think, dearest,' he said, but his face was not as cheerful as his tone. Eliza walked swiftly beside him as he swung his way purposefully across the great hall, still black and shadowed, and into the gallery whose portraits had frowned last year upon Eliza and her folly. Instead of going through the door at the end, James held open a double door set between two tapestries in the wall, and said:

'Captain Beaumont, sir, and Mrs Beaumont.'

Instinctively Eliza reached for Francis' hand, and then remembered he needed both for his crutches, and let hers fall back to her side. They were in an enormous low room, with an intricately plastered ceiling and great wide mullioned windows with deep stone sills and a view of the rose garden beyond. Sir Gerard and Richard had risen from tapestried chairs set together in one bay the of windows, and Richard was coming forward, his hands out in welcome.

'Ah, my dear brother, how welcome you are, how miraculous that you are alive! And little Eliza! We gather you are quite the heroine. There has been much talk of you in London you know, much talk!'

Eliza saw Francis flinch slightly as the proprietary tone in his brother's voice, and was herself aware of Richard's condescension in supposing that to be the talk of fashionable drawing rooms was the highest accolade anyone could wish for.

'I am surprised to see you, Richard,' Francis said, 'I hope – '

'Ah, there is a purpose, indeed there is!'

Eliza looked towards her father-in-law.

'I have to thank you for my gown, sir.'

He bowed.

'Will you sit down?'

Richard watched Francis propel himself to a chair and sit down.

'Quite the wounded hero, are we not, Francis? Are you to equip yourself with a wooden leg? I know of a capital fellow who would fit you out in a trice. He owes a great deal to me and would be honoured to perform a service for any brother of mine.'

Eliza gazed up at Richard in astonishment. She had expected to find a broken man, and here he was, expansive and self-satisfied as ever. She recalled how, once, he used to praise his brother, and even seemed to take a pride in Francis' distinction. Now it appeared that such generosity was gone for ever. She looked from his broad, insensitive, healthy face to Francis' fine one and wondered, not for the first time, how they came to be brothers.

'We have asked you here – ' Richard began ceremoniously, settling himself in the largest chair.

'Richard!' Sir Gerard's tone was horribly like the one he had used on Eliza in the library.

'Sir?'

'I have asked them here, not you. This is my house, and I summon here those I wish to see and shall do so until it passes to other hands.'

Richard looked discomfited and spread out his well-manicured hands as if the contemplation of them was the most important business he had.

'You may, however,' his father went on crisply, 'explain your own position. I find it distasteful to speak of it.'

Richard settled himself comfortably, looked at both Eliza and Francis to be sure he had their full attention, and took an elaborately deep breath.

'It is my misfortune to be the victim of the most unwarranted deceptions. I have given your cousin Julia,' he said, with an accusing look at Eliza, 'every benefit upon earth. No woman has ever had more to rejoice in. Not only did she have my undivided regard but every comfort she expressed the smallest whim for. However, she has proved herself unworthy of such priceless advantages, and has chosen to humiliate and alienate me in a way I feel no woman of true feeling could ever do.'

Eliza shifted uncomfortably in her chair. Something in his tone made a sneaking sympathy for Julia begin to spread itself in her heart. She might disapprove entirely of the method Julia used, but perhaps one could not entirely blame her for a desire to escape.

'You need not go on, Richard,' Francis said gently.

'Indeed I must. I have been profoundly wronged, and I wish that you should know how blameless I am in the matter. She has now gone away, I believe to France, with a man named Lennox, a man whom I once regarded as a close friend, someone who had the privilege of an intimacy with me. I shall not,' he said with emphasis, 'take her back.'

'But Richard —!' Eliza cried.

He held up his hand for silence.

'She shall not want. Lennox is clearly an adventurer, but I am not a man of stone.' At this point the memory of a certain adoring little actress who, only two nights before, had called him her saviour and only benefactor, caused a small and pleased smile to curve his lips. 'I shall provide for her. You need have no fear upon that score. I have no desire for vengeance. I am above such pettiness.'

His father sighed heavily.

'Will you hasten, Richard!'

'Sir. In short, I am now, to all intents and purposes, without a wife. However, life has not lost all its — its sweetness, and I still find very much that keeps me in London. I am well suited to urban living as you know, and find my talents best exercised among people of a certain sophistication. Therefore, I propose to divide my time between London and Bath – '

'And Julia?' Eliza said.

'I shall purchase a small house for her somewhere secluded should she need it. She will find me as large-hearted as ever.'

'Will you finish?' Sir Gerard growled.

'I have concluded, sir.'

Sir Gerard rose from his seat and came to stand opposite his younger son.

'In view of the changed circumstances in his life and tastes, Richard has, under pressure, decided to waive his right to Quihampton.'

Eliza saw Francis change colour, then blanch again. He leant towards his father.

'Quihampton?'

'Precisely so. The documents lie waiting for signature in the library. Life has been much altered by the last months, and I shall myself no longer be occupying this house. I am about to remove to the Dower House since I do not care to share my dwelling.'

'Share?' Eliza said stupidly.

'Quihampton is to be yours, if you will have it. I shall not interfere with your lives. You will be unaware that I am but a mile from you.'

Eliza thought Francis might be going to weep. His eyes were extremely bright. He was groping for his crutch to rise and go to his father, but he seemed unable to say anything. Eliza went forward quickly.

'Sir Gerard, I do not know how – '

For the second time only, since they had first met, Sir Gerard took her hand, so briefly that it was like being brushed by a dry leaf. He turned his unfathomable gaze upon her long enough to say, 'I want no speeches,' and then moved towards the door to the gallery.

Eliza looked back at Francis. He was sitting with his dark head in his hands, and he was shaking slightly. She put her hand on his hair and heard him say, muffled by his fingers, 'I believe I have nothing in the world left to wish for.'

By the spring of 1816, Quihampton was the talk of the neighbourhood. The new young mistress, of whom such amazing tales were told, had effected such changes that the place was hardly recognizable. She had temporarily imported an aunt, it was said, from somewhere in the south, and the transformation that resulted from that partnership made competition keen for invitations to the house to inspect the results. Successful visitors reported an effect of warmth and light, great fires and bowls of flowers everywhere, all of it much enhanced by the presence of that handsome and gallant Captain with his romantically tragic disability, and his wholly enchanting wife. Of the ferocious Sir Gerard the county knew little, but then, if it knew little, it cared less.

Eliza cared, however. He was as unobtrusive as his word, and as uncommunicative as ever, but she would wave to him when he walked or rode in the park, visit him with books or flowers from favourite bushes in the Quihampton garden, and despatch Francis to the Dower House at frequent intervals. They never ate together or saw each other formally, but it was hardly necessary.

Coming back from the Dower House one April afternoon after delivering eggs from the bantams Sir Gerald particularly liked, Eliza diverted from her usual path to approach Quihampton across the great greensward that swept up to the library and gallery windows. She could see no one, but the house had an air of animation these days even when its windows were closed. Francis would be in the stableyard, she supposed, trying out the saddle he had specially designed to compensate for the absence of his leg. He was so agile that she could sometimes hardly remember that he had once had both legs. She hoped he would not be long, she did not like to be apart from him for more than a few hours together.

She stopped in front of the house and looked about her with satisfaction. Daffodils were blowing in a great yellow sheet right up to the soft grey walls, and there were cushions of pale primroses around the mossy roots of the trees. She could see firelight in the library dancing rosily on the new white paint and the gleaming gilded backs of books. She hoped she would be able to eat dinner that day. Francis was bound to notice soon how little she liked food at the moment, and she did not want to tell him until she was sure. She patted a letter in her pocket. She had written to Mrs Howell a week before, and the reply had come that morning, warmly reassuring. Nausea was perfectly normal, Mrs Howell had written, but it was usually gone by the twelfth week. Eliza put her hand on her stomach beneath her cloak and smiled delightedly to herself. She looked about her again and thought how in a few years there would be a little Pelham perhaps, running among the trees, accompanied by others maybe – after all, Mrs Howell had successfully reared five –

'Eliza!' Francis was calling from the terrace, 'Eliza!'

Picking up her skirts, she ran swiftly towards him.